W9-AGI-415

THE MUSCLES OF HER BACK TWINGED IN ANTICIPATION OF THE SHOCK OF THE BULLET....

With agonizing slowness Sarah formed the thoughts: They've come back. They're shooting at me. Have to get out of the light.

She turned and ran.

For a moment she was in darkness, then the headlights in the glittering grille swung around on her. Each blade of grass stood out in brilliant outline, and her own shadow, eerily doubled, ran before her. She knew that they were aiming at her. When she heard the shots, she felt an overwhelming urge to throw herself to the ground. But she forced herself to run on, the soggy ground clinging to her at every step, almost tearing off her shoes.

The Book Rack
1000's of Used Paperbacks
Trade 2 for 1
3217 E. State Blvd.
3830 S. Calhoun
Ft. Wayne, IN
Other Stores Across the U.S.

BELGRAVIA

David Linzee

A DELL BOOK

Published by
Dell Publishing Co., Inc.
1 Dag Hammarskjold Plaza
New York, New York 10017

Copyright © 1979 by David Linzee

All rights reserved.
No part of this book may be reproduced,
stored in a retrieval system or transmitted in any form
by any electronic, mechanical, photocopying, or
recording means or otherwise, without prior written permission
of the author. For information address Seaview Books
(a division of Playboy Enterprises, Inc.),
New York, New York.

Dell ® TM 681510, Dell Publishing Co., Inc.

ISBN: 0-440-10472-6

Reprinted by arrangement with Seaview Books
(a division of Playboy Enterprises, Inc.)

Printed in the United States of America

First Dell printing—January 1981

To D.D.C.

ACKNOWLEDGMENTS

Many people helped me in researching this book, but I must offer particular thanks to C.B.D. of Hartford, who prefers not to have his name connected with computer fraud, and Mr. George Sandeman of London, who doesn't mind his name being prominently connected with sherry. Needless to say, they bear no responsibility for my errors and distortions.

I also wish to thank my aunt, Alice Linzee, for her heroic feats of typing.

—DAL

It was the worst debacle to befall a great multinational corporation since the payoff scandals of '73. It took four lives, and cut the value of RGI shares by a quarter.

In only one aspect of the catastrophe were the top men of RGI fortunate: It was so sudden and so total that there was no time for them to make things worse by attempting a cover-up. Before the murder case of the *Crown* v. *Lisle, Hardy, and Nicholls* got under way at the Old Bailey, and long before the first of the civil suits was heard at the law courts in the Strand, every ghastly detail had already come out. Unfriendly elements in the press and government assailed RGI with all the usual adjectives: "arrogant," "greedy," "callous," and "stupid."

With that last description, the men at World Headquarters certainly agreed. Walter Raspin, the Head of Operations for Europe, *could* have handled the matter more sensibly. And Christopher Rockwell and Sarah Saber, the two most prominent survivors of the affair, had made every possible mistake. They should be fired at the first opportunity, said the grumblers at WHQ.

The first opportunity was a long time in coming; Saber and Rockwell spent months testifying in London and Washington. As it turned out, Saber was not fired, while Rockwell resigned. His last comment was, "May trade's proud empire haste to swift decay." The *Wall Street Journal* got hold of this and identified it as a misquotation from Samuel Johnson;

they did not have to explain what Rockwell meant.
Like most disasters, this one had roots that spread
far and deep, but on one point everyone agreed: The
Dunbar fiasco had entered its final, fatal phase one
day in early January, on the island of Martinique.

Part One

Part One

Chapter 1

Almost as a gesture of defiance, Jack Wilson decided that he was going to enjoy this place, despite the reasons that had brought him to it. He dropped his shoulder bag, spread a towel, and settled down to admire the view.

In a life that happily included many visits to resorts, he had come across few beaches as beautiful as this one. The broad crescent of white sand was enclosed by tawny bluffs that were surmounted in turn by low green hills. A frothy white border like a lace frill marked the meeting of the land and the sea, an endless azure plane dotted with little gaily striped triangles that, on a closer look, turned out to be sailboats.

The beach was crowded, but Wilson decided that this too was a positive factor (he was a business executive, and he formed his thoughts in phrases like "a positive factor"). Most of the people were French, and he enjoyed the way the French behaved at the seashore.

They believed, for one thing, that modesty should not get in the way of a good tan. The women arrived in exiguous bikinis, cleared the straps away from their backs as soon as they lay down, and, as often as not, left their tops behind when they rolled over. Wilson's eye rested gratefully on the four teenagers in front of him, spread-eagled in a row like paper dolls, breasts bared to the midday sun.

The sun *was* fierce. Wilson dug into his beach bag for the cocoa butter and rubbed a palmful on his bald head. He did not want to go home to Connecticut with a scalp that was bright pink and peeling; he did not want to be asked any questions about this trip at all.

Unpleasant thoughts, and he steered away from them. The other amusing trait of the French was that they did not swim. There were dozens of people dabbling in the shallows—and giving cries of Gallic alarm whenever a languid Caribbean wave lapped higher than their waists. Only one man had ventured into the deep, and he had gone equipped with a styrofoam chair. Wilson stared hard at this diminutive figure, reposing in his throne just beyond the pull of the waves. He made a comic sight, but Wilson was not smiling.

The man raised his straw hat from his head, and Wilson's eyes left him to scan the beach. Thirty feet off to the right, a young man in white trunks stood up and strolled unhurriedly down to the water. Very nice, thought Wilson, very inconspicuous. Unless you knew what was going on, as he did, you would never have thought the young man was responding to a signal.

The man trudged through the shallows, dove into a gathering wave, and swam out to the man in the float. He trod water beside him for a minute or so, and then swam off. It was some time before he appeared again, wading back to shore far down the beach. Wilson studied him as he walked back to his place: Hadn't they met at a convention in Atlanta? He was too far away to be sure, and Wilson knew that if he approached the man, the proceedings could be canceled.

The man in the float took off his glasses and put

them on again. This time it was a woman in a sleek tank suit who rose and meandered down to the water.

Wilson reclined, propping himself on an elbow. Inconspicuous, but also time-consuming. Already he was losing a grip on his good mood, beginning to feel apprehensive. He wondered how long he would have to wait.

As it turned out, not very long. After the woman, another man went out, and then the man in the chair raised his arms above his head, as if stretching: the signal Wilson had been told to watch for.

He got up and padded down to the slick wet sand. A warm wave ran in and engulfed his feet. He dodged around a circle of children who were splashing each other furiously and shouting insults on the order of "*Salaud!*" and "*Tu m'enerves!*" The beach shelved quickly; in a few steps he was up to his waist. The water rose up in a long blue ridge, curled, and broke over his chest. He realized then why they had chosen this elaborate procedure: It was a precaution against listening devices. Wilson and the others could not possibly be wired themselves, and the noise of the surf and the crowds would play havoc with shotgun mikes.

He swam the last few yards and pulled up, treading water. "Hi, how are ya," he said genially. "I'm Jack Wilson."

The man in the chair sat with his arms folded across his pale, hairy chest. He wore thick bifocals and a neat white moustache. "Shall we call me Lisle?" he suggested.

"OK. Hey, you picked a beautiful spot."

"Neutral ground," the man replied, matter-of-factly. "The bid stands at three fifty."

Wilson's mouth dropped open and he swallowed salt water. "Three fifty!" he exclaimed, gagging. "You mean three hundred and fifty thousand?"

"Correct."

"U.S. dollars?"

"Correct. Come, come, monsieur. You are overdoing it. You know that the bidding will go far higher than that. The item—"

"Let's see the item."

"The vendor has custody of it, as usual."

"Then how do you know he's got the real thing?"

The man took from his watery lap a sheet enclosed in clear plastic, like the menu of a cheap coffee shop. Wilson snatched it and glanced over the half-dozen typed lines. The excerpts were well-chosen—tantalizing, meaningless in themselves. Meaningless to the other bidders, that is; Wilson knew them well enough, and he closed his eyes. The unacknowledged hope that he had carried with him—that they did not really have the goods—died. His spirits sank, and he nearly sank with them. It was not easy treading water with one hand.

"Yes," he said, thrusting the paper back at the auctioneer. "It's mine."

"I beg your pardon?"

"Oh, come on. You know who I am. The president of Atlantic Brands. I'm the cull—the guy this was ripped off from."

"Well, then," said the little man, imperturbably, "you should know what it is worth."

"Pretty rough—asking a guy to pay three fifty for something that was his in the first place."

"One might say just as well that it is decent of us to give you the chance to redeem what you have so carelessly lost."

"Three seven-five," said Wilson, biting off the words. He turned and plunged under water.

Following orders, he swam parallel to shore for a few minutes, turning in far down the beach. As his feet touched bottom he looked back. A man—the first bidder—was already on his way out to the auctioneer. Hoping that they would both drown, Wilson trudged back to his place.

As Lisle had guessed, most of Wilson's outrage was sheer bluster. He was an old hand at industrial espionage—or competitive business intelligence, to give it its newer and blander name. Only occasionally did he experience ethical problems with what he was doing, and he dealt with these by reciting the justifications that there were no black-and-white issues, and he had never done anything that others had not done to him first.

You slipped into it gradually. The first step was simply to invite your competitors' admen or market researchers out for a few drinks and a little shoptalk. Occasionally, these people were so bright that you hired them away. Then you set up a "research department" with files on competitors and potential target companies. Nothing illegal about that; all the information in these files came from annual reports and business magazines. At first, anyway. Then you would hear that your security chief, the man in charge of defending your own trade secrets, wanted to "go offensive." Once he knew how to beat them, he knew enough to join them. Sooner or later you would be contacted by a professional syndicate notifying you of an auction. Well, the item had already been stolen; it was *going* to be sold—if not to you, then to one of your competitors.

So Wilson had been to meetings like this one before. But it had never been his secrets that were on the block before.

For the next half-hour he gloomily watched the auction take its slow course. His only comfort was to see the man before him return to pick up his things and set off toward the bluffs. One down. Without waiting for the signal, Wilson strode across the sand and plunged in the water.

"Half a million even."

"Too high. Too damned high."

"Of course, you know best," said Lisle, with heavy irony.

"And twenty-five thousand," Wilson snapped.

The auctioneer looked down at him. The watery blue eyes were eerily magnified by his glasses. "Such a bid is really not worth swimming out here for."

"Twenty-five," Wilson repeated, knowing full well that the man was right. Ignoring instructions, he swam straight back to shore. He waded through the frolicking, laughing crowd with his head down and his hands clenched. They did not amuse him anymore.

His position, he saw with sickening clarity, was the businessman's nightmare: He *had* to have what they were selling; there was not an inch of bargaining room. "The item" was the marketing portfolio on his newest product line: Dunbar's ports and sherries. Whoever bought it would get not only the raw data —market research that had cost him tens of thousands of dollars—but also his conclusions, his own marketing philosophy, which he considered priceless. They could steal his advertising themes, reposition their own brands, and rework their distribution, so

that when he launched his campaign, they would
cut him to ribbons. It would cost Atlantic Brands
millions. It would cost Wilson his career.

Sooner or later, the truth would come out: that
he had let the most highly classified material imag-
inable get away from him. "First-rate manager, Jack,
but soft on security. And when a guy's soft on security, nothing else matters." That would be the
epitaph on Jack Wilson, once the fastest-rising man
in RGI.

He had to have what they were selling.

When his turn came round, he jogged out and
dove into the water, thrashed through the waves, and
surfaced beside the auctioneer.

"What's the bid?"

"Another big jump. I think the bidders are getting sunburnt," said Lisle, gazing down at his hir-
sute belly. "Six seven-five."

"Eight hundred thousand," said Wilson. His instincts told him that there was no point in being
cautious, allowing the bidding to rise steadily upward. He must crush the others, leave them behind
in one long bound. It was typical of Wilson that he
did not give a thought to how he was going to get
eight hundred thousand dollars together. The question was irrelevant just now. He had to win the auction; that was all.

The little man nodded. "A handsome bid, monsieur. It promises well."

Wilson turned and swam away.

For the next quarter of an hour he paced anxiously,
splashing through the froth of expiring waves. He
did not notice if any of the vacationers cavorting
around him remarked on his behavior; he was en-

tirely oblivious to them. He stared intently at the
man in white trunks as he emerged from the water,
tried to gauge from his stride or the set of his head
if he was beaten. The man quickly put an end to
his suspense; he picked up his towel and walked
away. Wilson's heart was thudding wildly as the girl
went out, conferred with the auctioneer, swam in—
and then she too gathered up her things and set off
down the beach. Wilson had won.

By the time Lisle waded in, clumsily dragging the
float behind him, Wilson was his genial self once
again. He even helpd Lisle shoulder his burden, and
they set off companionably down the beach.

"Congratulations, monsieur."

"Thanks. How about the payment?"

"Oh, you will be contacted about that later," said
Lisle unconcernedly. "You will not be put to further
inconvenience; you need only pay the amount into
an account number which we will give you."

"In a Swiss bank, natch," said Wilson.

The auctioneer nodded. "Once we hear from the
bank, we shall see that the item is delivered to you.
Of course, if you prefer, we can work out an arrangement under which you pay half the amount and receive the item before paying the second half—"

They had laid down no deadlines or ultimatums,
and Wilson decided to return the compliment. "That
won't be necessary."

"Good. Now if you will excuse me—"

Wilson stretched out a hand. The little man looked
at it in surprise, then took it. "Well, sir, I can't exactly say it's been a pleasure doing business with you.
But I feel a lot better than if you'd done business
with somebody else."

Lisle released his hand with a precise little bow; Wilson looked down to see that he was clicking—or rather thudding—his bare heels. Then he turned and walked away, carefully sidestepping the clumps of seaweed that the waves had brought in.

"Have a nice day," Wilson called after him. His pleasant manner was not a pretense; he felt no animosity toward Lisle or his organization. They were only the brokers in this transaction. Wilson's money, after they had deducted their commission, would go to the vendor—the little sneak who had stolen the marketing portfolio from him.

Characteristically, Wilson was still not giving any thought to how he would get eight hundred thousand dollars together, quickly and in secret. He was thinking about a counterattack. He had his suspicions about who had shopped him, and he meant to make sure.

Most executives, put in Wilson's position, would have reflected that in business spying the victim stood to lose more from exposure than the thief. They would have done nothing—certainly not until they had the secrets back again. But most executives were not Jack Wilson.

He strode back to the place where he had laid his towel, thinking. He could not risk going to his own security chief, of course. He would have to bring in somebody from outside—somebody who would conduct inquiries with utmost discretion.

The thought brought him up short. His mind was stocked with advertising slogans, and he knew that he had just stumbled on one.

He knelt beside his beach bag and rummaged through it. RGI deluged its affiliate heads with reports, newsletters, and circulars, and Wilson read them all religiously. He found what he was looking for at the bottom of the bag: a glossy little leaflet laid out like a travel agency brochure. The cover was taken up with a color photograph of a girl—a pretty blonde in a tailored suit. She was sitting at a desk studying a file intently and looking fearfully bright and competent.

Under the photo was a line of type: *Inquiries, Incorporated, One of the RGI Family of Service Companies. Our Byword Is Discretion.*

Wilson leafed through the glossy pages, glancing at the pictures of banks of computers, of a shooting range with somebody blazing away at a cardboard cutout, of a young man, just as sleek-looking as the girl, wearing earphones and writing on a legal pad. Inquiries, Inc., was the last word in "security specialists." Wilson reached the last paragraph, the one that had stuck in his mind:

To contact INQinc, establish a post office box, and then call our office at RGI Plaza, Greenwich. You will be sent a brief form. Fill it out and return it. Availability and suitability factors will be assessed by computer on the basis of your answers, and a member of our investigative staff will be dispatched to serve you. *Only* this person will know the nature of the case and your identity. Our byword is Discretion.

Ross Welch, Jr.
President

It sounded perfect. Wilson tucked the leaflet away

and lay back. Now, at last, he turned his attention to the little problem of the eight hundred grand.

The solution that eventually came to him might have been called "embezzlement." But, after all, it was for the good of the company.

Chapter 2

At Inquiries, Inc., it was so quiet that one could hear the Muzak— a sprightly, insipid drizzle from unseen speakers. Not a sound issued from behind the heavy wooden door of the president's office. In the reception area, Ms. Wexler was pivoting her chair slowly back and forth and reading *Cosmopolitan*. She had no telephone calls to answer, no letters to type. The hall that led past the offices of the investigative staff was silent and empty. In fact, only two members of the staff were in just now: the Number Two man and the Number Five person. They were in his office, where the Number Two man was nibbling on the Number Five person's earlobe.

"I just dropped by to borrow an eraser, actually."

Sarah Saber had a low, husky voice that, Chris Rockwell knew from long experience, became huskier still when she was in an amorous mood. "A likely story. Come into my den of iniquity."

She chuckled at this unlikely description of his little cubicle. He drew her around the Formica desk, gently pushed her into the plastic chair, and seated himself on its arm. The chair creaked and teetered.

"You'll have us both on the floor in a minute."

"My plan precisely." He kissed the crown of her head, laid his cheek against the thick, resilient cushion of her hair. "I love your hair," he whispered. "It's the color of . . . of . . ."

"Molten gold? Honey?"

"No, beer. German beer. Beck's, to be exact."

"Oh, Chris. That's the sweetest thing you've ever said to me."

"I've only begun. Now on to your skin." He kissed her forehead, her eyelids, the tip of her nose. Her lips parted, but he teasingly skipped them and began to nuzzle her throat. Her head sank back and she put her feet up on the desk. She was beginning to get comfortable. Very comfortable.

"Your skin is . . . perfect. Down to the last pore."

"Not so," she protested languidly.

"Don't contradict me, my love. I've been patiently searching every inch of the surface of your body for months now, and I have yet to find a mole, a scar, a freckle—" He ran his palm over the soft fabric of her blouse, over the shoulder and breast beneath.

"I have too . . ."

"Mmm?"

". . . got scars."

"Mmm."

"Vaccination marks on my arm . . . an old burn on my thigh . . ."

"Really?" Chris reached down and took hold of the hem of her skirt, gently drew it upward. Her legs were long and slender, with only a dimple halfway down to hint at the presence of a kneecap. "Where on the thigh?"

"Further up . . . Chris?"

"Hmm?"

"We're in your *office*, for heaven's sake." She gently but firmly removed his hand and brushed her skirt down.

"Let's go home early."

"We can't. We're supposed to be available for assignment."

Chris shrugged equably. "OK. Let's quit."

As if in protest, the intercom snarled. Reluctantly, Chris leaned across the desk and depressed the key. "Yeah?"

"Mr. Rockwell, Mr. Welch wants to see you in his office immediately," said the voice of Ms. Wexler.

"OK." But Chris had no sooner stood up than the intercom buzzed again. "What else?"

"Miss Saber, he'll be wanting to see you next."

Chris's finger jumped off the key as if it had suddenly become hot. He glanced nervously at Sarah. "Uh-oh."

"She has wonderfully sharp ears, Ms. Wexler." Sarah folded her arms and sat back. "Let's not give her the satisfaction of going out there together, at least."

Chris nodded and went out, straightening his tie. As he passed the reception desk, Ms. Wexler gave him a triumphant smirk. She was as sleekly turned out as ever, in a purple Qiana top the exact color of her eye shadow. "Go right in, Mr. Rockwell."

Chris glared at her and went through the door. Welch was standing with his back to him, looking out the window. His broad desk was bare but for two green-and-white strips of printout. Beside the desk stood a Securitco guard, in his natty black uniform, with a couple of manila envelopes under his arm.

Chris recognized the scene: He was going to receive an assignment. Not a pleasant prospect, but certainly more palatable than a warning not to fool around with Sarah during office hours. He advanced to the desk and waited.

Ross Welch let him wait. He stared out at the gently rolling hillside, littered with dead leaves and patches of dirty snow, which in summertime was one

of the fairways of the RGI golf course, and grasped
at the remnants of his good mood. He had been
delighted when the word arrived that two assignments
had come in. They were the first that day, and the
printouts bore the stars that designated them in-house
jobs. Mr. Welch coveted such assignments; he wanted
the fame of his agency to spread far and wide through
the RGI Family of Service Companies.

But then he had gone to Ms. Wexler, who kept
track of the staff. (The line in the brochure "availability and suitability factors are assessed by computer" was merely an impressive-sounding fabrica-
tion.) She had told him that only Rockwell and
Saber were in—and where Rockwell and Saber were
at the moment.

Welch pivoted slowly on his heel and gloomily surveyed Christopher K. Rockwell. Somehow or other,
Rockwell got results—he was the Number Two man
on the staff, after all—but from a corporate-image
point of view he was hopeless. He looked as if he
had just stepped out of the faculty room of a minor
prep school where he taught history and coached the
second-string basketball team. Rockwell was a big
man—just over six feet, just under two hundred
pounds—with a broad, bearded face and sleepy green
eyes behind horn-rimmed glasses. He was wearing a
tweed jacket that sagged under the weight of the
books in his hip pockets. The lapels were narrow,
in the latest fashion. It had also been the fashion
in the mid-sixties, when Rockwell had bought the
garment.

Welch sighed and dropped his gaze to the printout.
Some RGI executive had sent to him for a crack
security specialist, and Welch was sending him . . .
Rockwell.

"What would you say to a Special Assignment, Rockwell?"

"No, thanks."

"That's what I thought you'd say." Welch grinned to himself and flicked one of the printouts across the desk, the one that began SA 353. "Well, you've got one."

"Aw, Mr. Welch, the last SA I took I ended up spending two weeks in—"

Welch threw up his hands like a traffic cop, ordering Chris to halt. "You're not supposed to tell me *where* you were! All I am ever to know about any assignment is right here." He tapped the printout. "Which is: one person required, time frame five to seven days, operations area abroad. In-house job."

Chris glanced morosely over the line of numbers and abbreviations from which Welch had culled this information. Then he lugubriously extracted his hands from his trouser pockets and turned to the Securitco man, who smartly proffered the clipboard for Chris to sign. He scrawled his name and took the envelope, the familiar envelope sealed with a blob of blue wax and stamped "INQinc: Our byword is Discretion."

"Goodbye, Rockwell."

"So long, Mr. Welch."

As Rockwell went out and Sarah Saber came in, Mr. Welch's spirits rose. For here was his corporate image incarnate. Sarah was rather conservatively dressed, as usual, in a charcoal gray pleated skirt and white blouse. Her long blond hair was loosely gathered at the nape of her neck and bound in a pink-and-gray scarf. She wore no makeup, because her natural coloring could not be improved upon. What he liked most about her was her way of canting her head and looking at him down her long, straight nose. She looked cool, confident, sexy. She had class.

"Good afternoon, Sarah. We've got an assignment for you."

"OK." Without even glancing at the printout, she turned to the guard and took charge of the envelope. Mr. Welch dismissed him and watched him out the door. Then he came round the desk to take Sarah's elbow and lead her over to the little cluster of arm-chairs he called the "conference area."

"Like some coffee?"

"No, thanks." Sarah could see a heart-to-heart talk coming, and she made a feeble attempt to dodge it. "Shouldn't I be getting to the client's?"

"In a moment." Welch sat down and leaned for-ward, propping his elbows on his knees. The eyes behind his big steel-framed glasses were downcast, the broad forehead furrowed like a field in spring-time. "Sarah, John Morris and I played racquet ball the other day."

She nodded and said nothing. She knew that Welch wanted to talk about her "relationship" with Chris and waited patiently to see what bearing his game with the president of Securitco would have on it.

"He told me Inquiries was experiencing the high-est level of earnings growth of any division of Se-curitco. And the feedback he's getting indicates that the Discretion policy is our strongest selling point."

"Yes, Mr. Welch."

"Now, you know that it is the policy of all the RGI companies not to interfere in employees' per-sonal lives. But here at Inquiries, because of the Dis-cretion policy, intrapersonnel fraternization can be-come a problem."

"Yes, Mr. Welch."

Welch took a deep breath and arrived at the point in one long bound. "I haven't said anything about you and Rockwell, because I'm confident that one day soon you'll snap out of it. Still, I've got to ask you: When you two are working separate assignments, do you ever talk about your cases?"

She shook her head. "You're doing Chris an injustice, Mr. Welch. He never wants to talk about his cases." This was quite true, for Chris was so bored with the work that he could hardly bring himself to do the assignments, much less discuss them. She, on the other hand, was continually asking *his* advice, but there was no need to tell Welch so.

He shrugged and said, "Well, in any case, the problem won't arise at this point."

"Oh?"

"Your printout reads ar01—you'll be working right here in the tri-state area." Welch paused and glanced about the office, as if checking that Josh Morris was not in earshot. "And this much I'll tell you: Rockwell's assignment is ar07. Overseas."

Sarah could not help laughing. "You gave Chris a Special Assignment? How'd he take it?"

"Rockwell has serious attitude problems," Welch replied somberly. He got to his feet. "Well, I guess that's all. Good luck, Sarah."

"Thanks, Mr. Welch." She rose and tucked the envelope under her arm. As she opened the door, she saw Rockwell crossing the reception area, pulling on his down jacket.

"Bye-bye, Chris," she said, loudly enough for Welch to hear.

Chris gave her a quick, sly glance. Then he made an exaggerated wave, like a politician in a motorcade, and went out the door.

Chapter 3

Breaking the seal of his envelope, Chris had expected to find an airline ticket to some distant and dreary city. But there was only a note, asking him to come to Atlantic Brands, Inc., in Stamford, for a three o'clock appointment with John B. Wilson. The note was so wretchedly typed that Chris assumed Wilson had done it himself; most execs did not want even their own secretaries to know that they were dealing with Inquiries, Inc.

Atlantic's "design philosophy"—as the RGI jargon had it—represented quite a change from the sleek, chilly decor of Inkwink. Arising from the parking level in a glass-walled elevator, Chris looked out upon an atrium, furnished with a rock garden, a goldfish-speckled pool, and a waterfall.

The decor of the president's office, into which he was shown with the promise that Mr. Wilson would join him in a moment, was just as exuberant: blue walls, mustard-colored carpeting, and a huge desk trimmed in stainless steel.

Chris was just pulling a book out of his jacket pocket when Wilson appeared at the door. From his bald pate and lined face Chris guessed that he was in his mid-forties, but somehow he seemed younger. Perhaps it was the spring in his step and the grin like a good-natured boy's, uncertain, eager to please. He was wearing tan trousers and vest—no coat—and a strident yellow shirt with the sleeves rolled up to his elbows. He had the best suntan Chris had seen since last September.

"Hi, how are ya. I'm Jack Wilson."

"Chris Rockwell."

Wilson repeated Chris's name as he firmly shook his hand. It was the flattering trick of the salesman and the politician; Chris guessed that the man never forgot a name.

"Well. Care to join me for a little R and D?"

"Sorry?"

"Research and development. Let's go to the lab." He took Chris's elbow and led him to an alcove off the main office. It was a bar, the shelves lined with rows of tiny bottles.

"Our line," said Wilson with a sweeping gesture. "We import a full range of premixed cocktails, and import various wines."

"Oh," said Chris.

"This is our newest," Wilson went on, picking up a bottle and giving it a shake. "We call it 'Hooligan's Brew.' It'll be on the market as soon as the posters and T-shirts are ready."

"No thanks. It sounds kind of teeny-bopperish to me."

"Exactly. It's targeted for the eighteen to twenty-five age group. That's the fastest-growing segment of the market." He unscrewed the cap and poured frothy orange liquid into a glass. "See anything else you'd like?"

Chris scanned the shelf. Among the midgets there was one regular-sized bottle. It had an ornate label. The words "Upton Lawrence & Dunbar," "Select," and "Fino" emerged from a profusion of scrollwork and coats of arms.

"Ah. I'll have some of that Dunbar's, thanks."

Wilson handed the bottle to him. "You familiar with this brand?"

"Whenever I can afford to be."

Wilson nodded, beaming. "At this point in time, it's an appropriate choice."

"Oh?"

But Wilson did not explain immediately. He went over to a console in the corner and turned on the radio, then fiddled with the dial until he got a news show. He turned it up so loud that Chris could hardly pick his words out from the announcer's.

"We'll just listen as we talk, shall we? Find out what's going on in the world."

Chris poured himself a sherry.

"Say, Mr. Wilson—"

"Call me Jack, please, Chris."

"Say, Jack, if you think your office is bugged, how come you don't have Securitco down to run a sweep?"

Wilson's smile did not falter. "Very perceptive, Chris. I can see I've got a good man working for me. You're right, of course. This is a little precaution of mine whenever I'm holding an especially confidential meeting."

"Why don't you have the place swept?" Chris repeated.

"I do, but I don't trust the guys who run the sweep either."

Chris shrugged. Not for the first time he reflected that the RGI exec's mentality was not one he understood, or would care to. "OK, Jack. What's the job you want me to do?"

Wilson took possession of his elbow again and led him over to a couple of chairs on either side of the radio console. They sat down and leaned close, so that they could hear one another.

"Upton Lawrence and Dunbar—well, I don't have to tell you that it's a prestige name, a wonderful old firm. We've had the good fortune to acquire it recently. I want you to go there—"

"Where are they?"

"London, of course."

Chris nodded; the job was beginning to look better. His last SA had been in Detroit.

"I want you to check out one of their employees. She's an American, as a matter of fact, named Brenda Wertheim."

Chris nodded and got out a notebook.

"Uh—do you really have to write that down?" said Wilson.

Chris closed the notebook and put it away. "OK. I'll remember. Brenda Wertheim. What do you want to know about her?"

Wilson leaned back in his chair and crossed his legs. He made an offhand gesture. "Just check her out. I don't have to familiarize a pro like yourself with the procedures."

Chris stared moodily into his sherry. "If you've just acquired this company, Securitco will have a team there running screenings on everybody in the place."

"They do, and you're not to get anywhere near them. This is strictly between you and me."

Chris drained the glass and set it down. "Listen, Jack, I work a lot better when I know what the job is, OK?"

Still smiling, Wilson looked at him in silence for a long moment. At last he said, "OK, Chris." Leaning forward he went on. "It's a sad thing to say, but employee loyalty is a thing of the past. You can't just *trust* your people anymore. That's a lesson it's cost the managerial community millions of dollars to learn. If you've got a person who's experiencing financial difficulties, or a hostile person, or just a lax one, you'd better find out about it. Or somebody else will. You hearing me, Chris?"

"Uh-huh," said Chris wearily. "It's a Cobi job." This word, which sounded like the name of a cuddly Australian marsupial, was actually an acronym for competitive business intelligence. Chris had worked in the field more often than he cared to remember, and he automatically lapsed into the slang. "If this woman's a tap, or a potential turn, Securitco will find out about it. I wouldn't worry if I were you."

Wilson was shaking his head with mixed annoyance and amusement. "Say, what's with you? Trying to talk yourself out of a job? The fact is, I think we've gone beyond the 'potential' stage."

"Oh? Tell me more."

But Wilson clearly had not meant to tell him this much. The smile he had been wearing all along vanished abruptly. "For God's sake, Chris, do I have to lead you by the hand? I mean, if I knew everything I wouldn't need you. Just check out Wertheim, OK?"

Chris slowly got to his feet. He disliked nearly, everything about working for Inkwink, but most of all he disliked moments like this one, when he saw just how little his clients trusted him. If he wanted to know any more about Jack Wilson's case, he would have to find out for himself.

"OK. How do you want me to report? Am I allowed to write anything down?"

Wilson bounded out of his chair, smiling once more, and guided Chris toward the door. "No need. You'll report in person. I'll be arriving in England myself at the end of the week, for the Mid-Winter Conference."

"All right."

At the door, he grasped Chris's hand in both of his own and shook it. "Good luck, Chris, and I assure you I'll value your input. Of course, I don't have to remind you that this is a delicate matter, requiring—"

Chris recognized the beginning of a spiel he heard from every client. He cut Wilson off. "Yeah. I'd better get going if I want to catch a flight this evening."

"Have a nice trip," said Wilson, releasing him at last.

Chapter 4

Sarah had returned to her own cubicle and shut the door before opening the envelope. As usual, she nearly had to rip it to shreds to break the seal. Inside there was a single sheet of paper bearing the handwritten message: "Be waiting to left of doors in WHQ, at 2:30." This client carried Discretion even further than Mr. Welch; there was no signature.

She put on her raincoat and went out into the raw, drizzly afternoon. Flagging down one of the golf carts that ferried people across the vast parking lots, she asked the driver to take her to WHQ.

World Headquarters was a six-story block of steel and reflective glass, just like the building she worked in. Or so it seemed, until one entered the high-ceilinged lobby. Draped above the bank of elevators was an enormous banner, bearing the initials RGI in white roman capitals on a scarlet background. This was the prototype for a logo familiar throughout four continents; the research and design had cost RGI tens of thousands of dollars. Sarah paused beneath it to reflect, as did every employee below executive rank, that, given a scratch pad and crayons, she could have come up with the same result in about five minutes.

She showed her identification at the security console, a bank of television monitors watched over by half a dozen blackclad guards with holsters on their belts, and went to take a seat to the left of the doors.

Two-thirty came and went, and her client did not appear. She lit a cigarette and took the *Journal of*

Commerce out of her purse. She was reading the commodities market report when the squeak of tires made her look up.

A midnight-blue Cadillac had stopped at the curb. The doors opened and a trio of men scrambled out. They entered the lobby in a tight cluster, then broke like a football team at the snap: one for the security console, one for the elevators, and one for Sarah.

"You Mrs. Webb's two-thirty?"

"Well, I guess so."

"Come on."

He led her outside, where a woman was clambering slowly from the depths of the limousine's backseat. She was stout and middle-aged, with hard little eyes set in a pasty face like chocolate chips in cookie dough.

"Your two-thirty, Mrs. Webb," said the gofer, and left them.

"Sarah Saber, from Inkwink," Sarah supplied.

"I know where you're from," said the woman, shaking hands. Her voice had a harsh, metallic quality, as if one were hearing it over the telephone. "Well, my dear," she went on, "things are *chaotic* just now. It used to be you could count on some slack after the holidays, but not anymore. I got a call from my boss at six A.M., and I've been on the run ever since. Now I've got to get to Richmond in time for a meeting at one of the affiliates. And then tonight . . ."

Sarah nodded as Mrs. Webb continued to detail her evening's tasks. She was one of those people—so often to be met with in RGI—who tell you how tired and busy they are so as to convince you that they're very important people indeed. Sarah was convinced; she added up the limousine, the cadre of brusque aides, and the reverent tone in which the

woman said "my boss," and concluded that Mrs.
Webb was executive assistant to a very exalted per-
sonage. At last she interrupted to ask, "Who is your
boss?"

"Oh, it's Mr. Holman. Hal Holman, the VP (L) ."

These initials stood for Vice-President in charge of
the Leisure Group. He oversaw affiliates ranging from
sporting goods manufacturers to publishers, and reported directly to the CEO himself. Big stuff, thought
Sarah, and she asked what the VP (L) wanted her
to do.

"We'll talk about that on the plane."

"On the plane?"

Mrs. Webb heaved a weary sigh. "I told you I've
got to get to Richmond PDQ. Don't worry, we'll
have you back by dinner time."

The aides came sprinting back, and they all piled
into the car. During the short drive Sarah perched
on a jump seat and listened to the others discuss poli-
cies and regulations. Mrs. Webb did not introduce
Sarah or even speak to her. Sarah was used to this;
it went with the job.

At the airport the car swept round the terminal
building and onto the field, to stop beside a Learjet
trimmed with scarlet RGI markings.

The private jet, designed to carry a few people in
the utmost comfort, represented quite a change from
a commercial airliner. The narrow cabin was hand-
somely decorated and contained desks of real wood
and a scatter of comfortable armchairs.

Mrs. Webb seated Sarah at the back, as far as possible from her entourage, and told the pilot they
were ready to go. The whirr of the engines outside
Sarah's window mounted to a roar, and the raindrops
on the plexiglass veered crazily as they taxied and

took off—straight up, it seemed—into the overcast sky.

They were still climbing when she looked up to see Mrs. Webb making her way gingerly back to her. She leaned forward to glance at the *Journal* in Sarah's lap before lowering herself into the opposite seat.

"Commodities, Miss Saber?"

"Wheat futures."

"Long or short?"

"I'm going long."

"Are you in deep?"

"No. I've got the nerve, but not the money."

"Hell, in commodities, a few lucky breaks and you can retire early."

"That's the general idea."

She nodded. "Saber . . . any relation to James Saber, of International Harvester?"

"Daughter."

"Is that so?" Mrs. Webb looked her over with her beady eyes. "I've heard about Mr. Welch's concept—investigators with a solid business background, and I think it's a splendid idea. In fact, we wouldn't entrust this job to anyone else." She leaned over to a little refrigerator tucked against the wall and swung the door open to reveal shelves full of premixed cocktails.

"I'll have a Bloody Mary, thanks," said Sarah.

Mrs. Webb laughed, as if Sarah had meant this as a joke. She waved a hand over the bottles, without picking any up. "This is the product line of the company you'll be dealing with: Atlantic Brands, up in Stamford." She shut the door and leaned back to take a piece of paper from the pocket of her jacket. "And here, my dear, is the problem."

The paper was obviously one carbon from a thick form. It was a request from Russell Rabinowitz, of the Atlantic Brands Data Center, to take his vacation, originally scheduled for this week, in February instead.

Sarah looked up with a shrug. "I'm afraid the problem isn't clear to me yet."

Mrs. Webb took out a pack of cigarettes and lit one before replying. "The problem is, it's RGI policy for all data center personnel to take regularly scheduled vacations."

"Afraid they'll overwork themselves?"

Mrs. Webb laughed, and just as abruptly stopped laughing. "No," she said, "no, that's not the reason."

"Well, why then?"

They had broken through the cloud cover now, and sunlight gushed into the cabin. Mrs. Webb was silent a moment, peering at Sarah through a gray film of cigarette smoke.

"Now, there are perfectly valid reasons for keeping a programmer on at certain times," she continued. "Some of these damned programs are so complicated that anybody but the guy who wrote them would take weeks to figure them out. So naturally, the first time such a program is run, you want to have the programmer around. Understand?"

This was not the answer to the question Sarah had asked. But she got the distinct impression that it was all Mrs. Webb cared to tell her at the moment. She nodded and waited for her to continue.

"That's the reason Rabinowitz gives, as you can see: One of his programs is being run this week. He got the right permission too—and now we come to the really hellish part of the problem."

Sarah glanced at the signature on the form, a scrawl in which she could not distinguish a letter of the name typed below: John B. Wilson, president.

"You've heard of him?"

"Sure. They're always telling about his doings in the company newsletter, and I think I saw him on the cover of the annual report, chatting with some biggies in front of WHQ."

Mrs. Webb crushed out her cigarette. "Yes. Wilson is one of RGI's most promising people, and Mr. Holman doesn't want any friction with him, especially now, with the Mid-Winter Conference just around the corner."

Sarah had caught on by now; she had an inborn knack for corporate intrigue. "So what you want me to do is go up to Atlantic and verify that Rabinowitz really is running a program this week, without letting Wilson find out about it."

Mrs. Webb nodded.

"Because, if Wilson hasn't broken an RGI reg, you don't want him to know that you ever thought he did break it."

Mrs. Webb gave her another appraising look. "Exactly, my dear. I think you'll do. Rabinowitz works the four-to-midnight shift, by the way, so you should be able to wrap this up tonight—or tomorrow at the latest."

"Oh," said Sarah. She thought it rather odd that there should be so much urgency about a minor transgression of the regs. "Will I be reporting to Mr. Holman?"

"Oh, *he* hasn't got time for this," Mrs. Webb replied loftily, as if she had guessed what Sarah was thinking and wished to squelch any notion Sarah might be harboring about her own importance. "Now if you'll excuse me, I've got to go over some things with my people."

As she got up, Sarah took one more shot at it.

"Suppose I find out he isn't running a program? What does that mean?"

"We'll cross that bridge when we come to it," Mrs. Webb replied blandly, and then made her way to the front of the cabin. A moment later one of the aides came back to kneel beside Sarah's chair and tell her that they had made reservations for her on a five o'clock flight back to LaGuardia. First class, of course.

Chapter 5

Sarah's apartment was on Central Park South and commanded a fine view of the park. These virtues aside, there was little to be said for it; she suffered an appalling rent, indifferent management, and claustrophobia. As Chris Rockwell put it, he had been in phone booths that were more spacious than her bedroom.

He had said this last week, while she was trying to lure him down from his ramshackle farmhouse upstate to spend a few days with her. Chris had consented cautiously; the two had "conflicting life styles," as the cant phrase had it, and they both feared the arguments that could flare up between them.

But the visit had gone well. They enjoyed the commute: fighting their way through the throngs at Grand Central to settle on a nearly empty train bound for the suburbs and divide the *Wall Street Journal* between them—the wry, eccentric front-page stories for Chris, the market reports for Sarah. They enjoyed the nights, too.

The nights were much on her mind when she got home from the airport. Chris's things—he had arrived for a one-week stay with a change of shirt, a toothbrush, and ten pounds of books—were still there, and she hoped that he would be returning before he set off on his SA. She had no intention of going up to Atlantic Brands before she had laid some groundwork, and she waited in the apartment all evening.

But Chris did not come, and for the first time in three nights Sarah had to take off her own clothes.

* * *

It was a wicked morning in Manhattan. The wind was whipping a freezing rain to and fro among the skyscrapers. Streams ran in the gutters and litter was plastered to the grimy sidewalks. Skeletons of wrecked umbrellas protruded from the trash cans. From the sides of buses the airline ads—bronzed couples cavorting in the blue-green waters of the Caribbean—beamed down upon the wretched pedestrians.

At the corner of Park and Fifty-ninth a huge, oily puddle had formed. Sarah leapt over it and gained the curb. She tilted her umbrella and peered down Fifty-ninth. Sure enough, an impeccably nondescript black Chevrolet was easing out of the traffic to pull over beside her. Bill Chandler, the Number One man on the investigative staff, was as punctual as ever.

She waited for an opening in the traffic and dashed round to get in the car. "Morning, Bill."

"Good morning." Bill Chandler was fifty and looked it, with a seamy face and grizzled crew-cut hair—one of the last crew cuts in existence. "How are you, Sarah? And how's Chris?"

"I'm fine, and Chris is—out of town."

Bill pulled out, serenely ignoring the protesting bleat of the cab behind him. "Oh, they stuck him with an SA, huh? Well, I wouldn't dream of asking where he is—not that you'd know, of course."

"Of course." In fact, Sarah did know; her morning mail had included a letter from Chris, mailed at Kennedy the night before. He must have been taking off from one airport even as she was landing at the other.

Dearest Sarah,
I'm in London, England, U.K. If your assign-

ment takes you there, or to anywhere else in the eastern hemisphere, get in touch RIGHT AWAY.

Love,
C.

P.S. I'll bring you back gin and woolens.

Sarah had smiled to receive this; poor Chris had not yet recovered from their misadventure in Rome last summer. She had burned the letter and felt very foolish as she did so: Was she paranoid enough to think that Mr. Welch had men going through her garbage? But she had burned it all the same.

"What can I do for you?" Bill asked.

"Well, I've got this weird assignment, and I want to ask you a few questions about it. I thought it would be more—uh—discreet if we talked in your car rather than the office."

Bill shrugged. "A real private eye's car *is* his office."

She smiled; in Bill's case this was certainly true. Hats and caps were strewn across the back seat. ("Alters your profile," Bill had once explained. "Essential for tail jobs.") Tracing inquiries were neatly stacked on the dashboard, sorted by neighborhood. ("I can knock off a dozen skips on the way to a job. Saves you time, saves your clients money.") She glanced in the foot well—there was Bill's wide-necked bottle. ("For long stakeouts when you can't—uh—leave the car.")

Bill had been the Number One man at the Bronson-Whitman Agency when Securitco had taken it over and changed its name to Inkwink, and, to Mr. Welch's unending consternation, he was still the Number One man. Welch considered him an antique as well as a blot on the corporate image and wanted to fire him, but Bill had foiled his plan by rapidly transforming himself into Inkwink's crack expert on computer fraud. Thus he was essential.

"Here's the case," said Sarah. "This biggie at WHQ is all worried that a programmer at one of his affiliates has put off his vacation. Why?"

"Ah. Well, the vacation thing is a precaution against embezzlement."

"Embezzlement? I don't understand."

"You know anything about computers, honey?"

Bill always called her "honey"; he was that old. "Nothing, I'm afraid."

"Well, the problem is . . . money is blips."

"Blips?"

"How can I make this clear to you. . . ." Thinking it over, Bill took out one of his vile plastic-tipped cigars. Sarah surreptitiously cracked a window. "You know how Securitco pays you?"

"No, but I like it because I don't have to pick up a paycheck and take it to the bank."

"Right. In the old days there was an accounting department full of clerks making out checks. Now there's a computer, and the computer cuts a tape, and the tape goes to the bank. On it your name, account number, and the amount of your pay is expressed in a magnetic pattern. At the bank this pattern is converted to electronic pulses that run through a bunch of circuits and get turned into another magnetic pattern on another reel of tape. You have been paid. Money is blips."

Sarah stared at him and fumbled with her cigarettes. Her salary was very dear to her heart, and this seemed a pretty casual way to treat it.

"They're doing away with the paper work so money

can be moved around faster and easier," Bill continued. "And that makes it easier to steal, honey."

She nodded and waited patiently for him to get back to the point.

"Now, EDP's booming, and all kinds of clever, crooked guys are getting into it. If one of these guys gets into your accounts payable system, he can bleed you dry without your ever finding out. The only way to catch him is if something goes wrong. Companies lose a fortune every year—the scary part is they don't even know how much. Fortunately, things do go wrong a lot. Computers are finicky critters, and anytime a system is run there's a danger that it will bomb. If the operator thinks that it failed because of a bug in the software, he'll start looking for the programmer who's responsible for the module that bombed. And if that guy's not around, then any programmer will do."

Sarah could not understand all of the jargon, but she had grasped the general idea. "So, if you're a programmer who's running a fraud you want to be around all the time, to prevent somebody else taking your program apart and finding what you're up to."

"You got it. That's why they make 'em take regular vacations. If they know they have to be away sometimes, they'll think twice about embezzling from the company." Bill paused for a moment. "Say, honey."

"Yes?"

"That's a company-wide RGI reg. If a DPer wants to switch his vacation around, he's got to have permission from the president of the affiliate."

"He does. The permission slip says that one of his programs is being run for the first time and he's essential right now."

"Uh-huh. Well, if that's true, everything's fine. But if it ain't true, and the president okayed the request without checking, the president's in trouble."

"And what if Rab—if the programmer made the request because he's running a fraud?"

"Then the president's in big trouble. You know RGI, honey."

Sarah sat back and lit a cigarette. So the stakes were a good deal higher than Mrs. Webb had let her know. She began to consider ways of getting into the Atlantic data center without anyone suspecting who she was.

"In other words, you're sort of a corporate secret agent, and what you need is a cover."

"That's about it, Uncle Andrew."

Uncle Andrew was Andrew Morley, a vice-president of Dial-Rose Public Relations, one of the RGI Family of Service Companies. It was he who had gotten Sarah the job with Securitco, and he followed her new career with amusement. Morley followed practically everything with amusement, in fact; he was a charming, clever man, with the streak of frivolous cynicism common to people in his line of work.

"I figured I'd say I was from the company newsletter, doing a feature on computer people," Sarah went on. "Couldn't you have one of your friends there call Atlantic and arrange for me to get in?"

"Oh, I could fix you up with them, but . . ." Morley frowned. "The newsletter—the idea lacks panache, don't you think?"

Sarah sat back, grinning. "OK, Uncle Andrew. Lay some panache on me."

"Let me think." Morley left his desk and slowly

traversed ten feet of Persian carpet to the window. Outside, the sleet had turned to snow. From seven floors below, one could hear the protesting horns of cars snarled in a jam on Madison Avenue. The snow kept on falling, though, as gently and indifferently as ever.

When Morley turned around he was smiling. He came back to his desk, rummaged among the papers, and found a press release. "On April 10," he read, "RGI Family Theater will present a new production of Dumas's classic tale *The Three Musketeers*."

"Wasn't there a movie of that just a couple of years back?"

"Nobody ever accused RGI of originality, dear. ITT just did *The Count of Monte Cristo* and IBM has *Les Misérables* in the works, so we've got to do *The Three Musketeers*. It's one of those zillion-dollar things, shot in Europe, with every titled English actor playing a bit part."

Sarah nodded and allowed her uncle to approach the point at his own deliberate pace.

"Now, they're making a whole bunch of commercials, in which somebody comes on and says, 'Hi, I'm Faceless Nonentity, a clerk-typist at the Nebbish Corporation, and I hope you're enjoying this presentation from the people at RGI. Now I want to tell you about one of the things we do to serve you.'"

"You writing these things, Uncle Andrew?"

"No, the Dernham-Mufflin Agency is guilty of handling the whole business. They're sending their people out to look the proles over and find some just-plain-folks types to do the spots. You, dear, could be one of their people. How do you like it?"

"I love it," said Sarah.

"Good. I'll call Mufflin and have them clear you with Atlantic Brands. You just talk about 'the right facial planes' and 'a good on-camera presence' and refer to your subjects as 'the talent.' That's what they call anybody who gets in front of the camera, despite evidence to the contrary. Oh, and remember to dress like a creative person. You'll find plenty of examples in our outer office."

"Great. Thanks, Uncle Andrew."

"Glad to help." He rose and came round his desk to see her to the door. "Say, how's your boyfriend?"

"Fine. He's out of town just now."

"You know, I've been studying Rockwell for a long time, and I've arrived at a deep admiration for him. He really and truly doesn't give a damn. He'd walk out of Inkwink tomorrow, if he could only be sure you'd go with him."

"Well, heck, Uncle Andrew. I'm an eighties woman. I'm liberated, assertive, and all that. I'm not going to give up a meaningful career for a man."

Morley laughed out loud. "Oh, come on. All you want to do is cash in on the commodities market, quit, and take up a life of leisure in— Where is it again?"

"I want to become a citizen of Monaco—a *Monegasque*. They don't pay any taxes, because the casino supports the government. I think it's a great system."

"Somehow I can't see Chris taking to a life of water-skiing and roulette."

Sarah nodded sadly. "Chris's goal in life is to join his uncle's aluminum siding business in Middletown, Connecticut. He says it's a great business because it's not very successful, and he could sit in the office all day reading. He wants to read the unabridged *Pamela* before he turns forty."

Morley seemed to think it all over. "You two are

a very odd pair. How did you ever happen to fall in love?"

Sarah thought that over for a moment. "Head over heels, Uncle Andrew," she replied.

Chapter 6

At nine that evening, Sarah stepped out of the elevator on the first floor of Atlantic Brands.

The offices that gave on the atrium were dark, and the waterfall had been turned off for the night. Even the goldfish in the pool seemed to be asleep. Sarah crossed a miniature Japanese bridge and passed into a corridor that ended in a pair of glass doors labeled "Data Center."

She approached the clearance desk and gave her name to the man behind it. "I'm from Dernham-Mufflin."

The man checked a list before him. "Oh, sure. Wait a sec and I'll get one of the programmers to take you in."

Sarah set down her heavy shoulder bag and took off her coat. She was cleverly disguised as a creative person, in a work shirt over a turtleneck, designer jeans that fit her bottom as the peel fits an apple, knit leggings, and boots.

She hung up the coat and turned to find that the guard was back at his desk and a young woman was standing before her, casting a curious glance over her outfit.

"Hi, I'm Jill Markworthy. I understand you want to see the data center."

"Not exactly. I want to see the people." She launched into an enthusiastic account of her bogus task. Miss Markworthy heard her out in silence. She was about Sarah's age, with short curly hair and an alert, quizzical expression.

"I see," she said when Sarah was finished. "Never a dull moment here in the RGI Family of Service Companies. Well, come on in."

They went past the offices of the directors of the data center, which were dark and empty, and then threaded their way through a warren of little cubicles, which were also empty.

"Where is everybody?" Sarah asked.

"Oh, the big honchos have gone home. So have the medium honchos. The rest of us are in here."

They turned into a long room, with row upon row of metal desks. There were a couple of dozen men and women at the desks, their fingers splayed over keyboards, their eyes fixed on boxes like black TV screens.

Sarah had been a clerk at her father's company one summer, and in an instant this place brought the stale taste of paper work back: the big, windowless room with its blank, brightly painted walls; the fluorescent strip lighting that drained the color from people's faces; the clatter of typewriters, the hum and shuffle of machinery—and everywhere stacks of paper, orders, invoices, printouts, waiting to be copied, sorted, filed.

"I guess this looks pretty dreary, compared to your office?" said Jill Markworthy.

It was disconcerting to have her thoughts read so exactly. "I'm sure it's—uh—interesting work. Do you like it, Miss Markworthy?"

"Not enough to gush about it on an RGI commercial." She gave Sarah a sideway glance, and Sarah smiled.

"OK. Could you point out some of the other programmers to me, then?" She looked vaguely about the room.

"Well, that's Tim Nerman leaning over that CRT on the left, Sue Tallert just walking up the aisle, and over there is Russ Rabinowitz—" She indicated a tall fellow sprawling indolently at a desk across the room.

"Oh, I'd like to meet him."

This brought her another dry look from Miss Markworthy. "You want Russell to represent RGI to the nation? Well, come on over."

"What's the matter with him, Miss Markworthy?"

"Nothing. He's a very friendly guy." Sarah was reflecting as they came up to Rabinowitz's desk that Miss Markworthy had a capacity for irony that she would not have expected in a computer programmer.

"Russ?"

He gracefully uncurled his legs from the base of the chair and stood up to regard Sarah with a lazy smile.

"This is Sarah Saber. She's with the people who are doing this TV special. . . ."

Sarah looked him over as Miss Markworthy explained. He seemed very well turned out for an evening at work: a three-piece jeans suit with an open-necked, iridescent gold shirt that even the flat lighting could not subdue. His pants were as tight as Sarah's around the hips, and flared smoothly over his boots. The clothes set off the body to advantage: tall, long-limbed, too supple to be called skinny. His light brown hair was rather long, and so soft and shiny that it must have been washed a few hours ago. It fell in bangs over eyes that were returning her own close scrutiny.

"So you're gonna make me a star, huh, Sarah? Aren't you guys supposed to have casting couches? If not, I can supply one."

He chuckled richly, and she thought it would be politic to join in. Miss Markworthy looked at them as if they deserved one another, and excused herself.

"Have a seat." He wheeled a chair over for her.

"If I could ask you a few background questions—" She took out a notebook embossed with the name of the Dernham-Mufflin Agency.

"Shoot."

"How did you get into programming?"

"Chance, mostly." He slumped into his chair and stretched out his long legs.

"Chance?"

"Well, I don't really care what I do to pay the bills. Life begins at quitting time, you know." His grin widened.

" 'Course I won't say that on the air. Guess you'll write the copy, huh?"

"Yes, but we like to get a little truth into what we say, if possible." Sarah could almost see her Uncle Andrew chuckling. "Maybe you could tell me about your outside interests?"

"Tennis, skiing, dancing. Women. Especially blondes."

No danger of subtlety with Russell. She decided to edge around to the point while he was preoccupied with his own designs.

"I expect you're very busy just now?"

"Not too busy to sneak out for a cup of coffee—"

"Mm. There's no program of yours being run just now?"

"Nope."

She kept her eyes fixed on the notebook. "Oh? Then what are you doing?"

Russell hesitated. "Well, actually, I'm writing a

program. Or—uh—I would be, but the test data haven't come down from Distribution yet."

It was a good explanation, but Russell had taken just a moment too long to make it up. She snapped her notebook closed and got up. "Thank you! I've got all I need for right now."

Russell looked up at her from under his bangs. "Hey, I'll see you again, won't I?"

"You bet. I think you'll have a great on-camera presence." She turned away and went over to Jill's desk across the room.

"Miss Markworthy?"

She looked up. "Oh—you want to meet someone else?"

"No, I think I've found what I'm looking for in Russell. But I'd like to ask you something. What's going on just now? I mean, what program is being run?"

"A couple of things, but most of our capacity's tied up with FARTS."

"I beg your pardon?"

Jill made a wry grimace. "One of our dumber acronyms. Financial Accounts Rectification System."

"That's the one that pays the bills?"

"Right."

A ripple of anticipation ran through Sarah's insides. Holman might be right. Holman might well be right. She thanked Jill and went out.

Down on the parking level, Sarah moved her car to a space from which she could watch the elevator in her mirror. Then she got out the *Wall Street Journal* and her cigarettes and settled down to wait.

A few minutes before midnight the doors slid open to reveal those members of the evening shift who had been the quickest to leave. Sarah was not surprised to see the lanky figure of Russell among them. She put out her cigarette and started the engine; by the time she had reversed out of the space Russell was in his car, heading for the exit ramp. He had one of those overgrown Mustangs from a few years back, and she liked the color: a highly visible orange.

Sarah had come into detective work with the common misapprehension that following people was easy, as long as they did not "make" you and give you the slip. So naive was she that on her first surveillance with Chris she had been amused at his bad driving—he was always either riding the brakes or stamping on the accelerator. In fact, he was doing an expert job, managing to stay a good distance from the mark while keeping him in sight most of the time, but Sarah had failed to appreciate this until she had lost, within a few blocks, the first three people she had tried to follow.

The first part of this job was easy enough—Russell got on Interstate 95 and drove south. He drove south for quite a while in fact, and Sarah's excitement mounted as it became more obvious with each passing mile that he was not just going home.

He took one of the ramps for Port Chester, and immediately her problems began. At every red light she was either coming down right on his tail or so far back that she nearly lost him when the light changed. She began to run lights with abandon, and still she had to make blind guesses at a couple of intersections. Both times, luck was with her, and she saw the taillights of the Mustang—she had memorized their shape—as it idled peacefully at the next stoplight.

Finally, to her relief, Russell turned into an apartment building—one of those luxury buildings that sits on top of its own parking garage. She hesitated, then turned in after him.

He went up the ramp to the second level and parked. Sarah drove past and found a slot for herself half a dozen cars further on. She adjusted her rearview mirror and found that Rabinowitz was looking in *his* mirror, swiveling his head as he patted his hair into place.

He took a long time about it, and Sarah's eye wandered over to the car next to the Mustang. It was a long, low Mercedes-Benz—the 450SL model that carries two people at the price of $12,000 apiece. This was the car she planned to buy as soon as she cashed in on the commodities market. Even the color was perfect, a brown so deep and rich that one would think the car had been dipped in melted chocolate.

She was still gazing covetously at it when she heard the door of the Mustang slam—and she watched Russell turn, unlock the door of the Mercedes, and get in. The engine awoke with a roar that reverberated through the garage, then subsided to a rich purr. Russell flipped on the lights and pulled out smartly.

Sarah was so surprised that she just sat there for a moment. Then she reversed out of her space and went after him.

Chapter 7

For a long time RGI's European headquarters had been in Brussels. But when they saw the waves of industrial terrorism rolling west from Germany and north from Italy, the most kidnap-prone men in top management had decided to move. On the whole, they would have preferred to forsake this unstable continent and run European operations from Greenwich, Connecticut; failing that, they had put their faith in the English Channel.

RGI House—as it was called in the British fashion —stood on Victoria Street and was one of a row of concrete-and-glass blocks. Only the grimy spires of Westminster Abbey peeping over the flat roofs reminded Chris Rockwell that he was not in an American city.

Chris paid off his driver—who nearly sent him into a fit of giggles by actually calling him "guv"—and went into the lobby.

At the reception desk he showed his RGI identification and said that he wanted to see the Securitco field supervisor in charge of Upton Lawrence & Dunbar.

"Oh, that will be Mr. Nelger," said the receptionist, in her curious and lovely accent. "If you'll wait a moment, Mr. Rockwell, I shall ring him up." She picked up the telephone, and Chris wandered away toward the big windows.

He was, of course, disobeying Wilson's orders by contacting Securitco. But Chris had thought it over carefully on the plane and come to the conclusion that he didn't give a damn about this smiling, hard-eyed exec who would not even trust *him*. So he had decided to look over Securitco's file on Brenda Wertheim and from it compile his report to Wilson. That would take about half an hour; then he could begin his expense-paid vacation in London. As Mr. Welch said, Chris Rockwell had attitude problems.

He stood looking out at the passing traffic, the big black taxis, the red double-decker buses with conductors hanging off the back platforms. He had never been to London, but like everyone who read a lot, he had long lived here in imagination. Belgravia, Cheapside, St. John's Wood, Hyde Park Corner, High Holborn—every name struck sparks in his memory. This afternoon, as soon as he wrapped up the assignment, he planned to go up to Charing Cross Road and ransack the bookstores. Then he would take the Underground to Blackfriars and walk to Gough Square to pay his respects at Dr. Johnson's house. But first he would stop at a pub for a pint of bitter and shepherd's pie—for, as the doctor himself had said, "He who does not mind his belly will hardly mind anything else."

"Mr. Rockwell?" He turned to face the receptionist. "Mr. Nelger's not in the building just now, but you're to see Mr. Raspin. Tenth floor."

"OK. Which office?"

"Just the tenth floor."

Chris was puzzled. "Who is Mr. Raspin?"

The girl raised her eyebrows. "Mr. Raspin is the Head of Operations for Europe, sir."

Chris had a premonition that his plans for a literary afternoon were about to be torpedoed. "Are you sure he wants to see *me*?"

The receptionist nodded. "Directly, please. The lifts are to your right."

Five minutes later, he was seated in the HOE's office. It was quite different from any of the other RGI bigwigs' lairs he had seen. The big room looked more like the members' lounge in a Pall Mall club: big tufted-leather armchairs, rather anemic naval prints on the walls, and a mahogany desk the size of a Ping-Pong table, bearing a humidor and a couple of cut-glass decanters.

On the far side of the desk sat Walter Raspin. Chris had remembered, now, who he was: Though the line of succession at RGI was as jagged as that of the early Roman Empire, most people expected Raspin to be the next CEO. He was a tall, broad-shouldered man in his late fifties, with a magisterial slowness in his speech and movements. His pale blue eyes did not meet Chris's as he spoke.

"Just get in from Greenwich, Rockwell?"

"Yes. I came straight from the airport."

Raspin nodded ponderously. "I find that the time change doesn't catch up with me until cocktail time. Then it catches up with a vengeance." He fixed his eyes on Chris's forehead. "Better not plan a night on the town, Rockwell."

"No, sir. I wasn't."

Raspin took a piece of chocolate from his pocket and seemed to turn all his attention to peeling off the foil wrapper in one piece. "If you're free on Friday night, there's a dinner party at my place in Berkshire, for the people coming in for the Mid-Winter Conference."

"Well—thanks." Now Chris was sure that Raspin

had mistaken him for someone else, somebody important. But who?

Abruptly Raspin answered the question. "It's about time Greenwich sent somebody to take over for Nelger." He popped the chocolate in his mouth. "He's having a hell of a time at Dunbar's. Even worse than you've heard, I expect."

"Uh—I hadn't—I'm not—" stammered Chris.

"Who's that fellow in Shakespeare gets drowned in a butt of wine?"

"Clarence," Chris replied automatically.

"Yes, I think that's what's about to happen to Nelger." Raspin chuckled dryly. "He's over there now. We've already called to tell him you're on the way." The telephone buzzed and Raspin picked it up. "Good luck, Rockwell," he said, on a note of dismissal.

Chris could imagine the process by which his asking to see Nelger had passed from secretary to secretary until it reached Mr. Raspin as his arriving to replace Nelger. In the meantime he was in a company car, bound for Upton Lawrence & Dunbar.

They were in a busy, curving street, with shops on the right and a high wall on the left. Ahead of them the traffic slowed and clotted. Wisps of brassy music drifted through the thrumming of engines. Chris's driver glanced at his watch and said, "Bugger!" which Chris assumed to be an expression of displeasure.

"I'm sorry, sir. I should've gone round the other side of the park."

"What's happening?"

"They're changing the guard at the palace. We'll be stuck here for a bit."

"Have we got far to go?"

"Well, no sir, not at all. You can walk if you like—up The Mall and round the corner into St. James's Street."

Chris got out of the car and made his way to the sidewalk. The music grew louder as he skirted the flank of the palace. If Sarah—who had majored in art history at Vassar—had been there, she could have given him a quick lecture on rustication, pediments, and pilasters; on his own, Chris could only see that the building was gray, immense, and, well, palatial.

Glancing between the heads of tourists, he saw the little dark-coated figures of two marching bands square off in the forecourt of the palace. They were playing stirring but not very martial music; Chris thought it was "Cabaret."

He looked the other way and found that he was walking along the edge of a park. The lush, brilliant green of the lawns startled him. It hardly seemed right in January. The park gave way to a long, straight avenue. Chris stopped and thought for a moment, but he could not remember any novel in which a character walked from Buckingham Palace to St. James's Street. He was lost.

"Are you lost?"

It was a man with a bristly white moustache and a bowler hat. Chris was taken by surprise, but he was soon to learn that if you stood on a London street and looked bewildered, someone would quickly come to your aid.

"Well—yes. I'm trying to get to St. James's Street."

"Ah. You want to cross here and turn in at Stable Yard Road. Go round St. James's Palace and there you are."

Chris thanked him and the man wagged his umbrella and walked on.

Crossing the broad avenue was perilous. There were cars whizzing past on one side and a troop of cavalry in black capes and plumed helmets trotting along on the other. Chris gained the opposite side without being run down or trampled, and walked up to Stable Yard Road, a narrow lane that led through more stunning mid-winter greenery. Soon he was passing the brown brick wall of a venerable-looking but ugly palace that he took to be St. James's. A guard in greatcoat and furry black hat, who seemed as solidly rooted to the pavement as a lamp standard, abruptly sprang to life as Chris went by him and ran through an extraordinary display of stamping, wheeling, and strutting. When he was finished, he froze as if he had not moved, and never would.

Chris walked on, feeling rather bemused by all this. He had seen the airline commercials about the "pomp and pageantry" of London, but he had not expected them to go about it with such *conviction*.

Walking along the palace, he came into St. James's Street. It was a busy thoroughfare lined with shops that looked expensive and clubs that looked exclusive. He found Upton Lawrence & Dunbar halfway up the street, a three-story building made of mottled gray-brown brick. Its big windows displayed a handsome array of casks and bottles, and it was enclosed in a cage of scaffolding and steel supports.

Chris stepped into the front room. The walls were paneled in dark, lustrous wood, and the carpeting—suitably enough—was the color of ruby port. His eye wandered to a plaque beside the door that bore the royal coat of arms and the inscription:

By Appointment to
Her Majesty Queen Elizabeth II

Wine Merchants
Upton Lawrence & Dunbar
London • Jerez • Oporto
est. 1786

Beneath this another panel had been added:

A Division of Atlantic Brands, Inc.
One of the RGI Family of Companies

A receptionist, a pretty young woman who was wearing a suede overcoat and gloves, approached him. "Good morning, sir. May I help you?" Her breath misted. Chris realized that it was no warmer here than outside.

"Hi. Say, what's happening here?"

"Oh, I'm afraid our roof's fallen in," she replied blithely. "Or part of it anyway. May I help you?"

"I'm here to see Mr. Nelger—"

The woman's smile vanished. "Oh. It's Mr. Rockwell from RGI then. Follow me, please."

"Thanks."

"Quite all right."

There is no animosity quite as chilling as English politeness; every civility cuts like a knife. Chris gathered at once that Raspin had not been exaggerating Nelger's problems. People they passed on the stairs gave him quick, sidelong glances; looking through office doors he saw the employees gathered in listless groups, talking in low voices. They had the lost, passive look of refugees in old newsreels. And it wasn't just that they were all bundled in their overcoats.

The atmosphere seemed vaguely familiar to Chris, and abruptly he remembered: his own company, then called the Bronson-Whitman Agency, two years ago. That was just after Securitco had taken them over

and fired Bronson and Whitman, just before Ross
Welch had come sailing in amid a flurry of memos
about new procedures. Chris remembered Wilson's
words: "A fine old company that we've had the good
fortune to acquire." Chris had a feeling that the
take-over had not been as chummy as all that.

The receptionist opened a door and stood back to
let him pass. Then she left him without a word. Chris
went into a small, cluttered office, and a man sprang
up from a chair and approached him, thrusting out
a hand.

"Hi, Chris. Bud Nelger." He was a short, broad-
shouldered man, with dense brown hair falling over
his forehead and a dimpled chin.

"Hi, Bud. Listen, I—"

He was interrupted by a banging and clanging
from above. "Working on the roof, they tell me,"
Chris shouted.

"They've been working on it for the past three
weeks. Nothing gets done fast in this country," Nelger
shouted back. He gave Chris a quick, uncertain
look. "Not that I'm making excuses, Chris. It's just
that I'm experiencing problems with the personnel
here."

The racket on the roof let up. Chris nodded soothingly. "So I hear. Listen, I'm not here to take over
from you—there's been a mistake."

Nelger brightened immediately. "Oh? You are Se-
curitco/Greenwich, aren't you?"

"Inkwink, actually. I'm just here to run a spot
check on one of the employees, named Brenda Wertheim. So if you could just let me get a look at her
Security Personnel Profile, I'll be on my way. I'm
sure you're doing the best you can in this tough situation," he added, shamelessly.

"Well, that's the problem, Chris. There are no SPP's. On anyone."

Chris was so surprised that for the moment he did not even think about how much more difficult the lack of a profile on Wertheim could make his own job. "None?"

"Nope. I gave 'em—"

Behind Chris the door opened, and he turned to see a tall man in a tweed overcoat, who was speaking to someone in the corridor. ". . . bloody cold. Still, I don't know what we can do about it. Pass out a dram to warm the troops, eh?"

Nelger resumed, addressing Chris, but speaking loudly for the other man's benefit. "As I was saying, we're experiencing a very low level of cooperation at the managerial level."

The man approached Chris with a lumbering gait. He had thick white hair, ruddy skin, and brilliant blue eyes. "How do you do. I'm the managerial level. My name is Gordon Dunbar."

"Hi. I'm Chris Rockwell."

"Ah. Well, Mr. Rockwell, so far this morning you helpful chaps from Connecticut have lectured me on my receivables, my inventory, and my office procedures. Now what are you here to tell me how to do?"

Nelger stepped forward so that he and Chris were standing shoulder-to-shoulder, allies against Dunbar. "Chris is from Securitco/Greenwich. I was just about to tell him about the SPP's."

"Do go on, Mr. Nelger," replied Dunbar, turning away to sit down behind his desk.

"I gave them to Major Dunbar for distribution to personnel three weeks ago. Last week, he returned them—with a note that said, 'Can't see why all this information should interest you.'"

Chris laughed.

It would have been hard to say who looked at him with more surprise, Nelger or Dunbar. Chris cleared his throat. "Uh—sorry. Say, Bud, why don't I have a talk with the major? See if we can work things out between the two of us."

Nelger's puzzled expression acquired a few more wrinkles. "But I thought you were only here to—"

Chris cut him off. "We'll see what we can work out." He himself was puzzled at what he was doing; he supposed it was simply a matter of fellow feeling for a victim of RGI.

Nelger shrugged. "OK. Lotsa luck, Chris."

"Good day, Mr. Nelger," said Dunbar, as Nelger went out. Overhead, the racket resumed, and Dunbar waved Chris to a chair across the desk. They waited until the noise let up.

"Major, they're going to make you fill out those profiles, I'm afraid."

"Indeed?"

"If you don't cooperate, you know what they'll do?"

"Sack the lot of us?" suggested Dunbar.

"You don't get off that easy. Nelger will call in a Creative Conflict Resolution team."

"What's that?"

"It's a bunch of communicators, as they call themselves. They'll take you and your staff to RGI House and sit you down with Nelger's bunch. They'll call you all by your first names, and everything you say, they'll say they hear you. They won't let you go until you've . . . worked out your innermost feelings together."

Major Dunbar's ruddy face had lost a little of its color. He folded his arms across his chest, as if barring the way to his innermost feelings.

"When my company was taken over by Securitco—"

"Oh?" Dunbar interrupted. "I thought you were Nelger's superior."

"Not exactly," said Chris evasively. "Anyway, we fought those profiles too, but when they threatened us with an encounter group, we broke."

"I can well imagine. Mr. Rockwell, what's all this about? Why do they ask these odious questions?"

"Well, they're afraid that one of your competitors will try to bribe or blackmail one of your people to find out your—I don't know—your secret formula for sherry."

Dunbar grinned. "We don't have a secret formula. You're mixing us up with Coca-Cola. It's all in the heads of some wizened old Spaniards at our bodegas in Jerez. All trial and error, really, but over a few centuries they've gotten quite good at it. Do you like sherry, Mr. Rockwell?"

"Yes, I do."

Dunbar glanced at his watch. "Only an hour till lunch. Time to start drinking, I think." He got up and went to the sideboard, where he filled two tall thin glasses from a bottle of Select. "I'm afraid I've spoiled it for you by telling you what it is," he said, as he brought the glasses over.

"Oh?"

"Wilson tells me Americans don't like to think they're drinking sherry. How did he put it in that elegant way of his? 'Sherry is perceived as a drink for literary types and wimps like that.'"

"I'm afraid I am sort of a literary type."

"Really? Poor chap. I never would have perceived it."

"It's true." Chris raised the glass of golden liquid, and was suddenly overwhelmed by the urge to quote.

O, for a beaker full of the warm South,
Cool'd a long age in the deep-delved earth,
Tasting of Flora and the country green,
Dance, and Provençal song, and sunburnt mirth!
O, for a draught of vintage! that hath been
Full of the true, the blushful Hippocrene,
With beaded bubbles winking at the brim,
And purple-stained mouth.

Major Dunbar heard him out with a good deal
more tolerance than Chris usually received in his
native land. "A beaker full of the warm South—that
is good. Cheers."

"Cheers."

Dunbar did not drink immediately. He swirled the
glass, held it below his nose for a moment, then gently
tipped a little of the wine into his mouth. When he
swallowed, it was with a certain reluctance.

"We do make a jolly fine sherry. Even if I do say
so myself. There's a good deal of rubbish talked
about wine, but it's quite true that it's a living thing.
It's born, it matures, it dies. And once you get to
know it, it will tell you a lot about the land it comes
from, and the people who made it. We're having a
lovely Château Léoville-Poyferré at lunch, for instance
—Care to join us for lunch, Mr. Rockwell?"

It abruptly dawned on Chris that Dunbar had taken
a liking to him. Yet there had been no change in his
manner since he had come into the room thinking
Chris was yet another meddler from Greenwich: He
was still the same blend of poise, politeness, and
irony. Chris remembered something Sarah—who had
been in England often—had told him. "They're im-
penetrably civil. You could throw up in their laps
and it wouldn't blow their poise. You never know

what they're thinking." Chris decided that he might take a stab at his assignment, as Dunbar was in an expansive mood. "I understand you've got an American on your staff."

"Yes, Miss Wertheim. Works in the export department, responsible for Holland. Great sherry drinkers, the Dutch. You'd like to meet her? I shall ask her, then, but I'm not sure she'll join us."

"Oh?"

"Miss Wertheim usually lunches at her desk. She's the most diligent employee I've got."

In America this would have been high praise; over here, Chris was not sure how to take it. Dunbar leaned over his intercom and spoke clearly and distinctly to it, as if it were an aged and infirm aunt: "Oh, is that Hiller? Would you ask Miss Wertheim to come round to the dining room when she's free? Thank you." He straightened up and turned to Chris. "We might as well go on in—time to decant the Bordeaux. Also, they've got an electric fire going in there and it'll be a bit warmer."

Chris followed the big, lumbering figure down the hall and into the dining room. which had large windows giving a view of the august frontages of St. James's Street; a long, gleaming table set with half a dozen places; and a row of portraits on the wall—soldiers in the dashing garb of the Napoleonic era, dandies with extravagant neckcloths, stern Victorian gentlemen with muttonchop whiskers. Dunbar gestured at them as he passed. "Uptons—sold their shares for gambling money in Regency times. Dissolute lot. Lawrences—all killed off in the Great War and the flu epidemic."

"So that leaves the Dunbars?"

"I'm the last of them, actually. My son's in Toronto, running a string of discothèques." Shaking his head ruefully, he went on into the pantry. On the shelf were a couple of decanters and a row of wine bottles: sherries, whites, reds.

He thought of something Sarah had once told him. "I thought you weren't supposed to set wine bottles upright."

"Quite so." Dunbar was taking off his overcoat, and Chris followed suit, although it did not seem much warmer here. "Not until a day or so before serving. Then you want to get it upright by degrees, so that the deposit ends up at the bottom."

As far as the niceties of spirits went, Chris had only recently reached the stage of drinking his beer from a glass. Still, he was curious. "I thought that's why you decanted it, to get rid of the sediment."

Dunbar was stripping the capsule from a bottle of Bordeaux, without lifting it from the shelf. "Only partially. It's also to aerate the wine. The wine's been locked up in that bottle a long time, and it wants to be woken up a bit. Looks nice in the decanter, too." He glanced over Chris's shoulder. "Ah, Miss Wertheim. Mr. Rockwell."

Chris had not heard her approach. He turned to face a tall, dark-haired woman of about his own age. She was well-dressed in the latest fashion: boots, a long skirt with a ruffled hem, a soft, lustrous blouse with gathered sleeves. There were lots of things dangling from her neck and wrists: the knotted sleeves of a sweater, scarf, jewelry. Her coiffure and makeup were equally fashionable—short, fluffy hair and lipstick like wet red paint.

"Hi."

"Hi, Miss Wertheim. I—uh—thought that as we're countrymen, we ought to—"

"Where are you from?"

"Greenwich. I work for RGI," he said vaguely.

She watched him, intent and unsmiling. Chris waited for her to say something, but she did not.

He heard a soft "thunk" and turned to see that Dunbar had withdrawn the cork from the Bordeaux.

He bent over and sniffed. "Oh, dear."

"Something wrong, Major?"

"M'm. It's—" He glanced at Brenda. "Miss Wertheim, what do you think?"

Brenda was still staring at Chris. She started like a schoolgirl caught daydreaming. Dunbar offered the bottle, and she took it with visible reluctance.

"What do you make of it?"

"It's—um—it's gone bad."

"Oh? Do you think so?"

"I don't know. I mean, you tell me. I mean, you're the expert."

"Now how can I do that? With wine everyone must judge for oneself."

"Well, I don't like it," said Brenda.

"But that's not a very helpful description to the rest of us, is it? Come, Miss Wertheim. You've shipped tons of this stuff about Europe. You must have some opinion."

Brenda looked as if she were about to drop the bottle on the floor, turn, and flee. Chris, who had watched this odd little contretemps in bafflement, thought he had better intervene. He took the bottle and sniffed the rim.

"Smells like wood," he said.

The tension was broken. Major Dunbar nodded and took the bottle back. "Full marks, Mr. Rockwell. Yes, the fools didn't prepare the cask properly, and that smell will stay with the wine all its life. Not the wine's fault, but I'm afraid it's lost." He put the bottle aside regretfully. "Well, we shall have to send down for another bottle—"

"That's OK. I don't want any."

"Not at all, Miss Wertheim. It's no trouble. We do have plenty of wine about the place."

"I mean, I really don't have time for lunch."

"Nonsense. Shan't be a moment." Dunbar went through a swing door into the kitchen.

"Well—" said Chris, and broke off.

Brenda was staring at the floor as if into an abyss. "Oh, God," she said in a desolate whisper, "he's always doing that to me—giving me quizzes about wine."

Chris looked at her in puzzlement. First Wilson, now Dunbar. What did her bosses have against this girl?

And then she looked at him and said, "Do you have something to tell me—I mean, from Wilson?"

Chris jumped. "Wilson?" he echoed, taken by surprise and completely flustered. "You mean Jack Wilson, of Atlantic? Uh—no. Why?"

But already she was turning away. "No reason. Sorry. I've—I've got to get back to my desk."

Chris looked after her, thinking that she was an even worse liar than he was. He was beginning to take an interest in this job, after all.

Chapter 8

It was early in the morning. Brilliant sunshine angled through the glass roof of the atrium, through the picture window of the president's office, and fell mercilessly on Russell Rabinowitz. His eyes narrowed and finally closed.

Aside from his expensive and stylish casual clothes, Russell looked dreadful: face pale and drawn, fatigue showing in every line of his long body.

Jack Wilson took him by the elbow, just as he had Chris, but without the smile he had given Chris, and led him round the desk. Then he put his Dictaphone on playback, turning the volume high. Russell winced at the noise and put his fingers to his head, gently probing it, as a careful shopper handles a grapefruit.

"You look terrible, Russell."

"Yeah, well, I don't get off work till midnight, sir, and you called me at seven-thirty. Why the heck did you do that?"

"Because I wanted to talk to you, and I can't have you strolling in here during working hours."

"Yeah, yeah. Me, a mere programmer, getting a private appointment with the president." Russell had dropped the "sir."

Wilson jammed his hands in his pockets and began to pace, with little spring-heeled steps. "You don't look like you got seven hours' sleep last night. You're not doing anything dumb, are you, Russell? Anything that could make anybody suspicious?"

Russell sighed heavily. "Listen, man, we're safe. Or

practically. I mean, this is the very last day, remember? FARTS gets run with our little addition tonight, and that's it. Tomorrow I delete the command, and the money's *gone*. It wouldn't matter if anybody was suspicious, 'cause they couldn't find anything. The accountants could be up here dumping audit trails from now till doomsday, and they wouldn't find a trace, because there won't be any traces. So get off my case, willya?"

Wilson had stopped pacing. He switched on his smile, a smile as clear and brilliant as the sunshine pouring through the window. "OK, Russell, OK. Maybe I was overreacting. You've done a great job for me, and I'll remember it." Taking Russell's elbow again, he steered him to the door. "Now you go home and get some sleep, so you'll be a hundred ten percent sharp tonight, just in case—"

"Nothing'll go wrong. Nothing's gone wrong the other nights, and it'll be the same tonight."

"Sure, I know that," Wilson continued soothingly. "Have a nice day."

Russell nodded and went loping down the corridor, his head hanging and his steps wavering slightly.

Wilson returned to his desk and closed his eyes, dredging a telephone number up from his memory. It was a number he had never written down.

He picked up the receiver and punched buttons. As before, there was only an answering machine on the other end. The precise, faintly accented voice of Lisle told him to begin his message at the sound of the tone.

"Re Martinique transaction," said Wilson. "I'm ready for your account number now."

❖   ❖   ❖

Sarah Saber was having a pleasant and inconsequential dream. She was sitting under her favorite tree at Vassar, the huge and stately sycamore in front of the library. Her back was resting on the smooth bark of its trunk, her cheek on Chris Rockwell's shoulder. (She had not known Chris while she had been at Vassar, but trifles like this never trouble the subconscious mind.) Nothing whatever was happening in her dream, except for the wind rustling the leaves overhead.

The rustle grew louder and louder, until it turned into the buzzing of the house intercom. Sarah groped her way free of the covers and stumbled over to the little grille on the wall.

"Unhh."

"Miss Saber, there's a guy here wants to see you," said the doorman's voice. "Said to tell you he's your client and you'd remember who he is."

At the moment she could not even remember what line of work she was in. "Uh—ask his name, please."

A pause, and then the doorman said, "It's Mr. Holman."

"Oh. Oh, yeah. Send him up."

She turned to the kitchen sink and dashed cold water on her face. This did not do the trick—now she felt wet and sleepy. Crossing the living room, she pulled the draperies open. The vast white expanse of Central Park dazzled her. Halfway to consciousness now, she went to the closet and dragged a robe off the hanger. She struggled into it and glanced in the mirror. In her flowered granny nightgown and frilly peignoir, with her hair tumbled about her shoulders, she did not look like the model corporate security specialist.

She was still trying to find her slippers when the doorbell rang.

Hal Holman was leaning against the doorjamb with his ankles crossed. He was wearing Gucci loafers, dark-brown slacks and turtleneck, and a camel's hair blazer with Yves St. Laurent's initials on the buttons. His suede overcoat was draped casually over his shoulder, and the sheen on his Guccis revealed that he had not been obliged to trudge through the slush to get here.

"Sarah? Good morning." He reached out to shake her hand and smiled. His face positively glowed with a suntan, and he had magnificent curly gray hair. He was so vital and handsome that just looking at him made Sarah feel even more tired and feeble.

"Uh—good morning. Come in."

He pushed off from the doorjamb and strolled past her. Sarah looked out into the hall, expecting an entourage, or at least Mrs. Webb. But the VP (L) had come to see her alone.

Holman dropped his coat over a chair and swiveled gracefully on one heel, surveying her apartment. "Hey," he said. "Very nice. I like the ambience."

And then Sarah placed him. Her Uncle Andrew, who often regaled the family with tales of RGI, had mentioned Holman once. He had called him "the last of the Mellows."

Back in the late sixties, when RGI—like all the other conglomerates—was making money hand over fist and feeling defensive about it, a new breed of corporate leaders had come to the fore. They were chosen not so much for their administrative abilities as for their skill at looking into the camera and intoning that they too were concerned about the environment and the quality of life. In the hard, cold seventies, the Mellows had come to seem a luxury that RGI could ill afford, and they had been pushed out by the Bottom-Liners. Inexplicably, Hal Holman still survived.

Sarah offered this fragment of company history a seat by the window and slumped into the chair opposite him.

"I just got in from the coast," Holman said. "I called Thea—Thea Webb, that is—and she told me she found a message from you when she got to the office today. 'He's not running a program. Report to follow.' "

"Yeah. I didn't want to say any more over the phone."

"Sure, I hear you. But I thought I'd drop by and get the details. I don't mean to come on like it's a real heavy thing, but—"

"It is a pretty heavy thing, Mr. Holman."

"Oh?"

"I managed to pass myself off as somebody who could ask questions and went up to AB and talked to Rabinowitz. At first Rabinowitz told me he wasn't doing anything. Then he said he was writing a program. But I thought he was lying."

"I hope you've got something a little more substantive than that, Sarah. I mean—"

"Yeah. I followed him after work. He's got a brand new Mercedes-Benz stashed in a garage in Port Chester."

"Oh, wow," said Holman. His glasses apparently were light sensitive, for in the bright sunshine they were fogging over so that his eyes gradually disappeared from view.

"He came down here and started hitting the bars and discos. Spent a fortune just in garaging for the car. I thought I was going to freeze to death before he'd manage to score, but finally, about three, he left this place with a girl. Drove her back to her place in Queens. Apparently that was long enough for the car to work its magic, because he didn't leave until five."

"Where is he now?"

"I left him at his apartment in Stamford. I expect he's still there. Asleep. End of report."

Holman frowned and ran a hand through his mane. "Sarah, I hate to lay this on you first thing in the morning, but I'm afraid that what's coming down here is an attempt to defraud the company."

She nodded drowsily and propped her chin in her palm.

"Oh—you've—you've already flashed on that?"

"Well, I didn't think he got the Mercedes with Green Stamps, and if he had, he wouldn't hide it in a garage thirty miles away."

"Oh, right. Sure. But there are other factors entering into this situation." He then proceeded to tell her what she had learned from Bill Chandler. He seemed to think she was still in the state of ignorance in which Mrs. Webb had left her. It occurred to her that the VP (L) did not have brains to match his beauty.

"How 'bout that," she said when he was finished. "Better call Wilson and tell him to bring on the auditors."

"No," said Holman, "you're doing fine. I'd like you to stay on it."

"What for?"

"Try to find out how he's doing it. Try to find out where the money's going."

"It's going into a bank account Rabinowitz has set up somewhere, obviously."

"Try and verify that."

She felt her shoulders sagging at the prospect. "Mr. Holman, even when I've had a full night's sleep I'm no computer expert."

Holman was nodding and smiling. "I hear you, and of course I wouldn't want you to take on something that you don't feel is right for you."

"Thanks."

"However . . ." He got up and took another long look at the apartment. "No kidding, this is a great place. It must cost you a bundle, huh?"

Sarah nodded.

"How'd you like to make next month's rent—today? I have in mind a fifty-dollar-an-hour bonus. Starting" —he glanced dramatically at his watch—"now!"

"Fifty dollars an hour?" said Sarah incredulously.

Holman shrugged. "Why not? My analyst gets more than that, and he's never done anything for me."

Three voices spoke at once, from different corners of Sarah's memory. Mr. Welch: "You are salaried employees, and I need hardly emphasize that it is inappropriate for you to accept incentives." Chris: "If a client offers you a bonus, run like hell." Her father, the farming equipment tycoon: "Never try to talk anybody out of giving you money."

Sarah was a dutiful daughter. "OK. I'll stay on it another day."

"Say, that's just great," said Holman, beaming. "I've got to split for the airport right now, so you report to Thea. Tonight, OK?"

"OK."

Bestowing on her a last smile, Holman picked up his coat and sauntered out of the apartment, leaving Sarah to wonder if this bizarre interview was just a continuation of her dream.

Chapter 9

Four hours—or two hundred dollars—later, Sarah stood looking out over the playing surface of the New Rochelle Tennis Club. It looked like a vast pool table, on which someone had carefully chalked a half-dozen rectangles. Within each rectangle, four small figures in various pastel hues cavorted.

Russell Rabinowitz was on court number three. Resplendent in yellow warm-up jacket and tight blue shorts, he uncoiled smoothly through a serve and charged the net. His expensive aluminum racket glittered like a scythe as he knocked off the volley. His partner patted him on the behind as he strutted past her, and he turned to leer back at her.

Rabinowitz had the bottomless energy of a true hedonist. Sarah had no sooner arrived to stake out his apartment than he came bounding out the door and ran to his car. He went first to Port Chester, to pick up the Mercedes, and arrived here to meet his foursome (three of whom were female, of course) to take the court promptly at two.

He would be here until three, and then he would have to change clothes and cars swiftly to make it back to Atlantic Brands by four.

Not a lot of time to set things up, Sarah thought. She went into the pro shop and found a pay phone on the wall amid a thicket of rackets. She called Stamford information and got the number of J. Markworthy.

"Hullo?" said a sleep-throttled voice.

"Miss Markworthy? Sorry to wake you."

"That's OK. I should be getting ready for work."
There was the faint creaking of bed springs as Miss
Markworthy hauled herself into an upright position.
"Say, who is this?"

"Sorry. It's Sarah Saber."

There was a pause, during which she could imagine Jill's thoughts: Saber? Oh, yeah, that dummy in the tight jeans, from advertising. "So how's the great talent search going?"

She ignored the question. "I'd like to talk to you before you go to work."

"Go ahead."

"Well, can I come over?"

With some reluctance, Miss Markworthy assented.

The apartment was fairly pleasant, considering that it was a boxy one-room in a new building: There were throw rugs over the management's tan carpeting, art-show posters on the walls, lots of greenery. A bowl of cereal and a cup of coffee stood on the kitchen counter.

"Do you ever get used to breakfast in the afternoon?" Sarah asked, untying her scarf.

Jill laughed. "No. The worst part is arriving at work just when everybody else is leaving. Say, Sarah, if this is about those commercials, I thought I told you I didn't want to appear—"

She broke off, staring at Sarah, who had just shed her coat. Underneath, she was wearing not her creative-person outfit but her own clothes: beige herringbone skirt, cream-colored blouse, tattersall vest. Her long golden hair was gathered up more or less tidily atop her head.

"Well," said Jill. "I like the new you."

"I better tell you who the new me is."

"Oh?"

"I'm not from advertising, and I'm not interested in Rabinowitz for a commercial."

Jill looked utterly baffled for a moment, and then she grinned wryly. "So you did all this because you were desperate to get a date with Russ?"

"Give me a break, Jill."

"Sorry. So who are you, Sarah—if it is still Sarah?"

"Yes, it is. I'm from Inquiries, Inc., in Greenwich. It's part of Securitco."

Jill nodded slowly. "Inkwink, huh? I've heard of it, but I thought it was a joke. What are you doing in our place?"

"I'm here because I think Russell Rabinowitz is robbing Atlantic blind."

Jill stopped smiling. After a moment she said, "I suppose you've got some identification?"

Sarah handed over her Connecticut investigator's license and her RGI photo ID. Jill glanced at them and handed them back. "OK, so you're a real private eye. So how'd you catch on to Russell? How's he doing it?"

"I don't really know how. That's why I've come to you. What are the possibilities?"

"Oh, endless." Jill waved her to a seat on the sofa and settled into a creaking rocker. "The simplest one is this: He just inserts one bit of logic in the system—'pay ten grand to account number X'—and it goes on the tape the computer's cutting, and the tape goes to the bank."

"There's no paper work, no nothing?"

"Provided he deletes the command before the general-ledger tape is run, there's no trace anywhere. The money just disappears." Jill rocked meditatively back and forth, frowning. "But that can't be it—I mean, if he was doing that there's no way you could have caught on to him. How—"

"He's got a Mercedes-Benz stashed in a garage in Port Chester."

Jill chuckled maliciously. "Of course. He would."

Sarah got out her cigarettes and lit one, choosing her next words with care. "Jill, would you be willing to help me? Help me find out for sure if that's what he's doing?"

Jill stopped rocking. She looked at Sarah in silence.

"I work for a very big shot at WHQ. If you help me, you'll win his undying gratitude," Sarah went on.

"You didn't have to say that, Sarah. I'll help you—but not to make points with somebody in Greenwich."

"Oh?"

"For the pure, unsullied joy of nailing Russell."

They grinned at one another. "Great," said Sarah. "How are you going to do it?"

"I screw up another program so that it will feed bad data into FARTS. That'll halt the run, the operators will call for help, and I'll be there . . ." Her smile faded. "Damn it! The problem is, Russell's always there too."

"I'll see that he's not."

"Going to slip him a Mickey?"

"Nothing so drastic, I hope. How long will it take?"

Jill pondered, tugging at one of her corkscrew curls. "Let's see . . . the computer prints out the program. I get a copy from the production library and compare them. If he's slipped in a command that has no business being there, it'll be pretty blatant. I'll spot it right away. But Sarah, this is only one possibility. If he's got accomplices backing him up with forged purchase orders, say, I won't be able to spot it. You'd have to bring in the auditors."

Sarah put out her cigarette. "I'm banking on Russell's greed. I'll bet he doesn't have accomplices." She glanced at her watch and got up.

Jill rose with her. "Are you going to do something pretty nasty to waylay him?"

Sarah nodded.

"Good."

Half an hour later, Sarah was parked across the street from the apartment building in Port Chester, waiting for Russell. It had been a bright, bitterly cold winter's day, and as the afternoon waned the wind was picking up. Sudden gusts rocked her car and set the apartment building's canopy flapping like a sail. White wraiths swirled up from the piles of snow along the sidewalk. The unlucky pedestrians struggled along, bent over, hands on their hats.

The sign on the drive-in bank in front of Sarah read ten degrees. She watched as the digits blinked out, to be replaced by new digits expressing the temperature in degrees centigrade, which in turn were replaced by the time: 3:20. She lit a cigarette and sat watching the numbers change. Idly, she wondered how the responsibility for informing the public about the time and temperature had fallen upon banks. Stores and office buildings never seemed to have signs like this.

A wistful smile came to her face as she remembered that Chris had once told her that private eyes spent a good deal of time pondering dumb questions like that one. Investigation was the most boring work in the world—apart from the times when you were scared. When had he said this, exactly? She remembered—

on her very first job for Inkwink, two years ago. They
had spent the night watching a motel in New Jersey
—pointlessly, as it turned out. For the first few hours
they had played gin rummy, passing back and forth
a pencil flashlight with which to read their cards.
Toward three in the morning he told her that she
might as well get some sleep, that he would keep
watch. As she nestled against the door she saw him
train the light on a thick book—*The Anatomy of
Melancholy* by Robert Burton. Sarah had thought
that only doctoral candidates in English lit read
books like that one. She thought he was rather interesting, this lazy, kindly, eccentric man. Within a few
weeks, she had fallen in love with him.

The sight of Russell's Mercedes, its chocolate paintwork gleaming in the sun as it swung round into the
garage, jolted her out of her reverie. It was 3:35.
He was cutting it close.

She put out her cigarette and waited, picturing
Russell as he parked and locked the Mercedes, took
a last fond look at it, and got into his Mustang. Now
he would be turning the key—and receiving no response whatever. She wondered how much time he
would spend trying to figure out what was wrong.
The problem, in fact, was that the Mustang's rotor
was not in its distributor, but in Sarah's purse.

Even from across the street and through her closed
windows she could hear the squealing of tires as
Russell whirled onto the exit ramp. The Mercedes
shot into the street, skidded on an ice patch so that
Russell came within inches of crumpling one of his
beautiful fenders against a parked car, straightened
out, and disappeared round a corner. Sarah started
up and followed him, at a more deliberate pace. She
had a good idea where he was going.

Russell headed down the hill toward the Sound, passed under Interstate 95, and pulled into the parking lot of the train station. He had decided—as she had expected him to—that there was far less risk in being a little late for work than in showing his secret joy at Atlantic Brands. She had checked the time-tables and knew that Russell would wait fifteen minutes for the next train up, and that he would arrive in Stamford at 4:25. She made a U-turn and took the east-bound ramp of the Interstate.

At four-fifteen Sarah arrived at the Stamford station. She parked and went into a telephone booth to call the data center.

"Jill, how's it going?"

"Just fine. The system bombed and I stepped forward with my source codes and volunteered to fix it up. The program's printing out now."

"How long will it take you?"

"Sarah, I just can't say."

"OK. I'll give you as long as I can."

"Russell's not gonna come walking in here, is he?"

"No, no—I'll call. Don't worry about Russell. Bye."

Sarah was very worried about Russell. His train would come in just eight minutes from now, and there was a taxicab office right across the parking lot. And Atlantic Brands was less than five miles away.

She reached up and unpinned her hair, fluffed it out into a golden tumble about her shoulders. This was all she could do to restore her creative-person disguise; she hoped that she would not have to take off her overcoat.

The train came rattling in right on the dot, and Sarah cursed the New Haven line. Why couldn't they be late as usual? A minute passed all too swiftly, and the station doors swung open. Russell appeared at the head of a cluster of weary commuters. With an unaccustomed vigor that set his bell-bottoms flapping, he strode across the lot toward the taxi office.

Sarah let out the clutch and eased forward. When she was beside him, she tapped on the horn. Russell turned and peered in, not recognizing her until she leaned over to roll down the window.

"Hi, Russell. Thought I saw you."

"Sarah—you going out to AB now?"

"Yes—need a ride?"

Instantly, Russell's nervousness vanished. He swung into the car and, smoothing his hair with all his usual smug indolence, looked over at her. "Hey, thanks a lot, Sarah. I went down to Rye for a lunch date, and my damn car broke down."

"Gee, that's too bad." She slowed up as she approached a traffic light; it obligingly turned yellow and she stopped.

He swept her car with his gaze. "Nice car. BMW?"

"That's right."

The light changed, and Sarah took a left.

"Oh, don't go through town. It's quicker to take the highway."

Sarah swallowed. "Well, Russ—" She fine-tuned her voice, started again. "Well, Russ, the fact is, I'm not in any hurry to get to work tonight. I'm supposed to interview somebody else for a spot, but I just don't feel like it. I mean, I'm feeling pretty hassled in general, and—" She gritted her teeth, drew her lips back to show them, and turned to Russell. "What I mean is, how about us going to a bar instead?"

She was a little worried that since she had ducked his invitation the night before he might be suspicious at once. But she had underestimated his self-confidence.

He gave her a slow smile. "Hey, that would be real nice."

"Great. Where do you recom—"

"But I can't."

"*What?*"

A rush of embarrassment and anger swept through her, and for a moment she completely forgot the purpose of what she was doing. That a jerk like Russell should have the *nerve* to turn her down—

"Gotta work. How 'bout later on? I'll be free at midnight." He leaned toward her, rested his arm on the back of the seat, and examined her profile minutely. "You know I want to go out with you. How 'bout later on, Sarah?"

She could feel his breath on her cheek. Her limbs tingled with the urge to shrink back against the door. Instead she pulled the car to the side of the road and turned to him.

"How about now? Your place?"

Russell chuckled richly. His hand slithered across the seat back to settle on her shoulder. "Sarah, you really had me fooled. I didn't think you'd be that up-front with a guy."

"Why play games? What do you say, Russ?"

He was silent for a moment, staring past her, and she could follow his calculations exactly: Suppose something goes wrong? But the system's been run lots of times without a hitch . . . and this chick may not be in the mood later on. . . .

His eyes returned to hers. "Take the next left, and then it's just a mile up."

It took a long time to cover the mile, for traffic—to Sarah's delight—was horrendous. The vast parking

lots of Stamford's many corporate headquarters were
emptying into the narrow, inadequate streets, and
she crawled along in first gear. Russell did not bother
to converse anymore; he was busily fingering her hair
and kissing her coat's shoulder.

Inevitably, Russell's turnoff came up. He directed
her past a covered swimming pool to a row of "town
houses," as the developers call them. He told her to
stop before one of the houses.

He draped an arm around her shoulders, and under cover of nuzzling his wrist, she glanced at his
watch: ten minutes of five. How much longer could
she give Jill? And how was she going to call her?

His apartment was on the first floor. The draperies
were still closed, so that only a thin bar of light
fell across the unmade bed. Sarah winced and looked
away. God, this is sleazy, she thought. How did I
ever get into this?

Instinctively she turned back to the door, just as
Russell closed it. "Relax," he said, in a whisper.

He did not seize her and begin to maul her as she
had feared. He gently touched her hair, her face,
murmuring how beautiful she was. It was a long time
before he kissed her lips, and even longer before his
hand began, with extraordinary deftness, to undo the
buttons of her vest.

She felt the familiar stitch of tension, of want, in
her belly; felt her body begin to respond. He's very
proficient, she thought. He hits the right buttons,
and I turn on. It's just a matter of expertise. That's
the really horrible part.

She twisted away from him.

"Why don't I—why don't I just go in the bathroom
for a second?"

Russell seemed willing to humor her. He flicked on the light and pointed out the bathroom door.

She quickly crossed the room and went in. As quietly as possible, she locked the door, and then she sat down on the edge of the tub and stared at her watch. With infinite deliberation, the second hand circled the dial, twice.

Glancing up, she saw the door handle turning.

"Aw, come on, Sarah."

"I'll be right out."

"Why don't I come in?"

"I'll be right out."

Russell desisted. This is so ludicrous, Sarah thought. It can't go on.

It didn't. Just then she heard a sound that made her jump: He was dialing.

She stood up and put her ear to the door, listening for the muffled voice.

"Hi, this is Russ. I'm held up. Any problems with FARTS?"

Sarah twisted the lock open, flung the door wide, and rushed out.

Russell was standing at the night table with the receiver in his hand, stark naked. Sarah, her eyes on the floor, walked up to him and snatched it away.

"What the—"

"Jill Markworthy, please."

"Who's this?" said a startled voice on the other end of the line.

"Jill Markworthy please."

There was a moment's further confusion, and Jill came on.

"That you, Sarah? Where've you been? I found it ten minutes ago."

"You found it?"

"It couldn't have been more obvious if it had said 'embezzlement' in big red letters."

"So how much has Russell stolen?" She looked up at him. He had picked up his pants, and he was backing away from her, eyes wide open, mouth agape.

"Can't tell—I don't know when he inserted the bit."

"No problem. I'll just ask him," she said, smiling pleasantly at Russell.

"What do I do?"

"Just sit tight and I'll bring him down there." She hung up the receiver. "OK, Russell. Let's go."

"You a cop?" he said in a strangled voice.

"No, I'm from Inkwink, actually. Let's go."

But Russell showed no signs of moving. He was thinking hard. "No cops . ." he murmured, "and no auditors—so only you and Markworthy know about this?"

"For the moment, yes," Sarah replied, and then regretted it. She had watched altogether too much television, and she feared for a moment that Russell was going to leap on her and try to murder her.

What he did do was almost as surprising. He dropped his slacks on the floor and sat down in an armchair.

"You had me worried for a minute there."

Sarah stared; the shock must have unhinged him. "Will you get dressed?"

"Why? I'm not going anywhere."

"You are going to the data center," she said, slowly and clearly. "Ultimately, you are going to jail."

"Nope. You better get back on the phone to Markworthy. Tell her to get that program running and keep her mouth shut."

"Why should I do that?"

Russell sat grinning at her. She wished he would at least cross his legs. "Because you and I are going to make a deal."

"Russell, are you trying to bribe me?"

"Not money. Information. I'm going to tell you something, and you take it back to whoever you work for, and they'll be mighty interested."

Sarah leaned against the table and folded her arms. "OK," she said, "let's hear it."

But Russell was in no hurry. "Say—what made you suspicious in the first place? I mean, why did you come up to AB at all?"

"You delayed your vacation."

Russell snapped his fingers and tapped his forehead. "Of course. I completely forgot about that. The guys at Greenwich are a lot more on the ball than I thought. I figured that form would end up filed in the nearest wastebasket. But your boss actually followed up on it. Who is he, anyway?"

Sarah remained silent, waiting.

"OK. You don't have to tell me. Just go to him with the info I give you, and—"

"I'm still waiting for that info."

His grin grew broader. "I'm not stealing the money."

Sarah straightened up. "Tell it to the cops, Russell. Get dressed and let's go."

"I'm merely transferring funds on orders of the president."

She froze in her steps, staring at Russell, who grinned back at her."

"Wilson? No, I don't believe you. Sorry."

He went on, imperturbably. "First the money goes in my account in a bank in New York. I deduct a little commission for my trouble, then send it on to Wilson's bank in Geneva."

"How much?"

"By the day after tomorrow he'll have eight hundred grand. It's in Crédit Suisse de Genève, Thirteen rue Montaubin. Account number—" He broke off. "Aren't you going to take this down? Your boss will want to know."

Sarah shook her head. "It's not going to work, Russell. Swiss banks won't release the names of account holders. So how are we supposed to know that this is Wilson's account and not yours?"

Russell rolled his eyes. "Man, you are one stubborn chick. Why do you think Wilson okayed my delay of vacation if I wasn't working for him?"

A thin trickle of doubt found its way into her thoughts: Maybe, just maybe, Russell was not lying.

"I'd already slipped the bit into FARTS when the head of the data center comes around and reminds me I'm supposed to take off next week. Like I say, I'd completely forgotten about it. So I went to Jack, and we took care of it." He could see, now, that he was winning her over, and his tone grew still more confident. "Really bad luck, your boss dumping on us about that—I mean, it's strictly routine. Especially rotten luck 'cause tonight is the last time. Eight hundred grand was all Jack wanted, and like I say, the day after tomorrow he'll have it. And I'll bet your boss is going to want to know what he plans to do with it."

He raised his arms and stretched his long bare body. Sarah remembered to be embarrassed and looked at the ceiling.

"So this isn't just some crummy rip-off, is it? Now it's a high-level managerial problem. You call Markworthy and then run along to your biggie in Greenwich. And make sure to tell him how helpful I was. I expect to get a raise out of this."

"I don't believe you," Sarah said again, this time without any conviction at all.

"Can you take the chance?"

She couldn't, of course. She turned to the telephone and dialed the data center.

"Jill?"

"Sarah, what's happening?"

"Don't say anything about the system. Just fix it up and let it run."

"*What*? Are you crazy?"

"I can't talk now; I'll come right over as soon as I can." She replaced the receiver and turned back to Russell. "Just remember something, Rabinowitz: We've got you if we want you—I'm hanging on to that printout. If you so much as give Jill a nasty look—"

"Oh, knock it off. I won't do anything like that. I've changed over to your side, remember?"

Sarah turned away, shaking her head.

"Hey. One more thing."

Russell was standing now, hands on hips. "It really is too bad Markworthy worked so fast. I had you goin', Saber. You know where you would've been right now?"

"Yeah. Still locked in the bathroom." She went out and slammed the door, cutting off Rabinowitz's easy chuckle.

Chapter 10

"Well?"

"It's running. Another few thou are going down the tube."

Jill was leaning against one of the orange walls in the data center, her hands in the pockets of her jeans skirt, a thick ream of green-and-white computer print-out tucked under her arm. She made no move to hand it over to Sarah.

"I owe you an explanation."

"Right."

They went to her tiny cubicle. There was only one chair, so Sarah sat on the desk. As she recounted what Russell had told her, Jill's indignation gave way to astonishment.

"Well? What do you think?" Sarah said after she had finished her account.

Jill leaned forward, elbows on the desk, and dug her fingers into her short curly hair. "Gosh, Sarah. I don't know if he's lying or not. But . . ."

"But what?"

"Well, the fact is, I really wouldn't have thought that Russell was gutsy enough to do something like this on his own."

"And Wilson? What's he like?"

Jill straightened up, giving her a wry grin. "Can't help you there; I've hardly ever seen him. Presidents hardly know DPers are alive. Unless—"

"Unless they want help getting their hands in the till?"

"Well, yeah. Russell's sure the ideal candidate for that. But I don't know how you can prove it either way. Sorry."

Sarah stood, picking up the printout. "Well, I guess I'll go see what my client wants to do."

But as she turned away, Jill got up and caught her arm. "Sarah, one thing Russell said I absolutely agree with."

"Yeah?"

"That it's pretty odd that you came up here in the first place. That your boss followed up on that change of vacation. I mean, those requests are routine. It's almost as if . . . as if . . ."

"As if he had a pretty good idea what I'd find?" Sarah nodded. "Another funny thing is that he dragged me out of bed this morning and sent me up here . . . on what turned out to be the very last day I could've caught Rabinowitz."

"Gosh." Jill folded her arms and hunched her shoulders, as if a chill wind were blowing through the data center. "I think I agree with Russell again: Whatever this is, it isn't just some crummy rip-off. What the hell is your client up to?"

"I just have to try and find out. Clients have one big weakness." Sarah smiled as she quoted something Chris had told her. "They expect you to be smart enough to find out what they want to know, and dumb enough to believe any lie they tell you."

"Gosh," said Jill again, wagging her head, "I wouldn't have your job for anything."

Sarah glanced around the little cubicle: the flimsy yellow dividers, the metal desk with just room enough for a telephone, a calendar, and a stack of reports. "Funny," she said, "I feel the same way about yours."

Jill did not grin, as Sarah had expected; instead she put an arm around her shoulders and said gravely, "Sarah, be careful."

The lobby at WHQ was empty but for the Securitco guards and the cleaning women, who were mopping up a trail of ground-in slush and cinders that led from the doors to the elevators.

Sarah rode up to the fifth floor and went down the hall to the office of the Vice-President for Leisure. The door opened on a very flashy reception room, with smoked-mirror walls, carpeting in RGI scarlet, and a chandelier that looked like plastic but was probably crystal. There was no one at the desk, but she could hear voices and the clatter of typewriters from within. She turned down a corridor and immediately ran into Thea Webb.

"Oh, there you are, my dear. I was expecting you." Mrs. Webb sighed, heaving her considerable bosom. "What a day I've had! Mr. Holman leaves, and everyone expects me to—"

"Mrs. Webb, I'd better make my report."

The hard little eyes seemed to grow brighter. "We'll use Mr. Holman's office."

It was an enormous office, of course. A conference table stretched out from the desk. The walls were studded with photographs, of stars who had appeared in movies from RGI's studio, of athletes who endorsed one or another's sporting goods lines—all of them shaking hands with or wrapping an arm around the grinning Hal Holman. Sarah looked at them in surprise. You expected this sort of thing from a restaurateur or a hair stylist, but not from the VP (L) of RGI. It was rather pathetic, really.

Mrs. Webb sat down at the table and waved Sarah to a chair across from her.

"Now," she said, "let's have it."

"Rabinowitz is an embezzler, all right."

Mrs. Webb received this information as she would have news of the death of a distant relative whom she had not liked very much. "I see," she said, and got out her cigarettes.

"I confronted him, and he told me a pretty crazy story. Want to hear it?"

Mrs. Webb nodded.

"He claims that he was ordered to—uh—to misappropriate the funds by Wilson."

"By Wilson?" Mrs. Webb gave her harsh laugh. "A crazy story indeed, my dear. I suppose we can expose that quickly enough. Did you get the number of the bank account—Wilson's alleged account, that is?"

"I can get it, but it won't do us any good."

Mrs. Webb froze with the cigarette halfway to her lips. Her beady eyes fixed on Sarah. "What do you mean?"

"The bank's in Geneva. There's no way we can compel them to release the name. Everybody from the United States government to the Mafia has tried to get names out of Swiss banks, with no luck."

Mrs. Webb stood up, so abruptly that she tipped her chair over. She looked down at it, and back at Sarah. "This is going to be damned difficult—I mean, if we can't clear Wilson. Damned sticky."

Sarah decided that it was time to try a little test. "If you want my opinion, I think the account is Rabinowitz's. I think he made this whole story about Wilson up. I'd call in the cops."

Mrs. Webb did not reply at once. She carefully set

her cigarette down in an ashtray. "Where is Rabinowitz now?"

"Probably back at work as usual, watching over the embezzlement of the last installment. His story is that Wilson wanted eight hundred thousand, and by the day after tomorrow he'll have it."

"And no one else knows about this—misallocation?"

Sarah considered a moment and said, "No."

"You've done very well, my dear, very well," said Mrs. Webb distractedly. "Of course I must talk to Mr. Holman at once. Wait right here." And she went out.

There was a telephone on the desk, but obviously Sarah was not to overhear this conversation. No surprise there, she thought. She propped her chin on her palm and watched the smoke rising in a straight plume as Mrs. Webb's cigarette slowly turned to ash and expired.

Mrs. Webb, at that moment, was just leaving the building. Folding her arms and hunching her shoulders against the bitter cold night, she ran across the parking lot to her car at a lopsided trot.

She drove down the road about a mile to a shopping center and went into a drugstore. At the counter she bought a pack of cigarettes with a ten-dollar bill and asked for the change in quarters.

There was a telephone booth out in the parking lot. She went into it and placed a call to London. At the operator's order she poured about an ounce of change into the slot.

There was time to light a cigarette while her call ran through circuits and cables, up into space, bounced off a satellite, and came to earth again in London N.W.3.

She heard only half of a ring before Holman snatched up the receiver. "Hello?"

"It's me."

"Thea. About time. Man, I was popping Valiums all through the flight. So what's going down? You talk to Saber?"

"Yes, just now. Oh, Hal. What a day I've had. Do you know, the CEO's office called at four and wanted me to—"

"Thea," Holman interrupted in a low, urgent tone, "whenever you do this number about what a rough day you've had, it means bad news."

"No, Hal. Saber found out that Rabinowitz is stealing the money for Wilson, and—"

"Great!" The word was a gasp of relief. "Oh, that's beautiful. What a release."

Mrs. Webb gave one of her short, strident laughs. "There is one—uh—unforeseen element, but I've already worked out a way to—"

Holman broke in. "Unforeseen element. What the hell does that mean? Can we nail him, or can't we?"

"Of course we can. But we'll have to make a slight change in plan." She recounted what Sarah had told her. It took Holman a long time to grasp it.

"Oh, my God," he moaned. "Then he can pay off Lisle and get the portfolio back without a trace that the money ever passed through his hands. That bastard. Oh, my God."

"We can still get him, sir," said Mrs. Webb. She knew it soothed Holman considerably to be called sir. "What you have to do is—"

"Oh, I don't want to hear about it! I'm just too bummed out. Oh, my God."

"Sir, I've thought it over, and—"

"I don't want to hear what you think. This whole

damn thing was your idea, Thea. You pulled this manipulative number on me, and—" He broke off abruptly.

Mrs. Webb had served Holman long and faithfully, and she knew that he always dealt with crisis in the same way, passing rapidly through shock, reproach, and into despair. She had to catch him before he took the plunge.

"Sir, you've got to send a telegram to Lisle immediately. Tell him that you've changed your mind—you want the money in cash. Demand a meeting in England, on Friday night."

There was a long pause, and then Holman asked morosely, "What happens at the meeting?"

Mrs. Webb sighed noisily into the mouthpiece. Making an effort to keep the impatience out of her voice, she said, "The meeting will never take place, of course. That's the night of Mr. Raspin's dinner party—the one that opens the Mid-Winter Conference. Wilson will arrive, followed by Saber—I'll see to that. She'll report to you that Wilson's carrying a small fortune in cash. Naturally, you'll confront him—"

At last, Holman had caught on. "Nail him red-handed, right in front of Raspin and everybody! Oh, man, what a great scene that'll be. Anything the bastard says, he'll get himself in deeper trouble. Oh, that's great."

"Now you will send the cable right away? And you remember that address Lisle uses, in Brussels?"

"Yeah."

"And you start the telegram: 'Re Martinique transaction—'"

"Yes, yes. I know all that. You just make sure Saber stays on Wilson, got it?"

"Yes, sir."

"Oh, Thea. One more thing."

At that point the operator cut in to demand more money, and Mrs. Webb slipped a few quarters in the slot. "Sir?"

"Thea, I really feel that I should share my feelings with you on one point."

Mrs. Webb debated whether she should say, "Yes, Hal?" or "Yes, sir?" She decided on the former.

"The thing is, you came on like this was disaster, and it turns out it was something we could deal with easily. Your response was just—completely out of proportion to the problem, you know? You get where I'm coming from?"

Mrs. Webb smiled in relief. The fine, resonant voice was calm and authoritative now, with only a hint of petulance. Holman now believed that it was he who had come up with the plan. His splendid self-confidence was built upon an indestructible foundation of obtuseness.

"Yes, Hal. I'll watch that in the future," she said.

"OK then. Good night."

A gentle tapping on her shoulder roused Sarah. She raised her head from her crossed forearms. Mrs. Webb was standing over her, smiling as benignly as she could manage.

"Have a long day, dear?"

"Yeah. Also a short night." She rubbed her eyes. "Where have you been all this time?"

"Talking to Mr. Holman. He said to tell you that you're doing a fine job, and you're to stick with Jack Wilson."

"You mean he believed Rabinowitz's story?" She fumbled for her cigarettes.

"We can't afford to take chances."

"Uh-huh." Sarah had a good deal of trouble lining up the cigarette with the match flame; she was really tired. "What do you mean, stick to Wilson?"

Mrs. Webb circled the table and sat down. "You see, Wilson will be leaving the country tomorrow night. For Europe."

Sarah took this in. "How do you know?"

"He's scheduled to attend the Mid-Winter Conference." Mrs. Webb gave another bark of laughter. "We don't know what he's planning that isn't scheduled."

"Where's the conference being held?"

"In England."

England. Sarah gaped for a moment. Then, in an action as deliberate as smoothing icing with a knife, she set her features in a blank expression. "You want me to follow him to England?"

"Yes. And report to Mr. Holman—he's over there already, actually."

Sarah nodded and rose.

"One more thing, my dear: The bonus Mr. Holman mentioned to you this morning is still in effect. Good night, and get plenty of rest."

In the elevator Sarah pressed the button for the second floor. The doors slid open on a long desk marked "Information Center." Behind it half a dozen secretaries were consulting books or viewing terminals and talking on the telephone.

Sarah picked out one who was free. "I want to get in touch with a colleague of mine who's working in London," she said.

The secretary nodded and replied, "Just call the switchboard at RGI House on Victoria Street. They'll know where he's staying." She wrote down the number on a slip of paper. "I'm afraid they don't open until nine o'clock, London time, though."

Sarah glanced at her watch. That would be three in the morning, her time. She resigned herself to another short night. "Call me RIGHT AWAY," Chris had written, and she meant to take his advice.

Chapter 11

They had put Chris in a company flat in Kensington, near Holland Park. His street bore the plummy name of Duchess of Bedford's Walk, and lived up to it: big, bluff, handsome apartment houses, built of red brick and granite, with porters peering loftily out the doors, and a row of Bentleys in front. The neighborhood was studded with signs reading "private" and "no entry" and (Chris's favorite) "not to be used as a playground by unauthorized persons."

The flat itself was as spacious and luxuriously appointed as one would expect, but Chris had had little time to enjoy it. By seven-thirty that morning, he was up and out, bound for another day of tailing Brenda Wertheim. He knew by now that she left her place at eight, arriving at work a good hour before anyone else did. As Gordon Dunbar had said, she was a diligent employee.

Walking down Campden Hill Road, Chris thought back to his luncheon at Dunbar's two days before, to the point when the major had come lumbering back into the pantry, cradling the new bottle in his arm like a baby, and asked what had become of Miss Wertheim.

"Of course," he had said, when Chris told him that she had gone back to her desk. "First-rate businesswoman, Miss Wertheim—you ought to hear her haggling with the shippers to get the best rates. She's a Jewess, you know."

Chris had laughed; he thought the word Jewess

had gone out with Sir Walter Scott. But then the unpleasant thought occurred to him that Dunbar really was anti-Semitic.

Over luncheon the major made several other remarks in the same vein, jokes with an edge of rancor showing through. "Never have held with it," he said, when someone mentioned decimalization. "If we're to do that, what was the good of beating Napoleon?" Or later: "Don't like to see so many colored in London. Really, if they were so anxious for us to clear out of their countries, why do they want to come here?"

Finally he came to the conclusion that Dunbar was what he seemed, a cheerfully resigned reactionary. He had attained a certain equanimity simply because he disapproved of everything that had happened in the last forty years.

Whenever he spoke in praise of anything, he finished with the words, "But that's all gone now, of course." The firm's vaults beneath the City, full of bottles laid down for families who had given Dunbar's their custom for generations, were now replaced by an air-conditioned warehouse in the suburbs. The leisurely trips across France, stopping at château after château to sample the vintage, were now reduced to quick visits to Bordeaux to haggle with the *négociants*. The whole wine trade—once a matter of boozy luncheons and convivial tastings—was now transformed to a series of inventory and distribution problems little different in nature from the selling of deodorant or breakfast cereal.

There were four of Dunbar's directors at the table, and they exchanged tolerant smiles while he spoke, left a pause when he had finished, and then turned to Chris to ask for more information about the strange ways of RGI. (He had been introduced as "Mr. Rockwell—he's from Connecticut, but he's not one of them.") Chris felt sorry for Dunbar; it always pained him to see older people being pushed aside. There was nothing for it, though; the major did not understand Atlantic or RGI at all and looked gloomily at his plate whenever they were discussed.

The luncheon had been the last interesting event of Chris's assignment. For the past day and a half he had been following Brenda, an unrelievedly tedious chore. She had not left her office but to go home, and she had not left home but to go to her office. So Chris had spent most of his time lingering over cups of tea in cafés and reading *Humphrey Clinker*.

If Chris had really been serious about the case, he would have dropped surveillance and gone to talk to Brenda's landlord, her bank manager, her associates at work. But he had no idea what he was looking for, and he sensed that the English would resist this kind of snooping far more than people did back home. Chris did not much care for it himself, in fact.

He remembered her asking him if he came from Wilson, and regretted that he had been so flustered that he botched the opportunity. Had he played it smart, he might have found out what she expected of Wilson—and gotten some clue as to why Wilson suspected her. Now Wilson would arrive tomorrow, and Chris would not be able to tell him anything. Too bad.

Before going into High Street subway station, he glanced up at the pellucid gray sky, shot through with tendrils of orange in the east. At least, he thought, the weather looked promising.

*   *   *

The day ripened into a beautiful afternoon, one of those spells of Mediterranean weather that occasionally lighten London's mid-winter gloom.

Today, with the sun shining down on them and a clear blue sky as backdrop, the long white stucco facades of Belgrave Square looked outlandishly beautiful—too beautiful to last, like a snow sculpture or a confection in icing. Yet they had lasted; these houses were a hundred and fifty years old. Round the plane-treed square they marched, with their glistening black railings, columned porches, lines of pedimented windows, stately and serene.

This, the grandest of London's residential squares, had long ago become too grand to be residential. Some of the houses were now embassies, flying foreign flags. Others showed a discreet row of metal plaques by the doorbell, bearing the names of eminently respectable associations, boards, and councils.

It was before one of these houses that a taxi pulled up. From its spacious backseat appeared Mr. Lisle. Jack Wilson would not have recognized him in his handsome tweed overcoat, gray fedora, and red muffler knotted as meticulously as a huntsman's stock. He paid the taxi driver, went up the two short steps to the portico, and pressed the bell inside the big glass-and-ironwork door.

When the porter answered, he gave the name of an advisory board and was ushered into the vestibule. The porter led him across the long, high-ceilinged hall to a pair of sliding doors.

This, he thought, stepping past the doors, must have been the dining room. It was big enough to hold a table that would have seated twenty guests, with room left over for footmen to circulate around it. Now there were only a few chairs, a desk, a receptionist.

"Good morning. I have an appointment to see Monsieur Drucker. My name is Lisle."

The receptionist stared at him in silence as her hand slid to the intercom and pressed a button.

Two men in cloth caps and heavy woolen jackets appeared in the doorway beside Lisle. One was bulky and truculent-looking, the other tall, bespectacled, and impassive. It was the second man who spoke. "Right this way if you please, Mr. Lisle." He mispronounced the name, as Englishmen invariably did.

Lisle did not correct him. He passed between the two men, and they fell in step beside him. At the end of the short passageway was an office, which they entered. A swarthy man in shirt-sleeves stood before the desk.

"Monsieur Drucker?"

"That's right."

"I have come alone, as I said," observed Lisle pointedly.

"Just wanted you to meet two of my associates," Drucker replied. "Nicholls on your left, and Hardy."

"Messieurs," said Lisle, bowing to either side.

Nicholls, the taller one, gave him a half-smile, while Hardy continued to survey him as if picking a target for his first punch.

"You can wait outside," said Drucker, and the men withdrew. "Sit down, Lisle."

Lisle did so, looking about the room. In appearance it was a quite ordinary office. But Lisle knew that the filing cabinets to his left would be full of annual reports from corporations throughout the world: Drucker's organization, like his, owned a few shares in scores of companies, solely for the purpose of obtaining an annual report and the information it contained. The Rolodex on the desk would be stacked with the names of clerks, secretaries, charwomen, even airline stewardesses, who were paid a small retainer each month simply to keep their ears open. And the locked steel cabinet in the corner? Full of bugs, tape recorders in every shape and size, shotgun mikes—all the electronic tools of the trade. The safe behind the desk would contain dossiers listing the personal weaknesses of various executives, which might prove useful for leverage someday, and ready cash, and even—considering what he had heard of Drucker—a few firearms.

Drucker folded his arms and stood leaning back against the desk. He was in his late thirties, with dense black hair cut short, dusky skin, and dark eyes. His build was wiry, his manner nervous.

"I didn't think your lot operated in the U.K., Lisle."

"We do not," Lisle hastened to assure him. "Much to my surprise, I find that a transaction of mine seems to be reaching a conclusion in your territory. I thought the simplest and most proper thing to do would be to solicit your aid."

Drucker had been tapping his fingers on his biceps and his toe on the floor throughout this short speech, and now he began to pace. He seemed to be a very restless man. "Much to your surprise?" he said.

"A few weeks ago, a letter arrived at our Brussels office. It contained excerpts from an item in the vendor's possession, which he was asking us to auction. We had not solicited it; in fact, we have no idea who the vendor is."

Drucker nodded impatiently. "Baby on the doorstep," he said, using the jargon of the trade. "We get those all the time, with instructions to shop them and pass back the lolly, and never mind where it came from, thank you. We're happy to oblige, if the item's worth it."

"This one was. It was the marketing portfolio for the sherries of Upton Lawrence and Dunbar, for the American market, prepared by that firm's new owner."

"Jolly lucky for you. Who's the new owner?"

A smile was lurking beneath Lisle's white moustache. "Atlantic Brands, John B. Wilson, president," he said, and added, "as you well know."

Drucker ignored this. "I assume you invited Wilson to the auction?"

"Of course. He was the winning bidder, in fact. We have just heard from him that he now has the funds. All was going smoothly. Until I received a telegram this morning from the vendor. He wants a meeting tomorrow night. Wilson is to bring the money in cash, and we are to divide it on the spot."

Drucker perched on the desk again, shaking his head. "You don't still do that midnight rendezvous stuff, do you? That went out ages ago."

Lisle refused to take offense. "We prefer to keep personal contact at a minimum, and most of our clients see it our way. It is quite clear that in this case the source does not trust us."

There was no irony in Lisle's tone, for his business, curiously enough, was founded on trust. Having scouted a company for a take-over, he was trusted not to sell the information to stock market speculators. Having stolen documents on commission, he was trusted not to photocopy them and sell them elsewhere. Lisle's organization—and Drucker's—had thrived for years because they were known to be above such maneuvers.

"If you want my advice, Mr. Lisle, I'd say your source is an amateur—someone who doesn't know the rules. Some secretary or clerk who got lucky."

"Thank you," replied Lisle, as courteous as always. "Now would you be more specific?"

Drucker raised his heavy eyebrows and remained silent.

"Come, monsieur, I know that you scouted Dunbar's for Jack Wilson."

"Really? Who told you that?"

"Did you place a tap or did you turn one of his people?"

Drucker said nothing.

"Monsieur Drucker, I am asking you to help me complete the transaction. For a part of my commission, of course."

Drucker's hairy fingers beat a tattoo on the desk top. "We turned one of Dunbar's people," he said at last.

"By what means?"

"Cuddle job. And now you think she's gone into business on her own? Against Wilson, this time?"

"Turn once, turn twice," said Lisle. "It happens all the time."

"So it does." He went round the desk and opened a lower drawer, delved through it for a moment, and brought out a manila folder. "All right, Mr. Lisle. We'll see what we can find out, shall we?"

"What is her name—the one you turned?"

"Brenda Wertheim."

For Chris, one of the most endearing things about Sarah was that she never "went shopping." When she wanted something, she dropped in at Lord & Taylor and bought it. But she was not one of those females for whom trying on clothes was a favorite form of indoor recreation.

Brenda Wertheim was. She had left Dunbar's at lunchtime; apparently, this was her afternoon off. Chris had hoped she would do something suspicious, or at least something interesting. But she had spent the last four hours combing the stocks of the big stores of South Moulton Street and the chic boutiques of Knightsbridge.

At five o'clock Chris was plodding after her down Brompton Road, numb with tedium. Even the skittish English weather had turned on him; although it was April, the day had veered back into January. An hour ago the storm clouds had rolled in like a rock slide, and it had been raining ever since. The conditions were ideal for a tail job; everyone on the crowded pavement had his chin sunk in his collar and his umbrella open, so Chris's precautions to hide his face from Brenda were not in the least noticeable. He could stay close, so there was no chance of losing her—much as he would have liked to.

He noticed that they were walking along the flank of a huge, palatial store. The opulent show windows were topped by white-and-green awnings that bore the name "Harrods." He knew that the place was a "must see" ranking just below the Tower, and he hoped that Brenda would go in. She did not disappoint him.

The January sales were on, and Harrods was indeed a sight. The aisles were packed solid: the usual Arabs, along with shoppers from every country in Europe come to prey on the feeble pound. The merchandise lay in long troughs: scarves, gloves, shirts, stirred into an inchoate mess by thousands of probing hands. The sales staff were leaning against the walls with their arms folded, looking like bystanders at a road accident who preferred not to get involved.

It was a shadower's nightmare. Despite her encumbering parcels, Brenda oozed through the crowd with ease. Chris, bulkier and more polite, found himself blocked at one moment, carried away as if by a current the next. Then he would rush forward, to find that Brenda had halted three feet in front of him to pick through a bin.

After a long and expensive stay in a pink-and-white enclave called the "Perfumery," she passed under an archway labeled, with characteristic English forthrightness, "Food Halls."

It was a big room with a vaulted ceiling, tiled in lime and white. On all sides of Chris were carcasses sprawled across beds of crushed ice: plump pink chickens, emerald-headed ducks, russet-feathered grouse, and more exotic species of fowl that he did not recognize.

Brenda had paused before a six-foot-tall construction of seafood: tier upon tier of crabs, lobsters, trout, salmon. The couple in front of Chris turned away, and abruptly there was no one between himself and Brenda. By a piece of ill luck, she turned at that moment.

For a split second he considered dodging into the crowd behind him, but he knew he would not make it. Even as Brenda's eyes met his, he was advancing with an arm upraised and a smile on his face.

"It's Miss Wertheim, right? I just happened to—"

But she did not seem surprised that they should meet in Harrods; she simply greeted him and asked, with her grave and timid air, if he thought she should buy some trout.

"Well, it doesn't keep very well, you know," was the only reply he could think of.

Brenda pondered for a moment and turned away. "No, I guess not. I'm like really bummed out. I've been shopping all day."

"Have you?"

"Yeah." She looked up at him. "Are you busy? Like to have tea?"

Chris considered for a moment and accepted. Following Miss Wertheim had proved to be a waste of time; he might as well try accompanying her.

Chapter 12

M. Lisle was standing near the door of the pub in St. Martin's Lane. He was blocked in on all sides by a solid wall of damp raincoats. The pub was very crowded, and everyone in it seemed to be taller than he was. It was a famous, splendidly furnished pub, with big etched-glass windows, mirrored walls, red plush seats. Everywhere were golden statuettes of undraped girls, holding light bulbs aloft like votive lamps. Lisle knew that Salisbury's was reputed to have a theatrical clientele, but if Vanessa Redgrave had stopped in to quaff a pint before the evening curtain, he had missed her.

Drucker's swarthy face appeared over the nearest shoulder, and he held a hand high to beckon Lisle. Walking sideways, like men on a narrow ledge, they made their way to a red plush nook near the staircase.

A man was waiting there for them. He stood up, a pint in either hand. Lisle stared at him; he was not what Lisle had expected. He was forty and looked it, with hair going thin on top and gray at the sideburns, flesh bulging above the knot of his tie. But he met Lisle's gaze with a smile so amiable that Lisle could not help returning it.

"This is Mr. Sullivan," said Drucker.

Sullivan showed no surprise at this one-sided introduction. "How d'you do, sir. If I can persuade you to take one of these, we'll shake hands."

Lisle took a glass of beer and accepted the outstretched hand.

"Cheers," said Sullivan, and after they had drunk, he added, "now sir, what can I do for you?"

"Mr. Drucker tells me it was you who—er, contacted Miss Wertheim—"

"I seduced her, you mean. We all know it, and we might as well say it, eh?" He looked as if he were about to nudge Lisle in the ribs, but resisted the impulse.

"Quite so," said Lisle. "Now we want to know—"

There was an interruption as a few of Sullivan's mates hailed him loudly from across the room. Sullivan grinned and waved, then turned back to continue in an undertone: "I'm not ashamed of the word. When you come right down to it, that's the name of the game for everyone, isn't it? What do you think those blokes are up to, with their ads in the Underground, trying to part you from a few quid? If they're trying to sell you a bloody typewriter, they'll show you a girl in her knickers. At least I'm honest about what I do. Good at it, too."

Lisle and Drucker nodded in silence.

"I know what you're thinking." Sullivan's ever-present grin grew wider. "I'm not exactly your Robert Redford type, am I? Let me tell you, that's an advantage. I mean, here you are, some ordinary secretary or clerk, and along comes this handsome young bloke declaring he can't live without you. Go on! These people aren't fools." He broke off and scanned their glasses. "Another round, then?"

"Not just now, thank you, Mr. Sullivan. Please go on." In general the fastidious Lisle stayed away from this side of his business, but the seedy and jovial Sullivan interested him.

"Well, people have these daft ideas about it, right

out of Victorian melodrama. They think first there's this big struggle to entice the lady to lose her virtue, then once you've got her in the sack, you've got to be so wonderful that you make her your slave. Rubbish. The key to the lock is not the— If you know what I mean, sir."

"I gather it's a rhyme," said Drucker. He was staring into his empty glass and fidgeting as if he wished that he were somewhere else.

"Right you are, sir. Now the truth is, going to bed with 'em is just a way of making friends."

"Making friends?" echoed Lisle.

"Right. That's the point of it all. Now you take Miss Wertheim. Getting into her knickers wasn't difficult. She's a randy little bit, though you wouldn't know it to look at her. As a matter of fact, she taught *me* a few tricks." Sullivan chortled. "You ever heard of the knotted handkerchief routine?"

"Yes. Get on with it, Sullivan," said Drucker, much to Lisle's disappointment. He had not heard of the knotted handkerchief routine.

"Right, sir. Well, you know how it is: After you've rogered 'em, they always want to tell you about their problems. Most blokes just turn over. But that's where I go to work."

Sullivan drained his glass and set it down. "Now back home, Brenda's a fully qualified solicitor—a lawyer, as they say. But of course that's useless over here, so she's working as a sort of glorified clerk. And mind you, these stuffy chaps at Dunbar's make her feel it. She's a Jewish lady as well, and you know how these St. James's Street people are about that. Doesn't fit in. She's a bright girl, works hard—but it won't do her any good with that lot."

Lisle nodded. He could see how Sullivan did it. He spoke of Brenda Wertheim as if she were a close friend, as if he sympathized with her and wished her well.

"So one night she's complaining about her job, and I just out and say, 'I know there's an American outfit looking to take over Dunbar's, and it would be to your advantage if they did—'"

Drucker looked up sharply. "You told her that?"

"Not to worry, sir. I made up a long rigmarole about how I came to know it, leaving you gentlemen well out of it. So. A few rows, a few fits of tears, and, finally, she says I'm to collect her from the office one night, when she's working late. There's hardly a soul about the place, and she excuses herself to go to the loo. There were all sorts of papers on her desk, and I ran off the lot on the office copy-machine. After that it was easy—the ice was broken, as you might say. Anything Mr. Wilson wanted, he just passed on the word to Mr. Drucker here, and Brenda could get it for me. Bloody awful security they have at Dunbar's, like all these old firms."

"And after the deal went through," said Drucker, "when it came time to break off with her—"

For the first time, Sullivan lost his smile. "That part of it's always a bit tricky, isn't it, sir? But I tried to soften the blow by telling her I'd make sure Wilson knew how helpful she'd been. I did, too. Sent him a letter."

Drucker raised his eyes to the ceiling and began to fidget violently. "Sullivan, *we're* supposed to see to that, not you."

"But she's a very nice lady," said Sullivan. "I liked her."

* * *

"Stupid sod," said Drucker. "He told her too bloody much, even if he's admitted all he told her."

It was ten minutes later, and they were in Drucker's car, bound for Belgrave Square. It had been difficult to pry themselves loose from Sullivan before he bought them another round, but at last he had given up and gone to join a riotous circle at the bar.

"I'm afraid that is often the way with—with cuddle jobs." The brutal, facetious jargon of the trade came clumsily from Lisle's tongue. "While your man is working the turn, the turn is working him."

"Yes," said Drucker. He brought all his usual tenseness and alertness to driving: one hand on the wheel, one hand on the gear lever, eyes moving from mirror to road to instruments and round again. "Maybe Wilson hasn't been quick enough to reward her, and she wanted to get her own back, or maybe she just thinks it's a jolly easy way to make money."

"It would explain this rendezvous foolishness. She does not know the procedures, and she is afraid we will not forward the money to her. She wants the cash in hand." He stared thoughtfully out the window as they passed the floodlit fountains of Trafalgar Square. "But that she should risk a meeting with Wilson—unbelievably foolhardy. If he recognizes her, I fear that Wilson will become . . . obstreperous." He smiled to himself, pleased with this fine English word.

"We'll put a watcher on her tomorrow. See if we can make sure she's really the one."

"A team, I think," said Lisle. "And immediately, if you please."

Brenda lived in a pleasant street in Fulham: rows of small brick houses with outsized bay windows, all alike but for an intricate variety of paintwork, and the degree of enthusiasm with which each owner cultivated his tiny front garden.

Chris was sitting in her living room—she rented three rooms on the second floor—while she prepared tea in the kitchen. It was expensively and stylishly furnished; "wonderful use of texture and color" was the phrase from the magazines that sprang to his mind. She had refused his offer of help, so he spent the time perusing her library: cookbooks and diet books in equal numbers, the usual manuals of basic and advanced sexual technique. It seemed that everybody had these sex books now, he thought—except Sarah, who said that she "preferred to wing it."

The tray that she eventually brought in was splendid—three kinds of tea, buttressed by a wide array of biscuits and scones. Chris thought at first that all this hospitality was leading up to another question about Jack Wilson; that she still thought he, Chris, had something to tell her. But Brenda did not broach the topic.

She said very little at all, in fact. Conversing with her was like getting damp logs to burn; if he let up for a moment, she lapsed into an unsettling silence, staring at him with her dark, luminous eyes. She was like a child anxiously awaiting a parent's permission.

Chris fell back on compliments. He praised her flat, her clothes, her tea things. This did the trick; she brightened visibly, began to talk more easily.

He thought of Gordon Dunbar and his staff, with their centuries-deep incrustation of good manners and assurance. How totally unlike them was Brenda —high-strung, awkward, eager to please. The more anxiously she sought these Englishmen's approval, the more they would draw back from her. He wondered what on earth she was doing in this country.

He quickly found out. Brenda asked if he would like to go out to a pub—"I mean, if you can stand me any longer." It was an invitation that anyone— and particularly Chris—would have found difficult to turn down. So they adjourned to the local, where Brenda ordered gin and tonic for herself and a pint of Guinness for him. Chris knew at the first sip that this heavy black brew was lethal, but it was also very good.

Alcohol quickly dissolved the thin shell of her reticence. The somber, watchful expression turned to a lopsided, silly, rather endearing grin. Over the next hour, she told him her life's story.

She had married an Englishman in New York and accompanied him when he returned to London, giving up a prize job at a Wall Street law firm to do so. She was as uncomfortable here as Chris had thought. Dislocation and bitterness did their work, and the marriage ended.

Chris asked why she had not returned home immediately.

"Well, I meant to, and then I met this guy."

"I see."

"I was like really in love with him, you know? It was one of those really intense things, and, um—"

She broke off, and Chris supplied: "Intense things usually don't last."

She nodded. "After we broke up I was like really bummed out. I mean, I was too depressed to do anything but eat. I put on twenty pounds. I looked really terrible, and I couldn't go home and like face everyone until I'd lost weight, you know?"

By the time she lost the twenty pounds, a new love affair was blooming on the horizon.

So it had gone, for the last six years. Brenda lived
on the vacillations of her love life, and—understand-
ably but unreasonably—nursed a grudge against Dunbar because she was not earning thirty-five grand a
year as a corporation lawyer.

Her recitation made considerable demands on
Chris, since she wanted—needed—his sympathy for her
troubles, approval for her decisions, reinforcement
for her hopes. Yet she had just met him a few days
before, and knew nothing about him—for she seemed
to feel it would be presumptuous to ask him any
questions. On one of his frequent trips to the gentlemen's—a drafty shed in back of the pub, with a gut-
ter running down it—he reflected that Brenda, garru-
lous, trusting, and dissatisfied, was an ideal turn.
Wilson had good cause to be worried after all.

But, as usual, just when Chris thought he saw a
crack of light, the door was slammed shut in his face.

When he returned to the table, Brenda said at
once: "I'm going to be seeing you a lot, you know?
I mean, since you work in Greenwich."

"Oh?"

"Yeah—I'm going back real soon." She hesitated,
for the first time in the course of three gin and ton-
ics. "That's why I asked you, you know, if you had
a message from Mr. Wilson. See, he's got a legal department—ICC problems and stuff—and he kind of
promised me a job there. Um—don't say anything
about that, OK? I'm not supposed to mention it."

Chris stared at her. Was Wilson asking him for
nothing more unusual than a prepromotion screen-
ing? If so, why hadn't he said so? And what about his
reply when Chris had first asked if she might be a
potential turn: "We've gone past the potential stage."
Chris shook his head dizzily. His brain was awash in

Guinness and he could not fathom Jack Wilson's intrigues.

Abruptly, the landlord was making rounds, calling out that it was closing time. They had missed the last call for drinks. Just as well, thought Chris.

They stumbled home arm in arm, partly in boozy intimacy, partly because they both needed support.

On her front steps they broke so that she could get out her latchkey. As she opened the door, Chris stood wavering beside her, thinking that he ought to kiss her on the cheek. He knew that it was going to be awkward.

She turned; he leaned toward her. Sure enough, they could not get their noses aligned properly and he ended up kissing her mouth.

Her lips parted and her arms went round him. She squeezed him so tightly that he could feel her breasts against his chest even through all their layers of clothing. Trouble, he thought. He should have guessed that she would want the final proof that he liked her and found her attractive.

She rested her head on his shoulder and said, "Would you like to come up for coffee?"

He cast about desperately for an excuse. Fortunately, in London, there was one ready at hand. "The Underground stops running pretty soon. I've got to get going."

"That's OK." She whispered the next words into the lapel of his coat. "You can—stay the night."

Chris shifted uncomfortably in her embrace. "I'm sorry," he said, meaning it. "I should have said that—well, I have a girl friend."

"Oh." She broke from him and stood with her arms hanging and her head bowed. "I guess you're real tight? I mean, she'd be hurt if—"

"Yeah, and she'd hurt me, probably with a tire iron."

The little witticism brought no response from Brenda. She stood motionless, eyes on the ground, rebuffed and painfully embarrassed. It was a bad moment, and she hit upon the very question that would make it worse. "What's she like?"

Chris could not answer her, could not tell her that Sarah was blond, imperious, graceful—her direct opposite in every particular. Thank God, the two would never meet. He mumbled another apology, a few lame compliments, and turned away.

As he heard her door shut behind him, he thought: Well, I've resisted temptation and been faithful to my love, and I feel like a jerk. He regretted hurting Brenda's feelings; less worthily, he regretted that the one time in his life that a woman had propositioned him, he could not take her up on it.

He had a moment of tipsily intense nostalgia for the eighteenth century, which he visited so often in books. Things were simple then, by God: Virtue was virtue, and venery was venery. Of course, in the eighteenth century he would have been married to Sarah. He wondered if he *ever* would be married to Sarah. I'm having a *vin triste,* he decided. A *bière triste,* to be exact.

Occupied with such thoughts, he pursued a wavering course toward the subway station. The black pavement shone from the rains, and the sky had that odd rosy hue so characteristic of London, produced by the diffusion of thousands of sodium lamps in the mist. He reached the corner and found that he was not in the Fulham Road. Wrong way. He turned and retraced his steps.

As he passed Brenda's house, something went click

in his head. He stopped and looked about, waiting for his thoughts to catch up with his instincts.

There. Directly across the street, a closed van, unmarked, with whitewashed back windows. He walked over and glanced through the windshield. There was a blanket draped behind the seats.

Chris had spent many hours in the back of vans like this one, sitting on the floor and peering out the louvers, and getting cramps in his legs. Watching.

A wave of exasperation rippled through him. Nelger, of course. The indefatigable Nelger. Frustrated because he had no SPP's, and tipped by Chris himself that there was something to Brenda Wertheim, he had put a team of watchers on her. Chris thought of going round and hammering on the door until they opened up, and telling them to go home. But they would just say that they were following orders. He had better go straight to the top.

Everything was shut up and silent on the Fulham Road, and he had to go all the way to Parsons Green Station to find a public phone. After a bleary few minutes trying to figure out how the telephone worked, he got Nelger's home number from directory inquiries and dialed it.

"Nelger here." It was the weary, unsurprised tone of a man used to being awakened by telephone calls.

Chris put his two pence in the slot and said, "It's Rockwell."

"Oh, hi, Chris. How are you?"

"I've just left Brenda Wertheim's," he said, significantly.

He expected Nelger to begin pouring out excuses at once, but all he heard was a baffled, "Oh?"

"Come on, Nelger. Don't you take a certain interest in her yourself?"

Nelger laughed. "Hey, Chris, I'm a happily married man."

"Would you mind getting serious?"

"Oh. Sorry. Should I take an interest? I mean, what are we dealing with here? Is there a problem?"

The realization came upon Chris as slowly and chillingly as a winter's nightfall. "You're not running a surveillance on her?"

"Well, no. Do you want me to start one?"

"No—that's OK—sorry to wake you." He hung up the receiver, thrust the door of the booth open violently, and strode back toward Brenda's street as quickly as he could. Private detective work was far less dangerous than most people imagined, but it had its bad moments, and they always scared Chris Rockwell silly. His mouth felt dry and his heart was pounding violently; it stirred up turmoil in his beer-bloated innards, and he began to hiccup. Whatever's going on, he thought, I'm in no shape to deal with it.

At last he reached the corner of Brenda's street. He swallowed a hiccup and peered round the flank of a house. There was the high, bulky shape of the van, looming in the row of parked cars. His gaze moved across the street, in time to catch the light in Brenda's window going out.

He waited.

Nothing happened.

It was one of the most wretched nights of Chris's working life. He had no car, no place to sit down and read. Not that he was in any shape to read anyway. He passed slowly from drunkenness to hangover without the intervening sleep. It was a grim matter of his coordination improving slightly, his head beginning to ache, and his anxieties coming into sharper focus.

At times he tried to convince himself that he was imagining things; surely there were closed vans in the world that did not belong to surveillance teams. But his instincts told him that when Brenda left for work in the morning, someone would follow her.

In the morning? He could not assume that nothing would happen until then. Perhaps she had plans to go somewhere sooner than that, which the watchers knew about and he did not. One thing for certain: They knew something about her that he didn't.

He could not stand on the corner all night, of course. He wandered the streets of Fulham, returning to Brenda's as often as he dared, to peer around the corner and find that there were no lights showing in her place, and that the van had not moved.

Eventually he settled into an irregular circuit, shambling down to Parsons Green to sit on one of the benches for a while or to relieve himself behind a tree (the only pleasant moments of the night), then going up to Brenda's corner, then back to the green again. The mild, damp chill of an English night seemed to penetrate his clothes layer by layer, finally reaching the marrow of his bones.

Numb with cold, fatigue, and stale worry, he lost track of time. He was almost surprised when he perceived that the yellow glow of the street lamps was growing dimmer and the sky turning slowly from black to sullen gray. The swishes of passing cars grew more frequent, the pedestrians multiplied into a solid stream bound for the underground station. For the first time Chris allowed himself the luxury of checking his watch. His abstinence was rewarded: it was a quarter to eight. Brenda would be setting out soon. He trod back to her corner one last time, the soles of his feet and the backs of his knees aching.

Precisely at eight Brenda appeared, as beautifully turned out as usual in a white trench coat and soft beige boots. She walked away from Chris, toward Bishop's Road.

Chris turned his attention to the van, waiting for the rear doors to open. They did not. Instead a green Fiat sedan pulled up next to the van and three nondescript men got out. One climbed into the driver's seat of the van and drove it away, while the other two set off after Brenda. Changing of the guard, thought Chris, and went after them.

He turned the corner in time to see Brenda cross Bishop's Road and join a bus line. One of the two men walked on without a pause or even a glance; the other crossed the street and fell into the line.

Chris knew a first-rate professional surveillance job when he saw one. This man would stay on the bus when Brenda left it at St. James's Street; by that time the other two, in the Fiat, would have driven there and would be waiting to see her to Dunbar's.

They could follow her indefinitely without her catching on; but for ten years' experience Chris would never have spotted them himself. Whoever they were, they thought she was worth a lot of trouble and expense.

Chapter 13

Gordon Dunbar got down from the bus with difficulty. He had broken a leg parachuting into Arnhem in the last war, and on cold, damp mornings like this one the joints in his knee felt as if they had fused solid. The conductor watched his efforts indifferently. Dunbar could remember when the conductors—and everyone else—had helped old people. But then this fellow was an Indian.

Using his umbrella as a cane, Dunbar hobbled to the curb and waited to cross Piccadilly. He could quite easily have ordered a company car from RGI to drive him to work, but he had ridden the bus for thirty years, and he was a man of habit.

The lights changed. He crossed the street and was about to turn into St. James's when, out of the corner of his eye, he saw a man burst from the door of a café and rush at him. He froze and hunched his shoulders, with the old person's fear of being knocked over. But the man stopped beside him.

"Major—"

"Mr. Rockwell! Good morning." The American looked dreadful—hair and beard a damp tangle, the broad face pale and drawn, the green eyes behind his spectacles narrowed to red-rimmed slits.

"Major, I want you to tell me something."

"Of course."

"Does Brenda have access to any—any classified stuff from Atlantic Brands?"

"Miss Wertheim? Why, no."

"Are you sure? It's very important."

"Oh, quite sure. Ever since the merger we've had all sorts of fellows from Securitco about the place, seeing to it that nobody can get to anything. In the old days, of course, things were different—but then, what wasn't?" He chuckled, then broke off abruptly. "What is it, Mr. Rockwell?"

Rockwell had plunged his hands into the pockets of his dirty raincoat. He shook his head and turned away. "Sorry I bothered you, Major. I don't think there's anything you can do."

Dunbar laid a hand on Chris's shoulder. "I think you'd better tell me what's happened."

Chris hesitated a moment, then nodded. "OK. Wilson sent me over here in the first place because he thinks Brenda's a turn."

"A what?"

"That she's selling secrets to his competition. Or she's likely to, or— I don't know what the son of a bitch thinks. He didn't trust me either."

"Good God."

"Anyway, now there are some guys following her."

"*Following* her? Are you sure?"

"Yes. And they're not from Securitco. But they're pros, and there are a lot of 'em."

"What are you going to do?"

"There's nothing I can do. If I hang around any longer they're sure to spot me, and that'll only make things worse. I've got to talk to Wilson."

"He's to arrive tomorrow—"

Chris nodded dazedly. "Yeah. Sorry I bothered you, Major."

Dunbar watched him turn away and vanish into the crowds in Piccadilly. Then he made his way down St. James's Street—familiar, solid St. James's Street, with its rows of handsome shop fronts, ending in the

muddy-brown brick facade of the Palace, guarded by
the immobile soldiers in greatcoats and bearskin hats.
He stared about him in amazement. It seemed ludicrous that this place should be—should be "staked
out," as they said in the crook films. Such things did
happen in real life, he knew, but Major Dunbar's
mind had been cast in the thirties, and he believed
that they happened only among the "criminal classes."
Not here in St. James's, surely.

He entered his own building, acknowledged the
receptionist's salutation with a distracted wave of his
umbrella, and climbed the stairs to his office. He was
taking off his overcoat when he remembered how
cold it was.

His secretary rose as he entered. Out of the corner
of his eye he saw a trio of men take their briefcases
off their laps and get to their feet.

"Good morning, sir. These are the gentlemen from
RGI's accountancy group—"

Dunbar remembered vaguely that he was to be
lectured this morning on his cash-flow problems. "I
can't see them now," he said, and went on into his
office. As he closed the door, he could hear his secretary making flustered apologies.

All his employees treated him with bemused tolerance these days. "Poor old Dunbar," he had heard
someone say, "he was dotty to begin with, and he's
become dottier still since the take-over."

He understood; sometimes he even agreed. He had
been back on his heels ever since his first encounter
with Jack Wilson. Perhaps he ought to retire to a
seat on the board, go to Spain and live on the divi-
dends from the block of Atlantic Brand shares that
had come to him in the merger. He had been gener-
ous, Wilson had, with money. What prevented Dun-

bar from doing this was that he knew it was precisely what Wilson wanted.

It had all been very odd. Upton Lawrence & Dunbar was one of the last of the independent shippers, and about a year ago he had begun quietly looking for a congenial large corporation to take a block of his shares, in order to forestall unfriendly take-overs. He had settled on his American importers—but suddenly they had turned about and resold the shares to Atlantic Brands. Wilson had risen up before him so suddenly, armed with an extraordinary knowledge of who his other shareholders were, and the best times and ways in which to approach them. He moved so swiftly, so decisively. Dunbar had come to feel that he was overmatched. It was this as much as anything that had broken his resistance.

Now Wilson seemed to think that Brenda Wertheim was betraying him. Why? It was as inexplicable as everything else about that able, insidious man.

Dunbar sat down behind his desk, buttoning up his overcoat. His secretary buzzed him to say that one of his directors was here to go over the précis book with him, that someone from accounts wanted advice on a long-overdue bill, that the gentlemen from RGI were still waiting to see him. He told her that he could not be disturbed for the rest of the morning. He sat hunched in his chair, brooding, oblivious to the intermittent racket from the roof.

The answer came to him an hour later, in a cold, bright flash of insight. He ran over the jumbled, painful events of the take-over once more, and this time all was sickeningly clear. It was like watching the slow-motion film of an accident or an assassination on the television news. There was only one way in which Wilson could have known what he did, when he did: He had set spies on Dunbar's, and the spies had bribed someone. Not someone: Brenda Wertheim. It was obvious; looking back, he could even guess which letters she had stolen, which conversations she had repeated, and the times when she had done so. The only reason he had not seen it before was that he could not concede that such things were possible, that such things could be done to him. It was Rockwell who had opened his eyes.

But what was going on now? Why did Wilson think Brenda Wertheim had turned on him? In a cold fury, he attacked the problem, and eventually his intuition limned the shadowy outlines of an answer.

Major Dunbar's secretary had spent the morning apologizing to his appointments, and she was profoundly relieved when the intercom buzzed; perhaps he was ready to see people now. Instead he asked her to bring him two items from the files: the Securitco clearance sheet that set forth who had copies of Wilson's marketing portfolio, and a complete listing of those attending the Mid-Winter Conference.

Hal Holman was installed in the choicest of RGI's company houses, a tidy white stucco cottage separated by a high brick wall from Holly Mount, a genteel lane that climbed from Hampstead Village toward the Heath.

He was in the bedroom, having just awakened from his afternoon nap. He had once heard that President Kennedy had always taken a nap, so that he could start the second half of his eighteen-hour day fresh. Holman did not work eighteen-hour days, but nonetheless he thought the nap an excellent idea.

He was putting his purchases of the morning—a dozen shirts from a Jermyn Street shop—away in an elegant satinwood chiffonier when the doorbell rang. Automatically, he picked up a sheaf of papers before going downstairs. The papers were to give the impression that the caller had interrupted him in the midst of work. Such elementary tactics, if carried out shamelessly enough, could help take a man a long way in RGI.

He opened the door to find a tall, florid-faced man on the threshold.

"Mr. Holman? Good afternoon. My name is Dunbar. I wonder if you could spare me a few minutes."

It took Holman a moment to place the name; when he did, he felt as if he had been stabbed with an icicle. "Dunbar . . ." he murmured.

"Yes. Of Upton Lawrence and Dunbar," the man reminded him, politely.

"Yes, I know."

"Oh, good. May I come in?"

"No. I mean—I'll come out. I mean, I'd like to get some air." Holman did need air; he felt that things were closing in on him. He put down the papers and picked up his handsome suede jacket.

Side by side they climbed Constitution Hill. There were brightly colored kites dancing beneath the lowering clouds, and a dozen boys in yellow jerseys, strung out along the green brow of the hill, jogging. Central London, a blue-gray jumble, lay along the horizon below them.

"Lovely place, the Heath," said Dunbar. "Surprised they haven't managed to spoil it yet. Pity we haven't a finer day."

Holman mumbled an assent and waited.

"You're Wilson's superior, I believe?"

At that, Holman's last wan hope—that Dunbar's visit was purely coincidental, had nothing to do with the marketing portfolio—expired. His thoughts whirled dizzily. Usually, problems did not come to him until they had gone through layers of staff. By the time they reached his desk, they were attached to a "recommendation" from Mrs. Webb that made it quite clear what he should do. Now he was on his own. His anxiety level—as he would have put it—was high and rising rapidly. He wished he had taken another Valium with lunch.

"That's right," he finally said.

"Then I think you should know that he believes that one of my employees has stolen trade secrets from him."

"Someone in *your* company—" Holman broke off, giddy with relief. This was not disaster; on the contrary, it fit right into his scenario. It was an opportunity for a master stroke.

So, in a fit of glee, Holman set about committing his fatal error.

He stopped dead and snapped his fingers. "So *that's* it. Major Dunbar, this is not entirely a surprise to me. I'm already tuned in "

He was gratified to see that Dunbar looked astonished and impressed. "Indeed? Did you know?"

"Well, I've known something was up for a long time, and I've had my people on it. Now your input completes the picture. You did the right thing to come to me."

"Well, I'm glad to be of some help, but what is going on?"

"Wilson's misappropriated eight hundred thousand dollars from his company. He's arriving in England tomorrow, ostensibly for the Mid-Winter Conference. It's pretty clear now, the number he's really doing: He's going to pay off this employee of yours to get back the secrets the guy stole."

He looked up at the old man, who was obviously following him with some difficulty. "Good lord! Fancy that. Never heard of such goings-on. But Mr. Holman, what could these secrets be? What do we have at our place that's worth eight hundred thousand dollars?"

Holman ran his hand through his meticulously tousled gray locks, in counterfeit of thought. Then he snapped his fingers again. "The marketing portfolio on your line of sherries. That must be it."

"Ah. Yes, of course, that would be it." Dunbar's head bobbed slowly up and down. "Well, you do seem to have it all worked out, Mr. Holman."

"Call me Hal, please."

"Thank you. I expect what you're going to do now is let this—er—payoff take place, and then swoop down and bag the lot of 'em, eh?"

The first doubts began to slither into Holman's mind. Perhaps he had not been so clever after all. Perhaps he should have thought this through. "Well —uh—no," he dithered. "I mean, we can't take the risk . . ."

"Oh?" said Dunbar, perplexed. "Don't you want to catch Miss Wertheim too? She's the employee Wilson suspects, you see."

Holman cast about feebly for a pretext and found none. Like the good RGI exec he was, he made his stand behind a rampart of jargon. "The risk factors in such a situation would be unacceptable."

Major Dunbar raised his head and fixed Holman with his bright blue eyes. He smiled. It was an extraordinary smile; his lips drew back from his teeth as if he were about to take a bite from an apple. The teeth were large, uneven, and, despite his age, all his own.

"Now, Holman. What are you up to?"

The tone of his voice was entirely different now; it sent Holman's anxiety level right through the roof. He stared at the man and said nothing.

"Miss Wertheim has never gotten anywhere near that portfolio."

"Hey, now wait a minute. You just said—"

"I said that Wilson suspected her. As it happens, he's wrong. So that leaves us with the question: Who is he planning to meet and pay off? There were only four copies of the marketing portfolio made—I checked this morning. Two are at Atlantic Brands. One with me. And the other . . . with you."

Holman backtracked desperately. "Maybe I misspoke myself. About the meeting. I mean, I don't know if there's going to be any meeting."

"Really? But a moment ago you seemed so sure."

Holman squared his shoulders and made an attempt to sound indignant. "Look, Dunbar, I don't like this whole manipulative number you're trying to pull. You're trying to trick me."

"I should say I've succeeded in tricking you." Holman was about to speak, but the major held up his hand. "Now do be quiet and think for a moment, will you, Holman?" he said, in a schoolmasterly voice. "Suppose I go to—to what's his name, Raspin, and repeat to him what you've told me. That wouldn't be very satisfactory, would it?"

"You couldn't prove a damn thing." Holman winced and went on lamely, "I mean, there's nothing to prove."

"I'm beginning to think that you are an exceptionally dim fellow, Holman. Perhaps I should make it quite clear that I know you are plotting against Wilson—"

"That is absolutely—"

"—and I want to help you."

Holman froze in the midst of shaking his head in denial. He peered at Dunbar suspiciously. "Help me?"

"I loathe Wilson," he said distinctly.

"But—how come?"

"You've seen the marketing portfolio? And you don't know?"

Holman shook his head.

Dunbar shrugged his broad shoulders and turned away, to walk on with his stiff-legged gait. "Well, that's as may be. Tell me, what has Wilson done to you?"

Holman fell in beside him. "Wilson," he said, "is not planning to be president of Atlantic Brands much longer."

"Oh?"

"The son of a bitch is on a power trip that is not to be believed. Ever since the merger, he's been planning to slide into RGI to take my job." Holman's voice quavered; his handsome face had grown pale and strained. "And he's managed to get certain factions in WHQ behind him. He thinks—they think—that I don't perceive the situation. The bastards think they can go on smiling and patting me on the back right up till they stick in the knife. But I flashed on it right away. You hear often enough that the performance indicators on your companies are down and that 'Jack's going to grow with the company' and all that crap, and you know you're gonna get dumped on. So I decided to total the son of a bitch." In fact, it was Mrs. Webb who had flashed on what was going down, and had laid the plans for totaling Wilson, but Holman tended to make any good plan he had agreed to his own.

"Yes, I thought it might be something like that," said Dunbar with placid distaste. "But I don't see how your plan is going to effect that."

"My plan got royally screwed up," said Holman bitterly. "I passed the marketing portfolio anonymously to a Cobi outfit—"

"A what?"

"A business intelligence syndicate. Told them to auction it to his competitors. That would have been lingering death for Wilson. But the bastards—"

"They invited Wilson to the auction, of course. Figuring that since he had most to lose, he would bid highest. Jolly clever of them. So what did you do next?"

Holman stared at the big, white-haired man lumbering along beside him. "Hey, what's with you, anyway? You know a lot more about Cobi operations than you . . ."

Dunbar did not look at him. "It's vile and disgusting, but it's not particularly difficult to understand," he said. "What did you do next?"

"Well, I knew he'd have to get the price—eight hundred thou—together in a hurry, so I put my people on it, and they found out how he was embezzling the money. If I caught him doing that, it would wipe him out just as well. There was a slight hitch in that he was doing the whole deal through numbered accounts in Switzerland, but I cleared that up by contacting the Cobi outfit and demanding a meeting—"

Dunbar had stopped so suddenly that Holman broke off. The old man's gaze wandered vaguely across the London skyline. "A meeting? So Wilson's to be there. Alone. And these—these spies. They'll be obliged to send their top man, won't they? They can't very well trust just anybody with that much money. . . ." He smiled again, the gleeful, humorless smile that frightened Holman badly. "When and where?"

"I just told 'em tomorrow night, in Berkshire. That meeting's never going to happen, you know," he added, uneasily.

But Dunbar seemed not to hear. "Then they're waiting for further details, are they? I can specify them myself. That's excellent. Excellent."

"Look, Dunbar, it's not gonna happen. That scene is not gonna go down. Wilson will arrive at Raspin's country house for this big dinner party, my detective who's tailing him reports to me that he's got the money, and I confront him. He's totaled right there. His career is like *finito*."

"No," said Dunbar, "that's not enough." His hands behind his back, he started walking again. "Odd coincidence, Holman. These spies—these scum you're dealing with. They're the same lot that work for Wilson."

Holman shook his head vehemently. "No way, no way I'd take that chance. Wilson always uses an outfit based in Geneva and London. I went to a guy in Brussels named Lisle. He never works in Britain."

Dunbar merely shrugged. "They've joined forces then. You see, they're watching Miss Wertheim. They think she's the one who stole the portfolio. Just as Wilson does."

"Yeah. How come he thinks that?" Holman asked.

"Because Miss Wertheim is the one who betrayed me to Wilson. I couldn't understand that at first myself. But a treacherous man sees treachery everywhere. What a vile creature Wilson is. Vile."

Dunbar spat the word out; his shoulders were trembling with anger. Involuntarily, Holman stepped back. His gaze skittered across the vast green expanse of the Heath, as if he were searching for cover. This old guy is crazy, he thought.

"Do you know what he did to me?" Dunbar went on.

"Uh—no. I mean, I knew that Cobi aspects entered into the take-over process, but we feel that—I mean, we in top management don't keep a very close watch on things like that. We feel it's sort of—more ethical if we don't know."

Dunbar's fierce blue eyes met Holman's. For a long moment he was silent. Then he turned away.

"Yes, of course. More ethical," he said quietly, almost to himself. "It's quite wonderful, the way your squalid intrigues have set things up for me. There's a certain justice to it, really."

"What—what are you going to do?" Holman asked querulously.

"All you need do, Holman, is tell me how I am to contact this man Lisle with the final arrangements. Then, at Raspin's house tomorrow night, you call your detective off. Tell him you will deal with it. You can think of some pretext. That's all."

"What are you going to do?" Holman repeated.

"Wilson will not take your job, Holman. That's all that need concern you."

Holman stared past him, at the lush green hillside,

the line of bare, gnarled trees, the leaden sky. Just
then he was hardly aware what he was looking at,
but the view imprinted itself on his memory; it was
to stay with him, and make him shiver whenever it
reared up before his mind's eye, for the rest of his
life.

"You're gonna kill him. My God, Dunbar—"

"All of them," said Dunbar calmly. "You needn't
worry; I've worked it all out."

Holman wagged his head dazedly. "Hey, look, Dunbar. You're fixated on this moralistic thing—laying
all this stuff on me about it being disgusting and
scum and treachery. I mean, don't think I can't relate, but you're getting it all blown out of proportion. I mean, look at the other side. You got a lot
of AB stock, am I right? You know what AB stock
is worth?"

Dunbar did not even look at him. "The Wertheim
slut betrayed me, and Wilson and his hirelings stole
my company—a company that has belonged to my
family for two hundred years. And now Wilson's
wrecking it—wrecking it!" He broke off, closed his
eyes, and took a long breath. Then he resumed, quite
calmly, "But of course that wouldn't interest you,
Holman. Just tell me: How do I contact Lisle?"

Holman stared at him in stunned silence.

"You really have no choice, you know," Dunbar
pointed out, mildly.

Holman looked down at the dense green grass between his Guccis. This was, strangely enough, not
an unfamiliar situation for him. Throughout his in-
glorious but successful career, he had met many
people of greater weight and strength than himself,
and he had always yielded to them, gone where their
wills propelled him, while making the best he could

of it for himself. This astute pliancy was Holman's one great gift, and it had taken him a long way.

"You have to send a registered letter to Brussels," he said. "Like right away." And he gave the major the address.

Chapter 14

The day was gone already, thought Walter Raspin. He could hear the chat and laughter of his secretaries as they gathered at the cloakroom to bundle up for the trip home. Raspin himself would not be leaving for a long time. His vast desk, all the way from the telephone console to the humidor, was covered with reports from Greenwich, which he had to read. All of them concerned the rising power of the Japanese corporate state. It seemed to Raspin that all the people at WHQ did was worry about the Japanese corporate state, and how RGI could possibly compete if the antitrust division of the Justice Department kept getting in their way. Still, Raspin would read them all, and it would take him most of the night. He slowed himself down even further by correcting the grammar in the reports, referring to a copy of Fowler's *Modern English Usage* that he kept at his elbow. A concern for the language was so unusual at RGI that it added to Raspin's aura of enigmatic brilliance.

He was unwrapping a chocolate and shaking his head over a dangling modifier when one of the secretaries knocked and leaned in.

"Sir? We've had another change in the guest list for your dinner tomorrow."

Raspin sighed. This dinner was turning into considerably more trouble than it was worth. "Yes, what now?"

"It's Upton Lawrence and Dunbar—the wine merchants in St. James's. They say Major Dunbar is indisposed, and they'd like to send a Miss Wertheim, one of the directors in their export department. She's an American, apparently, and—"

Raspin had developed the skill for dealing with such minor matters without giving them any thought. "Yes, all right," he broke in. "Have somebody call Miss Wertheim and invite her. And call Mrs. Raspin and tell her she'll have to rearrange the seating." He had not looked up or paused in the careful unwrapping of his chocolate.

Brenda Wertheim was the last to leave the export department office, as usual. Standing in the doorway, Dunbar waited until she had taken her purse out of the bottom drawer and stood up. Then he approached her.

He noticed how fashionably and expensively dressed she was—the soft suede boots, the long, flowing dress in a muted Paisley. She looked as if she had stepped off a page in one of those women's magazines she was always reading. Those magazines. Dunbar was amazed, whenever he glanced at their covers, at the long lists of curt instructions: what you're to buy, how you're to look, how you're to live. It occurred to him that she was the "consumer" Wilson was always talking about. She lived to buy.

And she worked to make money—only to make money. It had long irritated him that she saw her job simply as a matter of shipping volumes of liquid, that she had worked in the wine trade for six years without taking any particular interest in wine. He should have guessed that she took no interest in his company, either. How foolish he had been to expect loyalty in a character of such mediocrity.

"Oh, Miss Wertheim?"

She turned her solemn, foolish face to him. "Oh hi, Major."

"Just going home, are you?"

She hesitated, as she always did when he addressed her, uncertain whether she should expect praise or prepare excuses. "Um—yes," she brought out at last.

"Oh, that's splendid. Would you mind terribly posting this for me?" He held out a letter. "It's got to go off tonight, registered mail."

"Oh, sure." Brenda took it.

"Thank you, Miss Wertheim. Good night." He watched her go out, noticing that she carried the letter in her hand instead of putting it in her purse, where she might forget it. The meek, diligent Miss Wertheim.

In a long file of Kensington gentry with bowler hats and umbrellas, homeward bound from the City, Chris Rockwell climbed Campden Hill Road to Duchess of Bedford's Walk. It was nearly thirty-six hours since he had left the flat, he thought wearily. Thirty-six hours without sleep, but for a nap this morning at the desk of a kindly secretary in RGI House.

He had spent the whole day there, trying to get in touch with Jack Wilson. Wilson's home number was unlisted, and there was no answer at Atlantic Brands until 3:00 in the afternoon—9:00 A.M. Eastern time. Then Chris had spoken with a resolutely unhelpful secretary, who told him that Mr. Wilson was not coming in at all today. He would be in meetings in New York right up until his plane left that evening. Chris tried to get some response by telling her his name, but Mr. Wilson had never mentioned it to her, of course.

By now, Chris was too worn to care. He trudged up the steps and into the creamy wainscoted foyer of his building.

"Oh, Mr. Rockwell."

He turned to see the porter—a cheerful, ruddy-faced man with a pronounced limp—coming toward him.

"Hi, Dutton. What's up?"

"Telegram for you, sir." He held out the long buff envelope.

Chris thanked him and walked toward the elevator, fumbling with the envelope. He stopped dead as he read the message.

TRYING TO REACH YOU FOR TWO DAYS STOP ARRIVE ENGLAND TOMORROW STOP SCHEDULE UNKNOWN BUT FOR RGI DINNER AT LEIGHTON HALL BERKS STOP BE THERE BANG

> LOVE
> SARAH

Chris sagged against the wall and closed his eyes. "Now what?" he said aloud.

It was early evening, the time when most of the transatlantic flights depart, and Kennedy Airport was busy.

Slumped in the back seat of his Cadillac, Jack Wilson looked out at that jumble of oversized clam shells that was the TWA terminal. To his right the taxi rank stretched out in a long, wriggling yellow line like a caterpillar, and in front of him the loading area was a hopeless tangle of cars and buses.

Wilson glanced at his watch. "Oh, what the hell,

Charlie," he told his chauffeur. "I'll walk it from here."

"It's OK, sir. You've got an hour till your flight."

"I'll walk," Wilson repeated. "So long, Charlie." In fact, he was not worried about catching his flight, but about making his appointment with the man who would give him the account number into which he was to transfer the money. It was typical of this outfit, he thought, that they would not give him the number over the phone. It was no less typical that they had known he was going to London, and even which flight he was taking. A very efficient bunch, these guys.

He stepped out of the car, into a howling gust of wind that bit his ears and cheeks, tore at his clothes, and nearly lifted his feet from the pavement. Hunching his shoulders, he jogged over to the terminal.

The vaulted roof of the main lobby resounded with the babel of hundreds of voices. The catwalks and steps leading to the restaurants were solidly lined with people, but the biggest crowd was the one keeping an anxious watch over the blackboard that announced, with a riffle of cards, the time and status of flights. Wilson noted that his own flight was boarding already, and walked on toward the International Concourse. He was to meet the man there. He reflected that it was smart of them to make him pass through the security checkpoint first; not many bugs were small enough to get past the metal detectors. A very efficient bunch, these guys.

As he walked through the long tubelike passageway that led to the concourse, he dismissed the whole matter of the marketing portfolio from his mind. Wilson's was a callous, ebullient nature; he was no more inclined to brood over injuries done to him than over the ones he inflicted on others. He was thinking, instead, of the Mid-Winter Conference. It was to be an important event for his future at RGI —a future that spread before him like a cloudless sky, now that the little embarrassment of the portfolio was taken care of—for there he would meet the celebrated Raspin. Success for an affiliate head demanded more than high earnings per share (Atlantic Brands *did* have the highest earnings of any company in the Leisure Group). It called for favorable personal interactions. Wilson wanted to make a good impression on Raspin; he was already looking forward to the day when Raspin would be CEO and he would be VP (L). Once he had lopped off that wilted flower child Hal Holman.

Thus Wilson was walking down the passage with an extra spring to his step, arms swinging with a military flourish despite the suitcase he carried, looking about him with a ready smile, as if he expected to recognize a friend or customer at any moment.

When the short man in a heavy black overcoat stepped up to him and quietly said his name, Wilson put down his suitcase and reached out a hand.

"Hi, how are ya?"

The man shook hands gingerly. "I have come about the transaction in Martinique," he said, in the same sort of faintly accented voice the auctioneer had.

"Yeah, I know. What's the account number?"

"There has been a change in plan," said the man. "There is to be an exchange—you bring the payment in cash, we bring the item."

Wilson's good humor vanished in an instant, as it was wont to do. "An exchange? You're not gonna

make me fly to Martinique or some goddamn place?
I haven't got the time."

"No, no. The exchange will take place in England,
tomorrow. It will not be inconvenient for you."

And then Wilson understood. England: not inconvenient for him, and not inconvenient for somebody
else, either. He put his hands in his pockets and
smiled. "You know, I'm going to have to transfer the
funds from Geneva to London damn fast—and that'll
be expensive. And if I convert them from francs to
pounds, that'll be costly too. Now I can't be expected
to make good the loss, can I?" And then he added,
easily, "Your vendor know about all this?"

The man nodded. "We are doing it at the vendor's
instructions."

Wilson's smile grew broader. "This vendor's a real
pain, isn't sh—isn't he?"

The man did not notice the slip. "We will give
you the final arrangements tomorrow—a letter left
at the desk in RGI House, Victoria Street. Make sure
you open it yourself."

"Right." Wilson picked up his suitcase. Whatever
the inconvenience of a meeting, it was worth it to
know for sure that Brenda Wertheim was the one
who had shopped him. "Have a nice day," he told
the man, and turned away.

This brief meeting had of course meant nothing
to Sarah Saber, who caught glimpses of the two men
between the intervening figures of passing travelers.
As Wilson walked on, she quickened her pace, keeping approximately fifty feet between them.

At two o'clock the next afternoon, M. Lisle entered the house in Belgrave Square. He could hear

the floorboards creaking in the next room as he passed the receptionist's desk, and he entered Drucker's office to find him pacing with his usual energy.

Seeing Lisle, Drucker stopped and swung round. "You've got it?"

Lisle held up the envelope. "Such a waste of money," he said. "One of my people had to fly over from Brussels with it the moment it arrived. A pity your Monsieur Nicholls could not have walked up to Miss Wertheim at the post office and taken it."

Drucker was in no mood to heed Lisle's playful speculations. He snatched the envelope, slit the flap, and dumped the contents on his desk: a typewritten sheet and a piece of a royal ordnance map.

"Berkshire," said Lisle, looking over his shoulder. "Of course." He tapped a spot on the map labeled "Leighton Hall." "This is Walter Raspin's house. Wilson is to attend a dinner there tonight. I would not be surprised to learn that Miss Wertheim will be there too." His finger slid over to an X in red ink, not five inches—five miles—away. "And this indicates the rendezvous?"

Drucker was reading the sheet of instructions. He gave a harsh laugh. "Never saw such a lot of complicated rubbish in my life. Follow this if you can: We're to tell Wilson to arrive promptly at half past ten, turn off the road at a sort of track to the left, and drive until the track ends, and stay in his car. 'Our representative' is to arrive five minutes later and stop a hundred feet short of Wilson. She'll arrive immediately after and hand over the item. Then 'our representative' goes to Wilson's car and makes the exchange. Wilson waits where he is while we divide the money at Wertheim's car, and we leave in the order in which we came." He tossed the paper down on the desk. "No lights, she says. If she sees the headlamps of a car, or even a torch beam, the thing's off."

"She does not want Wilson to see her face, of course."

"There'd have been a damn sight less chance of that if she'd let us handle the whole show our way. Silly bitch."

M. Lisle winced at the rude language. "You ought to be grateful, Monsieur Drucker," he said. "But for Miss Wertheim's eccentricities, you would not have had the chance to handle this matter."

"Yes, that's another thing." Drucker went round the desk to fling himself down in his chair. He folded his hands behind his head, showing the dark sweat stains beneath his arms. An extremely nervous man, thought Lisle.

"I will be handling this matter, Lisle. Let's have that straight."

Lisle peered at him expressionlessly through his bifocals.

"I think we should have reinforcements at hand, just in case. So I'll have Nicholls and Hardy waiting in the van a few miles down the road."

"Just as you say," said Lisle.

"You'll be waiting with them." His dark face creased in a saturnine smile. "Doesn't matter which of us goes, does it? So I think it should be me."

It did matter, of course: Drucker preferred to take charge of the money himself, while Lisle waited under the watchful eyes of Drucker's men. Lisle said nothing.

"I know you'd never just piss off with the lolly, Lisle, straight to Heathrow. But it doesn't hurt to be careful, does it?"

Lisle shrugged. "No," he said, "I suppose it does not matter who goes to the meeting."

Major Dunbar was very different today than he had been yesterday, his employees noted with relief. All day long he was seeing callers or phoning people; he even skipped luncheon to spend an hour with the accountants from RGI. He was almost frenetically active, as if he wanted to keep his mind off some worry or other. Mind you, as his secretary told everyone, it was a good job he'd gotten over his funk, as there was a great deal that wanted doing.

He left at six, but instead of walking up Pall Mall to his club, where he usually dined, he went directly back to his house in Knightsbridge.

After rummaging in the attic for half an hour, he came down with his old army rucksack. From it he took something wrapped in grease paper. It was a Webley service revolver. He hefted it, looking it over in the light. Nearly forty years old, but there was not a freckle of rust on its blued surface. Still he tore it down and examined it. He took a long time over this. Once he would have been able to fieldstrip the weapon in under a minute, blindfolded. But tonight his hands were shaking.

Part Two

Chapter 15

At four-thirty the same afternoon, Walter Raspin was standing on the front lawn, looking at his house. Soon it would be dark; soon after that the hordes of guests would descend to cluttter up the sweep of his drive with their cars. But just now, all was tranquil. The silence seemed to deepen as night fell; Raspin could hear the clinking of silverware from the dining room windows, where his servants were setting the table.

The house was at its best. In the thickening dusk (quite literally thickening—it was going to be a foggy night) the buff stucco facing took on a richer, more mellow hue, and the lighted windows and the big lamp hanging over the front door bore aureoles of diffused light.

Leighton Hall was bracket-shaped, a long central block flanked by short wings. It had been built in the middle of the eighteenth century, and since then no additions had marred its spare, symmetrical elegance. Three clean-lined rectangular blocks; straight rows of unadorned windows; a quartet of Doric columns raising a pediment above the entrance. Neither forbiddingly large nor overbearingly opulent, it was still a great house—one of the dwindling number of great houses that were neither open to the paying public nor owned by an Arab.

It pleased Raspin enormously that he had rescued Leighton Hall from such fates, for he was a thunderous snob. He felt that since so few Englishmen had the will or the means to keep Edwardian splendor alive, it was a good thing that he did. Too bad about this party, though. The trappings would be splendid indeed, but the guests . . . He would have to suffer RGI executives, who would call Leighton Hall "a real nice place." Their wives would ask Mrs. Raspin where she had bought her china, while they talked across the dinner table of performance indicators and earnings per share and sales vitality. Raspin shuddered; he had lived in England long enough to acquire the attitude that business was something one left behind at the office.

Clasping his hands behind his back, he crossed the lawn with his heavy, deliberate stride. How had he gotten into this? Oh, yes, the conference planners had said that since his house was convenient to Heathrow Airport, and most of the executives were flying in today, it would be pleasant for them to come here for a meal and a night's sleep. Tomorrow, refreshed, they would head for London and the day's meetings. There was the further, unspoken assumption that Raspin would want to show off the house, impress the minor nobility with the style in which the crown prince of RGI lived. This irritated him. He liked to impress people, but he did not like to *try* to impress them.

He passed between the lofty columns, and the twelve-foot-tall front door swung open as he approached it. He knew that he would find his butler—who bore the wonderfully butlerish name of Blandford—behind it. Blandford saw to it that the master never had to open a door, or search for an ashtray, or pour a drink, and that his coat pocket was stocked with chocolate candies.

Blandford was the only one of Raspin's own servants in the long, simply furnished entrance hall. The rest were from RGI House: men to take coats and carry bags; a receptionist at a desk, to assign rooms, and, inevitably, Bud Nelger with a trio of Securitco guards lurking unobtrusively in an alcove. Nelger in his evening dress was not half so smartly turned out as the guards in their tunics trimmed with scarlet piping, their leather holsters protruding from a slit at the right hip. Raspin remembered how much trouble the arming of these guards had given him. Her Majesty's government thought it inappropriate for company guards to have guns when the metropolitan police did not, and Raspin had been obliged to call upon the Home Secretary himself about the matter.

Raspin conferred briefly with Blandford, with the receptionist, and with Nelger, and found that all was in readiness. Then he walked on, through an arched doorway and into the library.

Leighton Hall was the work of Robert Adam—of course—and he had established a chaste, plain style for the rest of the house solely to burst gloriously through it in this room. Directly before Raspin two white columns rose twenty feet to explode in gilt Corinthian capitals, on which rested a lintel inset with panels of muted pink. A carpet in a matching shade stretched away the length of a tennis court to another pair of columns. Beyond them the room rounded out in an alcove lined with books and furnished with a large mahogany desk. Raspin did his best thinking at that desk.

He walked along, eyes raised to the barrel ceiling high above his head, contemplating the panels of pink and light blue, set off by floral plasterwork of astonishing intricacy. Raspin had spent hours staring up at them, following each swirl and flourish. Men would never build anything as solid and exquisite again.

Leighton Hall was as far beyond the resources of the twentieth century as—well, as RGI had been beyond those of the eighteenth.

Raspin decided he would like a drink now, and to be sure, he turned to find Blandford at his elbow, bearing a glass on a silver tray.

"Ah. Dry sherry?" he asked, unnecessarily.

Blandford nodded gravely. "Yes, sir. Dunbar's."

Two hours later the great room was nearly filled. There was a contingent of wives, and a smaller contingent of women executives, but they were only occasional bursts of flesh and evening gown amid the milling black-clad figures of the men. Raspin, in his lord-of-the-manor wine velvet smoking jacket, stood in an alcove with his gaze fixed on his shoes, as if he preferred not to see what was going on. Perhaps this was just as well. Some of the guests stood back and "appreciated" the room, with the dutiful blank faces one sees in museums, but most were circulating obliviously, looking for familiar faces, as if they were at a suburban party. There were hearty greetings, vigorous handshakes, explosive laughs.

"Jack!"

"Hal!"

They stood beaming at one another. Holman, with his tanned face and gray mane, looked even more handsome than usual in his severe, elegant evening clothes. Wilson, his velvet-collared jacket open to reveal a ruffled blue shirt, looked as if he were about to mount a stage and start telling jokes.

"Good to see you!"

"Good to see *you*!"

"It's been a long time."

"Months," agreed Wilson. "Our offices are twenty

minutes apart, and it takes a conference in England
to get us together."

"We'll have to do something about that in the
future," Holman replied.

"Really—" Wilson was about to say more, but then
he glanced over Holman's shoulder and said, "Looks
like you're wanted."

There was a servant waiting beside the VP(L).
He shook his head ruefully. "Probably another damn
phone call from Greenwich. It's a real hassle working
at WHQ—you never get a moment's peace."

"I'm sure. I don't envy you."

They nodded to one another, and Holman turned
to the servant.

"A young lady to see you, sir."

"Lead on," said Holman. As he followed the servant
across the room, he was running over his lines in his
head. He had to play this scene just right, for, after
what was going to happen tonight, his words and
actions would be subjected to close scrutiny.

The hall was crowded too, and it was a moment before he saw Sarah Saber. When he did spot her,
slumped in a chair with a cigarette in her hand, he
felt a deeper stab of nervousness. There was something formidable about this slender young woman,
with her pale, willful face and smoke-gray eyes. He
thought: Christ, I'll never put this one over on her,
she's too smart.

But just then he caught sight of himself in a mirror
on the wall, and noted that there was not a trace of the
uncertainty he was feeling in his handsome, authoritative face. Role playing was something Harold Holman
had a knack for—after all, he had pretended for dec-
ades that he was a capable executive—and so he advanced, confident that he could carry off the scene.

"Well, Sarah?" His expression as she rose to face him was calm and grave.

"He's got the money with him, Mr. Holman."

He closed his eyes and shook his head. "*With* him. In cash, you mean?"

"Yes. In a British Airways flight bag. It's upstairs in his room right now."

"Are you sure?"

"When he got in this morning, he went straight to the main branch of the Midland Bank on Lombard Street in the City. He went to the manager's office, and he was there a long time. They had an armed guard see him to his car—and in England you don't get an armed guard for nothing."

Holman put his hand in his pockets and looked at the floor. He stood "lost in thought" for a count of fifty.

"A first-rate manager like Jack," he said. "Doing something like this. I just can't get my head around it." He shrugged heavily. "Well, I've got to have a frank discussion with him the first chance I get. The first chance I get," he repeated, to fix the words in her memory. "Obviously he's gotten himself in some kind of trouble, but I'll try to be as supportive of him as I can—provided, of course, he hasn't gone off the deep end already."

"I'm sure you'll do whatever you can for him, Mr. Holman," Saber replied.

This was even better than the line he had expected of her, and he smiled warmly. "You know, you look really out of it, Sarah."

She nodded. "Time change, plus running all over London after Wilson."

"Oh, yeah," said Holman sympathetically. "Listen, you want to—like—crash? I mean, Wilson's staying the night here—he's not going anywhere. You could just go back to your hotel."

Sarah nodded again. "Thanks a lot, Mr. Holman. I really appreciate that."

"Not at all, you've done a great job." He patted her on the shoulder and turned away, smiling to himself.

The talk had gone beautifully. With a slight twist of emphasis, he could make it seem that she had come to him dead-tired, begging to be let off for the night.

I shouldn't have let her talk me into that, he would say. God, that was a mistake.

Yes, his interrogators would reply, but a perfectly understandable one. After all, you couldn't know. . . .

Had he looked behind him, he would have seen that Sarah, who had resumed her seat and was lighting another cigarette, was showing no eagerness whatever to leave Leighton Hall.

Wilson saw Chris Rockwell standing against the mantel. His black satin tie was crooked and his dinner jacket much too tight across the shoulders. He seemed lost and ill at ease.

Wilson came up beside him, clapped him on the shoulder, and grasped his hand. "Chris! Hi, how are ya?"

Rockwell swung round in alarm; his large hand was limp in Wilson's. "She's *here*, Jack."

Wilson was still grinning. "Wertheim? Where?"

Rockwell pointed. Brenda Wertheim was standing across the room, listening attentively to a man who was making expansive gestures as he spoke. She was wearing a beautiful gown of deep blue silk. It was slit up to the knee on one side, and the neckline was rather low for her small bosom.

"Jack," Rockwell went on, as urgently as before,

"do you have anybody watching her—I mean, besides me?"

"Somebody's watching her, huh?" Wilson nodded slowly: a precaution taken by Lisle's bunch, no doubt. They did not like this rendezvous business any more than he did.

"I can't believe she knows what she's gotten herself into."

She sure doesn't, thought Wilson. Little bitch, trying to shop *me*— He grinned at Rockwell and clapped him on the shoulder again. "OK, Chris. Thanks for your input. You've been a big help."

"Help? I don't know what the hell is going on."

"Yeah, but now I do, and that's the important thing, right?" He laughed. "Thanks again, Chris. And you have a nice evening, now."

Wilson turned away. Out of the corner of his eye he caught a glimpse of the big man gaping at him, but before Chris could say anything, Wilson had moved on to greet a colleague from Cleveland.

Chris had a flare-up of ill-temper that burned right through his usual equanimity. He felt frustrated, lost, foolish. Wilson had dispatched him to another continent to inquire into a stranger's life. Chris had gotten to know that person well enough to be puzzled and worried for her—and now Wilson dismissed him, like the hired hand he was.

He stalked into the hall with his eyes on the floor and asked one of the servants for his coat. As he stood waiting for it, he felt a touch on his arm.

It was Sarah. Without saying a word, she embraced him. He had never been happier to see her, which was saying something, and for a moment he thought of nothing but her slender, pliant body in his arms, her warm mouth against his.

Eventually they separated so that they could look at one another. She was wearing a dusty-pink shirt dress with a thin gold chain beneath the collar. Her long blond hair was parted at the center and swept back into a chignon at the nape of her neck.

"My, you look handsome, Mr. Rockwell," she said in her husky, sardonic voice. "But your tie's crooked. Let me fix it up."

"It doesn't matter; I'm leaving." His own words brought it all back, and his elation shattered like glass, leaving nothing but jagged edges. He turned to see the servant coming back with his overcoat. Chris took it and thanked him.

Sarah was frowning beside him. She touched his face gently. "Really a rotten job, huh? Who's your client?"

"His name's Wilson—"

She closed her eyes and nodded. "John B. Wilson, President, Atlantic Brands. Of course. What were you doing for him?"

Chris did not even ask her how she knew Wilson. "Snooping on an employee of one of his affiliates. Wilson thinks she's a turn. I think he thinks that. I don't know. Anyway, the son of a bitch has discharged me, so I'm going home."

Sarah fumbled for her cigarettes. "How interesting. I've just been discharged too. And the woman—the one he thinks is a turn—is she here?"

"Yeah." Chris was putting on his coat. "Well, if your job's over too, shall we go home?"

She gave him a sly glance from under her eyebrows. "No, I don't think so. My client's Holman, a guy at

WHQ, who set me on Wilson. Wilson's embezzled eight hundred grand from his own company. He's got it with him now. In cash. Holman's a snake. He hasn't told me one straight thing since he hired me. Now he wants me out of here. So I'm staying."

"Why? I mean, who cares?"

"Oh, Chris. Are you in one of your moods again—where you want to go back to Middletown and sell aluminum siding? Come on, you'll feel better when you've got your tie straight."

"Don't knock aluminum siding," Chris protested listlessly, as she dragged him by the arm into an alcove off the hall. "You just hose it down every spring, and it'll last forever. Neither marble nor the gilded monuments of princes shall outlive aluminum siding."

Sarah pulled his tie loose and began to retie it. "Chris, don't you *see*? They want us out of here because the curtain's going up on the last act. This woman stole something or other from Wilson. Wilson's here with a fortune in cash. Holman knows that—"

"I don't care," Chris replied stolidly, lifting his chin as her fingers worked deftly beneath it. "People in Middletown don't care about stuff like that. They worry about important things, like how to keep the rabbits out of their tomato patches."

"She's *not* a turn—she's shopped him, and tonight's the payoff. Don't you think that's it? I mean, what else would he be doing here with eight hundred grand? And Holman— God, I can't figure what he's up to. Do you—"

"I don't care," Chris repeated. He looked about the hall, with its fluted columns, its marble-topped tables, its mahogany desks. "I'm fed up with these rich, duplicitous people and their rotten schemes. I mean,

I can see why *you're* interested. Your relatives have been giving you stock for your birthday since you were two. The first year you could vote, you voted for Nixon, and you can knot a black tie backwards in ten seconds flat. Where did you learn that anyway, weekends at Yale?"

Sarah's hands dropped to her sides. "You mean I'm one of them? The people you can't stand."

At the uncertainty in her voice, all the rancor drained out of Chris. He ran a finger lightly along her hairline.

"Dearest Sally, no."

Cautiously, coaxingly, she said, "We're so close, and it would be so easy. They'll probably—"

He shook his head, marveling. "Sarah, you'll sink to anything! Trying to lever me into this scheme by—"

"*I'll* sink to anything? What do you call reminding a person that she voted for Nixon?"

They embraced, laughing. She kissed his cheek and whispered, "Do you mind if I go on? Please?"

Chris released her, nodding. "OK. Go on."

"It'll be so easy. They'll probably just sneak up to his room, he'll give her the money, she'll give him the goody she stole, whatever it is. We burst in and nail them. Plaudits for us. Consternation for RGI big shots."

Chris thought for a moment. "No, it's not going to be that easy. There's another party in the deal."

"Who?"

"I don't know. But there's somebody running a surveillance on Brenda. Some big outfit."

"Brenda?" said Sarah, smiling. "Leave it to you to be on first-name terms with this crook."

"She's not like that. I just can't believe she knows what she's doing—" He broke off and took a deep breath. "OK. I'll stay on this job—but only to keep an eye on Brenda. I don't want her to get hurt, if I can help it."

Sarah stood on tiptoe to kiss his cheek. "Softy," she said. "Then you think they'll go someplace else to meet these other guys, and do the deal? So I better wait outside to tag Wilson—you stay here and keep an eye on your friend Brenda. OK?"

She was about to turn away, but he caught her arm. "Sarah, this stuff about bursting in and nailing them —forget that, will you? Just stay back and keep an eye on 'em. We don't know who these other people are, but they probably aren't very nice guys."

Sarah nodded, kissed him one last time, and was gone.

Eight miles down the road, Drucker's sleek Jaguar was pulling into the parking lot of a pub. It stopped beside the black van.

Drucker and Lisle got out. Drucker was wearing jeans and a heavy leather jacket, Lisle his usual fedora and tweed overcoat. His only concession to this wet night in the country had been to tuck his pinstriped trousers into Wellington boots.

Nicholls and Hardy were lounging against the side of the van. They straightened up as the other two approached.

"Well?" snapped Drucker.

Nicholls adjusted his spectacles and peered at a note pad. "Subject departed her flat at half-past five—"

"All tarted up in her best," Hardy threw in.

"Proceeded to neighboring mews to collect her car, a black Austin Mini, registration—"

"Never mind that, Nicholls."

"We followed subject up Great West Road to M

Four," Nicholls continued. "Due to conditions on motorway, and bearing our instructions in mind—"

"Traffic was bloody awful, and we knew where she was going, so we didn't close up on her," Hardy finished for him.

"End of report," said Nicholls imperturbably, and put away his notebook. "I've brought the things you asked for, sir."

"Good man." Drucker stepped closer to him, taking a quick look round the parking lot.

Hardy took from his pocket a gadget like a tire gauge. "If you want help, sir, just press this down. We'll pick up the signal on the receiver in the van." With his other hand, he took out a small pistol, which he offered Drucker in silence.

Drucker took the two objects and stowed them away in his jacket pockets. "Right. What time is it?"

"It hasn't gone eight yet, sir."

"Oh," said Drucker, deflated. "Bit of a wait then."

The four men stood about silently. A light rainfall, invisible in the darkness, began to patter on metal and concrete.

"I think I should like a small cognac," said Lisle, and turned away, toward the pub. After an exchange of glances, the others followed him.

But for the predictably low level of the conversation, the dinner was coming off well, Walter Raspin thought.

He looked down the long table. The cloth was Irish lace, over dark red satin. The china was Wedgwood— a blue, white, and silver pattern so beautiful that Raspin hated to see it smeared over with food. Not that the food was anything less than splendid: smoked salmon, green salad, rack of lamb with new potatoes in cream sauce, and broccoli in hollandaise sauce. A traditional English meal, save that the vegetables were not overcooked.

Raspin ate slowly and thoughtfully, enjoying the complex, unobtrusive activities of the servants, and nodding his head while not listening to Holman's conversation. The Vice-President for Leisure had flown over a day early for "preliminary conferences," and Raspin had quickly discovered that he had no more depth than a birdbath. Still, he was the second-ranking man here, so he had to be placed at Raspin's right.

Halfway down the table, Chris Rockwell was forcing down the marvelous food course by course, and trying to prevent the waiters from refilling his glass. He had attempted to quell conversation with his neighbor, a wife from Tulsa, by answering her first question with a terse "I work in Greenwich." A bad move; saying "Greenwich" to anyone in RGI was like saying "Rome" to a priest. He was continually fending off her questions as he stared across her bosom and down a row of elbows at Brenda. She was seated near the end of the table, directly across from Jack Wilson. They were laughing and talking animatedly. Chris tried desperately, and in vain, to catch a little of their conversation.

Wilson had been stunned when Brenda Wertheim had walked up to him in the library and reminded him of his promise to transfer her to Stamford. That, he thought, took real gall. Was she already thinking of the secrets she could steal from his legal department? Of course he had smiled and said that, yes, she could count on the promotion coming through any day. When he found himself seated across from her at dinner, he continued in the same vein. He joked about the snowy winters in Stamford, discussed her salary, her office, her full range of perks. He wanted her to have something to remember, once he had fired her and sent the word around about her. Better not spend that eight hundred grand too fast, Wertheim, he thought, smiling at her, because I'll see to it you never make another dime in your life.

When the main course was finished, the servants cleared the table so smoothly that it was as if the plates and glasses had evaporated into thin air. Cheeses the size of drums were brought in, and humidors and decanters of port. At the far end of the table, Mrs. Raspin rose.

The ladies did not take the hint, so she announced, "Shall we leave the gentlemen to it?"

Chris stood up with the rest of the men and watched helplessly as the women—and Brenda—went out. He had not foreseen this last Edwardian touch of Raspin's. Now what the devil was he going to do?

He swung round and looked at Wilson. But the man glanced at his watch and then resumed his seat, to rummage about in a humidor. Chris sat down slowly and passed the port without taking his eyes off him.

The room grew smokier, the laughter more boisterous, the conversation coarser. At the head of the table, Raspin, who had refused both cheese and cigars, sat unwrapping chocolates and popping them into his mouth. When there were six squares of foil in front of him, he looked up and surveyed the table with his cold blue eyes.

"Well."

Conversation lapsed instantly.

"Let's join the ladies for coffee in the library."

With scraping of chair legs and patting of cummer-

bunds, the men got to their feet and filed out of
the room. Chris hung back far enough to see Wilson
veer down the hallway toward the stairs. Toward his
room, and the money.

Almost at a run, Chris went on to the library. He
passed between the towering columns, sweeping the
room with a glance, just to make sure that Brenda
had gone.

She had not. He saw her near the far end of the
long room, comfortably ensconced in a wing chair,
listening to Mrs. Raspin, a Wedgwood demitasse bal-
anced on her knee. He advanced slowly into the room,
trying to blend into the nearest group, and waited
for Brenda to make her move.

Five minutes passed, and Brenda did not get up.
She did not even glance at her watch.

Chapter 16

Sarah was sitting in her rented car, near the end of the long uneven row that lined one side of Raspin's drive. She was a good hundred yards from the noble portico of Leighton Hall, but still she recognized Wilson the moment he stepped out of the door: spring-heeled gait, light gleaming on his bald head, bulky shoulder bag slung under his left arm. He passed between the columns and disappeared from view. A moment later she heard a starter grind and catch, and his car swung out of line. She ducked as it went past and watched in her mirror until it turned out of sight round a bend in the drive.

Then she started up and went after him. She felt elated. This job had seemed to consist mostly of boring waits in chilly cars, and now the last one was over. Now things would happen.

She rounded the bend in time to see Wilson pass the gatehouse and turn left onto the main road.

It was a bad road for her purposes: lightly traveled, so that she had to stay well back, and with so many hills and turns that she caught only occasional glimpses of Wilson.

Fortunately, he did not go far. Just a few minutes after leaving the house, she topped a hill to see Wilson turning off below her. In the beam of his headlights she saw a broken wooden gate, a section of fence, and woods.

She stepped on her brakes and crawled down the hill as slowly as possible. Wilson was moving into the woods at a worm's pace. When she reached the turning, she could still see his lights through the trees; she had no choice but to turn off her own.

The darkness was abrupt and total; she could not even tell where her hood left off and the road began. Sarah had forgotten how dark it was in the country on a moonless night. She could not possibly drive on. But Wilson was moving slowly: She could follow on foot.

Have to hide the car, though, she thought. Gently, she let off the clutch, steering toward the side of the road. Suddenly the rear end broke and slued around, the wheels spinning uselessly. The car tilted, and she found herself sliding slowly, helplessly down a muddy grade. Her fender clunked a tree trunk and she stopped. Well, the car was hidden. She hoped she would not be needing it again.

She got out and scrambled up the bank to the road. It was not a road at all, but a muddy, rutted track. At her first step her foot sank into a depression; she heard a squelching noise and felt cold water soaking through to her toes. Even looking straight down, she could not see the puddle. Visibility: less than five feet, she noted.

But there was no problem spotting Wilson's car; the red spots of his taillights and the pale wash of his headlights were flickering through the trees ahead. She could just hear the drone of his engine through the steady patter of rain.

Chris's mark—what was her name, Brenda?—would be coming along at any moment. Sarah had to move. She started down the track at an unsteady jog.

Wilson was no more than a couple of hundred yards off the road when he turned. The mist swirled like smoke in his headlight beams. Sarah half-ran, half-fell off the road and into the woods, and crouched behind a tree trunk. Light coated the branches around her like a sudden frost. Then there was darkness once more as Wilson switched off the engine and lights.

She got slowly to her feet. There was no danger of being seen now. No chance of seeing anything, either. Looking up, she could discern the delicate filigree of tree branches against the overcast sky, but ahead of her, where Wilson was, she saw nothing but impenetrable gloom.

Minutes passed. Then she heard the other car and turned to see headlights wavering as the car bumped along the track toward her. She started to move further into the woods, trying to edge round and to get nearer to Wilson. Branches stabbed at her face, undergrowth tripped up her feet. I'd never make it as an Indian, she thought; even in these wet woods I can't move quietly. At every step she heard twigs snapping. She had a humorous image of Chris, who even now must be stumbling along a few hundred yards away. He would be even more ungainly than she.

The second car was stopping now. Its headlights struck a glitter from the grille of Wilson's car, then went out. Sarah was blind again. She was looking right at the cars, but she could see nothing. She strained her ears, vainly trying to pick up the sound of voices through the rain.

As the third car came into view, its headlights winking between the trees, she was feeling acutely frustrated. Stay back and watch, Chris had said. Watch what?

The car came right at Drucker, so that he was dazzled and could not make out the driver's face. But he could see the front of the car plainly enough: It was an old one, with an upright radiator grille and a battery of white and amber lights. Nicholls had said that Wertheim was driving a Mini. . . . His hands sank deeper into his pockets, closed around the gun and the transmitter.

The engine and the lights died. Drucker heard the door slam, and as his eyes adjusted he made out the man's shape—for it was a man, a big man. Drucker's thumb snapped the transmitter into life.

"Good evening."

"Who the hell are you?"

"My name's Dunbar. You do know it, don't you?"

"Oh. Oh, I see." Drucker had his gun hand half out of his pocket. He let it slide back in. So it was Dunbar shopping his new boss. He felt foolish and angry at himself. They'd seen Wertheim post a letter, that was all; the rest was that fool Lisle's conjecture. Well, no harm done. "Have you got it, then?"

Dunbar was standing before him, towering over him. Drucker could see his white hair, his teeth, the whites of his eyes, but still was not able to discern his features.

"You're an Englishman—you're not Lisle."

"No. I hope I'll do," replied Drucker sarcastically.

"Oh, you'll do admirably."

"Let's have the item then, shall we?" Drucker was vibrating with nervousness now; he wanted to get this bloody exchange over with before Nicholls and Hardy came charging in.

Dunbar offered a thick sheaf of papers, and Drucker took it. "I'll have to verify this—I'll want a bit of light. Don't worry," he added, "we won't let Wilson see you."

He turned and placed the folder on the hood of his car, then examined it briefly with a pocket flashlight. Yes, this was the marketing portfolio, no doubt about it.

"Quite a slick operation, Dunbar," he said, flicking off the flashlight. "What you're doing to Wilson, I mean."

"One might say the same about what you did to me," Dunbar replied, and shot him twice in the back.

The impact knocked Drucker over the hood of the car as if he had been kicked by a horse.

Dunbar stepped back, startled by the reports and the muzzle flashes. He stood blinking for a moment, eyes readjusting to the dark, as Drucker's body slid off the fender and collapsed at his feet. He had killed before, in the war, and he found it much easier this time. After all, this was a man he hated. He turned and walked toward Wilson.

Jack Wilson might possibly have had a chance to get away, except that he was in an English car. Instinctively, desperately, his right hand scrabbled over the dashboard, but the ignition key was on his left. Before he realized his mistake, the door beside him swung open. He gave a strangled cry and his arms flew up, uselessly, before his face.

A voice said mildly, "It's Dunbar, Wilson."

Even now, Wilson's gift for names did not desert him. "Gordon—what the hell are you doing?"

"I'm going to kill you, you thieving bastard."

"No!" Wilson shrieked. "You're—you're one of my stockholders!"

Dunbar thrust the gun at the vague shape of Wilson's head and fired. In the muzzle flash he had a horrid glimpse of the bullet's impact, a sight that made him gasp and turn away.

But he swallowed hard, and then reached into the car, across Wilson's body. His hand fumbled at the strap of the shoulder bag, closed round it, and he dragged the bag out of the car.

He walked quickly back to the other car, hastily running down a list in his mind, making sure that he had remembered everything. He had a sense of rehearsal; he had thought it all through so often and so intensely that he could not grasp that this was the real thing, that he had done it.

The portfolio—he must remember that. He found it still lying on the hood of the car, snatched it up, and hurried back to his own car.

There was no way Sarah could tell the direction of the gunfire. She saw only the muzzle flashes and, in a moment of terror, thought they had been aimed at her, that she had been discovered. Her limbs quivering, she sank to her knees staring into the darkness that yielded nothing to her senses. At the next shot she threw herself to the ground and covered her face with her hands. A scream tried to tear its way from her throat, but one last shred of rationality told her that silence was her only hope of safety. Another dreadful lull, and then she heard an engine start up and saw the lights of the car; the car was turning, going back toward the road.

Feeble with shock and confusion, she would have remained motionless behind the tree but that a fresh horror reared up in her mind: Suppose Chris were out there, wounded or dead?

She rose stiffly and ran through the woods, stumbling at every step, her hands stretched out and groping to keep the branches from her eyes.

At last she came to the clearing, but she ran on. She did not see the car until she was a few paces

from it. She looked down—she had nearly trod on a
pale, still hand. Bending over, she thrust her own
hand against the warm, wet skin of the face. It was
not Chris.

She straightened up and ran on, peering into the
gloom until at last she discerned the darker shape
that was the other car. She ran up to it, probing
desperately for the door handle.

Then light fell on her. The brightwork of the car
glittered and her own shadow sprang up before her,
and she was looking into the face—Wilson's face,
thrust back, mouth agape, the whole right side a sheen
of blood.

She heard shots, and then the thunk of a bullet
punching a hole in safety glass. She stood frozen for
a moment, staring stupidly at the bullet hole in the
window not a foot away from her. With agonizing
slowness she formed the thoughts: They've come
back. They're shooting at me.

Have to get out of the light.

She turned and ran.

For a moment she was in darkness, and then the
lights swung round on her. Each blade of grass stood
out in brilliant outline, and her own shadow, eerily
doubled, ran before her. She knew that they were
aiming at her again; the muscles of her back twinged
in anticipation of the shock of the bullet. When she
heard the shots, she felt an overwhelming urge to
throw herself to the ground. But she forced herself
to run on, the soggy ground clinging to her at every
step, almost tearing off her shoes.

There was another sound behind her now, a high-
pitched whine. In a dazed, vague way she realized
that the car's wheels were spinning: It was stuck in

the mud. Hope and determination flooded through her. They have to come after me on foot, and they're not going to catch me.

Now her shadow was growing dimmer, merging into darkness. She was beyond the lights—they could not see her anymore.

Then she was stumbling through bracken again, batting tree branches away from her face. The trunks were upon her almost before she could see them and maneuver around them.

Suddenly she was out of the trees and climbing a bank. The surface beneath her feet changed. Now it was hard and smooth: a road. She was across it in six paces, sliding down the bank and into the woods again.

It was easier going now: big trees spaced far apart with little undergrowth. She ran even harder.

Her fear was abating and she grew conscious of the effort of drawing breath, of the painful stitches in her sides. A root snatched her foot from beneath her and she plunged forward full length onto the soggy ground. She tried to rise but could not. She lay trying to ease her gasping breath, straining her ears for footfalls. But she heard only the soft, steady tapping of the rain.

Lisle was standing at the edge of the woods. He heard a racket of snapping branches and swung his light round.

"It's me!" shouted Hardy. He was stumbling forward, breathing hard. He had lost his cap and his wet hair was plastered to his forehead.

"Well?"

"Lost her—never saw her, even. But there's a road back there away—"

"A road—"

"She had a car there, I'll wager. Gotten clean away by now."

"We must get away from here in any case," said Lisle. "Someone will have heard the shots."

They ran down the hill side by side.

"Mr. Drucker?"

"Dead. As is Wilson. And the money is gone, of course."

"Bitch."

Nicholls was standing beside the van, playing his light over the wheels, which were sunk to the rims in mud.

"We can get it out in reverse, easy enough," he said in his stolid way, as if this were their only problem. "Here, Hardy, give us a hand."

"I will help you," said Lisle. "Hardy, it will complicate things badly if the police find Drucker. Get the body into the boot of his car. You will drive it. Meet us at—"

"Look, who says we're taking orders from you? You got us into this lot." He raised his gun hand so that the muzzle was pointing at Lisle.

Lisle ignored it. "What do you wish to do?" he asked, in his polite tone.

"We haven't time for this, Hardy," said Nicholls.

Hardy stood wavering for a moment, then shoved the gun in his pocket. "Right. Where do I meet you?"

"Heathrow," said Lisle. "I assume that Wertheim will run as far and as fast as she can now."

"We haven't a chance of catching her."

"We shall catch her," Lisle replied quietly, turning to put his shoulder to the van.

* * *

The highway unfurled before Chris, an endless curling string of yellow lamps. Brenda was a hundred feet ahead, doing a cautious forty in the far-left lane.

This was wise of her, for she was pretty drunk. Chris had spent the half-hour after Wilson had left in ever deepening bewilderment, sitting in a wing chair with his back to Brenda, listening to her giggle. As one of the few unattached women at the party, she was getting a lot of attention from the execs, and reveling in it. Finally, at midnight, she had gone swaying out the front door, with Raspin looking frostily after her.

There was a great tangle of cars in the drive, and for a moment he was afraid he would lose her. But there was no mistaking her car, which was shaped like a station wagon, but so tiny that Chris thought he could have laid planks and driven it right into the back of his own wagon back home. It was called a Mini, and there were thousands of them in London, but no other ones here tonight. He kept sight of it easily among the larger white-and-red RGI company cars.

When she climbed the ramp to get on the M4, bound for London, he let go his last wisp of hope that she was heading for the rendezvous with Wilson. He was following her now simply because there was nothing else he could do. He was worried sick about Sarah, but he had no idea where she was or how he could get in touch with her.

They went through the dreary industrial fringe of West London and got onto the Great West Road. Soon Chris recognized the streets they were passing, streets he had paced the other night, when he had kept a confused and anxious vigil over Brenda. Just as he was doing now.

She turned into a mews and slid her car into a garage. Then she made her way, with wobbling steps, around the corner and into her own street.

Chris parked on Bishop's Road and watched her let herself in—saw her lights come on, and then go out. He was sure that no one else had followed her. Had they finished with her? Had she done what they had been expecting?

What?

Chapter 17

Hal Holman was kneeling on the bed in his darkened room, peering out the window. He had retired early and had not stirred from this position once—except for a trip to the bathroom to take another Valium.

It was long past midnight when he saw what he was waiting for. A long white Rover bearing the seal of the Berkshire County Constabulary pulled up before the portico. Two men—one uniformed, one not —left the car and went up to the front door. Holman was too far away to hear the ringing of the doorbell—to hear anything at all, in fact. But he saw bars of light fall across the gravel drive as lamps were turned on in the front rooms, and saw two more cars—unmarked ones—arrive.

Another anxious quarter of an hour. Finally, steps approached and there was a knock.

"Yeah? Who is it?" Holman tried to sound sleepy.

"Sorry to disturb you, sir," said the voice of Blandford. "Mr. Raspin asks that you join him in the library."

"O.K. I'll be there in a minute." He took off his dinner jacket and tie, put on slippers, mussed his gray locks, and went downstairs.

There was a policeman conducting interrogations on the steps, another writing in his notebook at the inlaid marble table, and three more clustered about the telephone at the receptionist's desk. The hall was full of bleary-eyed people in various stages of undress, the most prominent among them being Nelger,

who was trying to look cool and efficient in a raincoat over striped pajamas.

Holman hurried through into the library. The
long room seemed even longer now, as it was entirely dark but for a light at the far end, where
Walter Raspin was sitting at his desk alone. Holman
marched down toward him, his insides quavering.

Raspin was wearing a blue robe the exact color of
his cold eyes. His gray hair lay in lank disorder,
and there was an angry crease across his cheek, like
a dueling scar, left by his pillow. He was unwrapping
one of his damned chocolates and did not look up
as Holman approached.

"Mr. Raspin—what's going on here?"

"It's Wilson. He's been murdered." Raspin said
this as if he thought it a very inconvenient thing for
Wilson to have done.

"My God! When—"

"An hour or so ago. About five miles from here."

"Do they have any idea who—"

"No. There are a lot of tire tracks they're making
casts of, all that sort of thing, and an abandoned car
they're looking into, but no, they don't have any
leads."

Holman gave a long, drawn-out sigh of relief, which
he hoped Raspin would ascribe to shock and regret.
He sank into a chair before the desk and passed his
hand across his face.

"Sir—I feel, like, partly responsible for this tragedy."

This was the first line of his carefully prepared
speech, but Raspin threw him off immediately by his
reply. "You should."

Holman gulped. "What do you mean I should?"

"You're his superior. You're supposed to know if
he's gotten in trouble."

"Oh. Well, sir, I do know. We're going to have to work together on this problem. It could impact very unfavorably on RGI."

Raspin popped the chocolate in his mouth. Let's have it, Holman."

"The fact is, Jack was up to something questionable. I don't have a clear perception of all the factors in the situation, so I don't want to make any value judgments, but—"

"Let's have it, Holman."

"Yes, sir." He ran through the scenario, starting with Rabinowitz's change of vacation, and ending with his interview with Sarah Saber a few hours before. He played it perfectly—but Raspin failed entirely to respond the way he was supposed to.

"You took her *off* the job?"

"Sir, she was really bummed out. Could hardly put one foot in front of the other. I can't tell you how I regret—"

"You should."

"Well, it's easy to say that now," Holman protested. "Mr. Raspin, I'm trying to cope with some heavy guilt feelings right here, and I really feel that you could be more supportive."

Raspin was so astonished at this speech that he actually looked Holman in the eye. Meeting Walter Raspin's gaze was a sensation akin to putting one's hand on a block of dry ice, and Holman looked away and mumbled, "I just thought I ought to—you know —share my feelings with you."

"Keep your feelings to yourself, you nitwit. My God, I always thought Leisure Group was nutty as a fruitcake, but this . . . Why the hell didn't you confront Wilson and find out what the son of a bitch was up to?"

His gravelly voice resounded through the gloomy library. Holman gulped. "Sir, I've already explained that. I needed time to evaluate the situation in terms of a response—to come to a full awareness of Jack's needs. I mean—discretionary funds, large cash payments—these are sometimes legitimate tools. No one who's in touch with what's happening today in the business environment would deny that."

"I do," said Raspin. "Wilson was a crook." Before Holman could say anything, he bellowed, "Wells!"

There were footsteps, and after a moment a figure in a raincoat materialized out of the gloom. He was a bland, balding man, his face distinguished only by heavy black-framed spectacles.

"Sir?"

"Superintendent Wells, Mr. Holman. Holman is—was—Wilson's superior. Tell the superintendent what you've told me."

Holman quailed. "Sir—are you sure this is . . . er . . . wise?"

"Tell him."

Holman repeated the story once more. The policeman listened attentively, but without any response. When Holman had finished, he said, "Well, it seems we've got something now, sir."

"Oh?"

"We finally got through to the hire-car people, got them to check through their records. That car we found off the road, some three hundred yards from the scene—it was hired this morning by a Miss S. Saber."

"She was—she was *there*?" Holman's innards felt like coils of steel tubing, and his throat had constricted to the width of a straw.

"You haven't heard from her since, sir?" Wells said to him.

"No! Of course not."

"This agency in Connecticut—are they a reputable firm, would you know, sir?"

"They're an affiliate of RGI," said Raspin.

"Well, that's as may be, sir, but private investigators are an unsavory lot by and large."

"Come now, Wells," said Raspin, "you don't think she bumped off Wilson and stole the money?"

"It's a possibility we can't afford to discount at this stage, sir."

"It's the only possibility you've got, as a matter of fact."

"Well—yes, sir." He turned to Holman. "This embezzlement business is more a matter for the American authorities, of course, but we shall be wanting you to come round to the station and make a formal statement, sir."

Holman dragged himself from the chair and accompanied the policeman across the long, dark room.

"The thing we need straightaway," Wells went on, "is a description of Miss Saber."

Holman nodded, and uttered a silent and fervent prayer that when Sarah Saber was found, she would be found dead.

A few minutes later Raspin also left the library. He shuffled across the crowded front hall in his slippers and stopped beside Bud Nelger, who was using the telephone.

"Nelger."

"Hold, please," said Nelger into the receiver. He turned. "Sir?"

"What do you know about an outfit called Inquiries, Inc.? Division of Securitco, I think."

Nelger nodded vigorously, so that his heavy shock
of brown hair fell in his eyes. "Of course. You want to
know about Rockwell, right? I'm sorry, sir. He completely slipped my mind."

"Rockwell? You mean Rockwell is from Inquiries,
Inc.?"

"Well—yes, sir. He came to check out somebody at
Dunbar's— you know, Wilson's affiliate here."

Raspin grunted. "Is that so? Nelger, find out where
Rockwell's staying. Call him. And keep trying until
you get him."

"Yes, sir."

Raspin grunted again and turned away, back to
the library.

Seven-thirty Friday evening, and Ross Welch was
still at his desk. He was leaning back in his chair,
telephone cradled on his shoulder, talking to Josh
Morris. (After all, what was the point of working
late if your boss did not know that you were doing
so?) Thus he was extremely annoyed to see one of
the buttons on his telephone console flash. Ms. Wexler knew perfectly well that she was to hold all calls
when he was talking to Morris. He made a mental
note to rebuke her, filed it away, and ignored the
button.

His door flew open and Ms. Wexler ran up to him,
gasping for breath, as if their desks were separated
by a mile, not twenty paces.

"Sir—sir, I'm sorry. But you've got a long-distance
call—"

Welch waved his hands as if brushing a fly away

and swiveled his chair away from her. He was far
enough up the ladder not to jump when someone
said "long-distance."

". . . from Walter Raspin."

Welch froze. Then he slowly swiveled back. "Excuse me, Josh," he said. "Seems Raspin's on the line
from London." How well that sounded, he thought.
As if it were routine for the HOE to call him. And
Morris was impressed—he could tell by the haste with
which he cleared the line.

Welch punched the button. "Ross Welch here. Can
I help you?"

"You are the president of Inquiries, Inc.?" said the
slow, gravelly voice.

"That's right, sir."

"You have a couple of people on your staff named
Chris Rockwell and Sarah Saber?"

Welch riffled through his memory. Rockwell was
on an ar07—in Raspin's territory. But Sarah wasn't.
Trouble.

"That's correct," he said cautiously.

"Have you heard from either one of them recently?
Have they reported in?"

"No, sir. They're on assignment. They're not supposed to report in."

"What?"

Welch straightened up and drew a memo pad
toward him. "Sir, if you could familiarize me with
the nature of the situation we're dealing with—"

"There's been a murder here. Wilson, of Atlantic
Brands. It looks like both your people are mixed up
in it somehow. And they've both disappeared."

Welch's thoughts tumbled and whirled as if a
strong wind were blowing through his ears. One thing

was fixed and certain: Somehow, this fiasco was Rockwell's fault.

"Now, how much do you know about the cases they were working on?"

"Uh—nothing, sir."

There was an ominous silence on the other end of the line.

"I take it you're not familiar with our philosophy here, sir. . . ." Welch went on to explain about the Discretion policy. He had never done so with less enthusiasm.

"See here, Welch, what kind of outfit are you running over there?" Raspin bellowed. "For your information, Saber is working for Harold Holman, on some embezzlement scheme over at Wilson's place, and Rockwell—we think—was working for Wilson. You take it from there."

"Uh—take it where, sir?"

Raspin gave a long, impatient sigh that reverberated over the earpiece. "Find out what the hell your people are *doing,* Welch!"

Welch groped through his confusion and fastened on the tenet he lived by: in any situation, he must appear a can-do exec. "I'm on it, Mr. Raspin. We'll be getting back to you."

Raspin hung up with a resounding click.

Welch replaced the receiver and got shakily to his feet. He began to pace up and down his office, watched in silence by an anxious Ms. Wexler.

As he reached the desk and pivoted for the tenth time, he looked through the open door of his office and caught sight of Bill Chandler, who was crossing the reception room, wearily peeling off his raincoat. Welch froze and watched him disappear down the corridor.

"Ms. Wexler, buzz Chandler's office—" He broke off. "No, never mind. I think I'd better go to him."

He walked hastily to his employee's office, tapped at the door, and leaned in. "Evening, Bill. Mind if I come in?"

Chandler was sitting in a miasma of cigar smoke, laying out tracing inquiries on his desk in neat rows, as if he were playing solitaire. He looked up in surprise. "Well, sure—er—Ross."

Welch removed a couple of beer cans and a pile of papers from the chair before Bill's desk and sat down. It crossed his mind that it had been a long time since he'd been on the other side of someone's desk.

"Bill, I want you to know that I realize the contribution you make to this company."

"Contribution?"

"Yes. I know that the younger members of the staff respect you. They call you 'the Sage of Inkwink.' "

Chandler's mouth dropped open and his cigar nearly fell in his lap. In the two years since it had been coined (by Rockwell), the nickname Inkwink had never passed Ross Welch's lips.

"Oh, that's just a joke the young fellas have," he replied cagily.

"No, no—I realize that they're always coming to you for help, for advice with their cases."

Bill shook his head. "Absolutely not. They used to, but since I got that memo from you about the Discretion policy and all that, I've told 'em I can't talk to 'em, just like you said."

"C'mon, Bill," said Welch, grinning with all his might, "I know you have a pretty good idea what goes on around here."

"No, sir. I just look after my own—"

Welch cracked. He slid forward in his chair as if he were about to go down on his knees. "*Please,* Bill. Rockwell and Saber have gotten their assignments crossed and somebody's been killed. You've got to help me. Please, Bill."

Bill Chandler gave him a slow grin. He removed the cigar from his mouth and carefully dumped the ash. "I see," he said. "Well, as a matter of fact, I did have a few words with Sarah the other day. . . ."

Chapter 18

Sarah's clothing was soaked through, and she felt every stinging, chilling raindrop as if it were falling on her bare skin. She was dead-tired. What energy she had left was being sapped by convulsive shivers that seemed likely to shake her bones apart. She could not even keep her head up to look where she was going, and when she stumbled she could not regain her balance. Gratefully she sank down to the soft, rich-smelling earth.

She was lost.

The first time she had fallen, she had lain motionless for a long time, recovering her breath and listening for any sound of pursuit. When at last she was satisfied that they had given up, she set her mind to calculating the way back to Leighton Hall. But in her frenzied flight she had lost all sense of time and direction. She set off at random, confident that she would come upon a road before very long.

She wandered for hours in the rainy, pitch-dark night, never seeing a light. Once she found herself in a furrowed field and set off across it, looking for a farmhouse, only to end up back in the woods once more. Then she thought she heard the whisper of a car passing in the distance and headed toward the sound. But she could not find the road.

This was Berkshire, she kept reminding herself, not some trackless wilderness. She could not be more than six miles from Raspin's estate, and she had crossed a road just a few minutes before her fall. How could she be so utterly lost? She realized, with bitter frustration, that she was going around in circles. Still she trudged on until she collapsed.

When she came to her senses, it was still raining and the night was as black as ever. As she got up, a fit of dizziness swept through her head; the solid ground beneath her feet seemed to roll like the deck of a storm-tossed boat. She leaned against a tree until her head cleared. Then she raised her wrist up to her eyes, trying to read her watch. It was six o'clock. Dawn would not come for another two hours. Doggedly, she trudged on.

Presently she was confronted with a steep gravel bank. She scrambled up it to find herself on a railway line. Thank God, she thought. This is bound to lead somewhere.

It took all her concentration to walk along the tracks without stumbling over the ties, and the first time she lifted her eyes it was to see, with infinite relief, lights ahead. She walked on, and the low, boxy outline of an old station emerged out of the gloom. The last twenty steps seemed the longest of the whole night, but at last she reached the flight of steps that led to the platform, climbed them, and pushed through the glass doors into the waiting room.

It was as if she had been blind all her life, and the power of sight had just been bestowed on her. The electric light revealed a big, plain room: a ticket grille with no one behind it, a yellowing schedule pinned to the wall, rows of long wooden benches. There was a young man, a student on holiday perhaps, sprawled along one of the benches. His head resting on his knapsack, he was snoring peacefully. At the end of another bench was an old couple, upright but equally dead to the world.

Sarah sat down. She decided to make what repairs

she could to her appearance. Her stockings were
beyond hope, and she knew that if she bent down
to scrape the mud from her shoes she would keel
over. She dug a scarf out of a pocket and covered her
hair with it. Then she took off her mud-stained trench
coat; it was soaked and useless anyway.

Now, she thought, I'm ready to face civilization.
But what shall I do? She tried, for the first time in
hours, to think, to make some sense of what had
happened. But the mental effort was beyond her.

Slowly she got to her feet and crossed the room
to the street door, in the faint hope of finding a taxi.
If she did, she wondered where she would tell the
driver to take her.

She was saved from dealing with the question;
there were no taxis, no vehicles at all, parked before
the station. She was in a wide street that curved
away before her and climbed a hill. The street was
lined with low buildings, all of them dark. No; there
was a lighted window, a yellow square of steamy
glass, bearing the letters CAFÉ. A few cars and trucks
were parked in front of it.

At the renewed touch of the cold damp air Sarah
began to cough. She coughed until bright flecks
danced before her shut eyelids. Tears slid down her
cheeks.

"What I need is a cup of hot tea." I said that
aloud, she thought. She wondered, in a detached way,
if she was becoming delirious.

She crossed the street and went in. She recognized
the place at once: a fine specimen of the dreary
English "caf": peeling linoleum floor, pocked and
dented plaster walls, a clientele of truck drivers and
commercial travelers sitting about one to a table
and reading their newspapers. A radio played incon-

gruously sprightly pop music. No one even looked at
Sarah except for a man in an apron, who came forward with an air of craven politeness that put the
final touch to the desolate atmosphere of such a
place.

"Good morning, miss . . . anywhere will do. . . .
Shall I get you a menu, miss?"

"No, thanks. I'll just have tea."

"Thank you, miss."

The tea, when it arrived, tasted of soap. But it was
hot and strong, and she felt better at the first swallow.
After finishing the cup, she would be ready to prod
her brain into action.

". . . murder of John B. Wilson, an American
company director, last night . . ."

With a start, Sarah's attention fastened on the
radio news broadcast. Straining to catch the announcer's words over the rustle of newspapers and
clatter of plates and silverware, she heard a story
that only deepened her bafflement. There was no
mention of the other man who had been killed. Were
the police withholding that information?

"Police are seeking to interview Sarah Saber, who
is believed to have been on the scene. She is an American, in her mid-twenties, blond, and of slender build.
She was wearing a beige raincoat. The Berkshire
County Constabulary ask that anyone having information about Miss Saber's whereabouts ring them at
Reading 02843."

That was all; the announcer went on to tell about
the latest bad economic news.

Sarah swallowed hard and kept herself still with
an effort. She glanced quickly about the room, without raising her head, expecting to meet an alarmed

pair of eyes. But still no one looked up from his paper; apparently, no one had been listening.

She took another gulp of tea. The police wished to "interview" her. Sarah knew that in England that bland phrase could mean what it said, or it could mean that they suspected her of murdering Wilson. If they had found no trace of the killers, had found only her car—what would she expect them to think?

And how could she prove that she was innocent? She imagined herself in the police station, saying, "I didn't do it." And then answering "I don't know" to every question they asked.

She stroked her forearm absently, searching for the strap of her purse. She must have lost it somewhere in the woods. She delved in her pockets with stiff fingers and, luckily, came up with crumpled pound notes and silver. She dropped a few coins on the table and went out into the dark, chilly street.

She hesitated only a moment before starting back to the station. Chris. She had to find Chris. The idea no sooner came to her mind than it was a resolve. She shut her eyes and thought hard, and came up with the address to which she had sent the telegram: Duchess of Bedford's Walk, W. 8.

She was in the waiting room, trying to decipher the schedule, when she heard a rush and a mounting clatter and turned to see the blue-and-yellow train slide in beyond the dirty windows.

In the Atlantic Brands Data Center, the eight-to-midnight shift was just getting off. Papers were being shoved into folders and jackets pulled from the backs of chairs, tired limbs stretching and yawns no longer being suppressed.

Bill Chandler was sitting in one of the little cubicles, across the desk from Russell Rabinowitz, who
was sprawling sideways in his chair, his long legs thrust
out before him.

"So you say you were working closely with Sarah?"

Russell nodded. "Hand in glove. Now what can I
help you with?"

"Russell, get out of here."

Bill looked around. A young woman with a pert,
pretty face was standing in the doorway.

"Oh, hi, Markworthy. I was just telling Sarah's
colleague here—"

"Out, Russell."

Rabinowitz frowned, got to his feet, and ambled
out of the office.

"I'm Jill Markworthy," the girl said. "You're from
Inkwink?"

"That's right. Bill Chandler." He grinned. "I'll bet
that real cooperative guy is the embezzler Sarah caught,
right?"

Jill stood in the doorway, looking at Chandler warily and toying with one of her corkscrew curls. "Sarah
said I wasn't to talk about this with anybody."

"Oh, sure," said Bill, nodding sympathetically. "But
you see, Sarah and I discussed this job, and I have a
pretty good idea what went on. I just want you to
tell me if she said anything about her client, Holman."

"Holman," said Jill. "So that's who it was." She
sat down across from Bill, still frowning. "Look, I
don't want to get Sarah in any trouble—"

"Honey, Sarah is in trouble. I'm trying to get her
out of it." Jill looked up in alarm, and he leaned
closer to her and spoke more quietly. "Your boss has
gotten himself killed."

"Wilson?"

"He was shot, over in England, a few hours ago. Sarah was following him, and now she's disappeared."

"Oh, gosh," Jill said, her eyes wide and worried. "OK. Um—Sarah thought Holman wasn't telling her all he knew."

Bill nodded. "That's fairly typical. What did she say, exactly?"

She was only one step from the door of the VP(L)'s office suite when she heard the receptionist: "Mrs. Webb? Call for you, ma'am."

She reluctantly withdrew her hand from the doorknob. It was now five hours since she had heard that the meeting in Berkshire that was never supposed to happen had indeed taken place, and with such disastrous results. She had spent the time lighting one cigarette from the end of another while trying to reach Holman. At last someone told her he was unavailable: He was in a police station just now. When she heard that, Mrs. Webb resolved on a course of action: She would go home and take the telephone off the hook; she would leave it off except when she was trying to call Holman. She did not care to talk to anyone else before she talked to him.

"Who is it?"

"A Mr. Chandler. From Inquiries, Inc."

Mrs. Webb trod across the crimson carpet as if it were quicksand and cautiously accepted the receiver.

"Hello?"

"Mrs. Webb? Chandler here," said a cheery-sounding voice. "I guess you've heard about that mess over in England."

"Yes. A shocking business."

"Right. And you know about my colleague from Inkwink, Sarah Saber?"

Mrs. Webb did some fast thinking. "Well, I haven't talked to Mr. Holman. Is she the one who's disappeared—the one the police are looking for?"

"That's right. She was working for your boss—but of course you know that too."

"Well . . . as I say, I haven't talked to Mr. Holman. All I know is what I got second-hand from Mr. Raspin's people."

"Oh, sure. But did he say anything about Sarah before—I mean, before he went to England?"

Mrs. Webb squirmed on the end of the line as if it were a hook. Falling back on her last line of defense, she said, "I don't recall."

"You mean, he hired her himself, and didn't tell you anything about it?"

That sounded very good to Mrs. Webb. "Yes, that's right."

"Yeah," said the affable Mr. Chandler, "that's the way clients usually do it. Thanks, Mrs. Webb. So long."

Mrs. Webb handed back the receiver, turned, and fled the office as quickly as she could.

Chris heard the high-pitched whirr and turned to see the milk truck glide past him and turn down Brenda's street. It stopped and the driver got out, swung a wire carrier full of bottles off the back of the truck, and strolled over to the pavement to start distributing them on doorsteps.

Chris shook himself. He had not fallen asleep, but he had sunk into the stupor that comes over watchers when they have nothing to watch. No one had gone

into or out of Brenda's house; no lights had shown;
not even a shade had been raised.

He glanced at his watch: It was nearly twelve hours
since he had talked to Sarah at Leighton Hall. Twelve
hours of futile vigil, of probing listlessly at the problem and getting no answers. Abruptly, an inspiration
came to him: He would ask Brenda what was going
on.

He got out of the car, walked down to her house,
and rang the bell.

There was a moment's silence, then lights went on.
He heard Brenda's step on the stair, saw her shadowy
form on the other side of the frosted glass.

"Who is it?"

"Chris."

She opened the door with a smile. "Oh—Chris. Hi."

Without foundation cream, blusher, lipstick, eye
shadow, and with no lashes except her own, Brenda's
face looked naked. Still, she was quite pretty in her
diaphanous pink nightie, her short hair tousled from
sleep.

"Sorry to wake you, Brenda—"

She reached out to take his hand. "That's OK. You
don't have to explain. It's OK."

Oh, hell, he thought, what do I expect her to
make of this? When I show up at her door at this
hour, wearing last night's tuxedo and looking nervous?

He withdrew his hand. "There's trouble, Brenda.
We've got to talk."

She dropped her eyes and drew back. "Trouble?"

"Let's go upstairs."

He followed her up the steep flight of steps. At
the top she looked at his grim face and then down
at the flimsy negligee she was wearing. "I'll—um—get
dressed, OK?"

She went in her room and closed the door. Chris leaned against the wall outside and said, "Do you have any idea where Wilson went tonight?"

He could hear the surprise in her muffled voice. "Where he went? You mean after the party? No. Wasn't he—like—staying there?"

"He left before coffee, didn't you notice? And Sarah —she's my girl friend—was following him."

There was a moment's silence, and then she came out wearing jeans and a turtleneck jersey.

"I don't understand. I mean, I don't know why I should know anything about this."

"Tell me about you and Wilson."

"I told you, he offered me a job." She blushed a vivid pink and looked past his shoulder. Once more, he thought that she was the most pathetic liar he had ever seen.

"The first time we met, you asked me if I'd brought you word from Wilson."

"Right—that was, like, about the job—"

"As a matter of fact, I did come from Wilson. He wanted me to check you over. He thought you were selling him out."

Her surprise at this was as transparently genuine as her earlier confusion had been false. "No!" she exclaimed. "You must have got it wrong."

"That's possible. Wilson isn't a model of candor. But I don't think so. He suspects you of something, Brenda."

She sank down on the arm of a chair. "Oh, God. He was real nice to me last night—and all the time he was thinking—Oh, God." She covered her face with her hands. "Everybody lies to me. Everybody—"

Her shoulders heaved as she took a long, shuddering breath and swallowed to keep herself from cry-ing. "The guy I was going out with. I thought he was a real nice guy. Really fun to be with. He said he had—like—contacts. And he needed the money and it would be better for me and stuff if an American company took over. But as soon as he had what he wanted, he just dropped me. He went with me only so he could—" She broke off, fighting away another sob. "Anyway, I know Wilson was told that I'd—like—helped him. He said I'd get a promotion back to Stamford. And he thinks—"

It took a moment for Chris to grasp the meaning of this vague recitation. Then he cursed himself for his thickheadedness. He would have seen it before, but that Wilson had sent him into the case looking the wrong way. Clever Jack Wilson, who did not trust anybody. "You turned on Upton Lawrence and Dunbar? You scouted them for the take-over?"

"Well, they're real mean to me," said Brenda despondently. "I work so hard, and I get paid so lousy, and they treat me like—"

"Never mind that. What are you up to now?"

Her head jerked up abruptly. "Now?"

"I told you, Wilson thinks—"

She shook her head violently. "He's wrong! I don't know why he—look, I worked *for* him, don't you understand? That's the only time I've ever done anything like that."

Chris believed her. He stared at his feet, furious with himself for having wasted so much time only to come to this dead end.

In the momentary silence, he heard a clink of glass. Somebody had knocked over a milk bottle—somebody standing on Brenda's doorstep.

"Where are your roommates?" he asked.

"Away—away in Spain."

Chris swung round and leaned over the banister. He could see two shadowy forms through the frosted glass. He waited for them to ring the doorbell. They did not.

He turned back. Brenda was now standing next to him. "Have you got a back door?"

She nodded shakily. "Who—who do you think?"

"I don't know, but we better get out of here." He thought swiftly. "Where are your car keys? We'll need 'em."

Brenda looked about dazedly, then snatched the keys off the edge of a table.

Suddenly they heard glass cracking and the sound of slivers raining on the floor. Brenda gasped and fell back against the wall, staring at Chris wildly.

Grabbing her arm, he pulled her into the living room and ran to the window. He looked out at the rain-slick flagstones of the back garden. Fifteen feet down.

He jerked the sash all the way up. "We'll have to jump," he said in a strained whisper. "Try to roll when you hit."

He swung his legs over the sill, considered briefly and feverishly whether he could turn and drop the length of his arms before letting go, and realized there wasn't time. He slid off the sill and fell.

The pains shot up from his ankles as he hit and went sprawling. He was just getting to his knees when Brenda landed beside him, stiff-legged, badly. She gave a cry of pain and toppled over, and as he turned to help her he found himself looking into the face of a man behind the ground-floor windows. A gun came up in front of the face and the pane shattered. Chris's mind registered: no report—silencer.

He whirled around. There were brick walls as high

as his chest on all sides. He picked Brenda up, crossed the courtyard in two long steps, and heaved her over the wall. As he vaulted after her, a jet of pink dust sprang up from the bricks a foot from his hand.

Bent low, he grasped Brenda's arm and pulled her to the French windows at the back of the neighboring house. Smashing a pane with his elbow, he reached through and twisted the lock. He swung the door open and pulled Brenda in after him. It was the kitchen; a rackful of plates on the sink exploded into fragments at another flurry of muffled shots from behind them. It occurred to Chris that this guy was very good, and they'd had their quota of near misses.

They ran out of the kitchen and through the hallway. There was a woman in a dressing gown standing halfway up the stairs. Seeing them, she shrank against the wall.

"It's OK," Chris called out, stupidly. "Call the cops!"

He yanked the front door open and, supporting Brenda as best he could, ran down the pavement toward the mews where she kept her car.

The doors of her garage were open. Chris pulled up short.

A small man was crouched beside the Mini, gently working a probe through the rubber molding round the front window. When he heard them he stood up, looking at them through thick spectacles. Smoothly, unhurriedly, his hand moved toward his coat pocket.

Chris lunged forward and slugged him.

He had not hit anyone in years, and he missed the little man's chin, landing his fist on the collarbone. Still, the blow had all of Chris's considerable weight behind it, and the man fell over backwards and slammed against the brick wall.

Brenda stood staring at him.

"Get the door open, for God's sake!"

She fumbled with the keys for an agonizing second and pulled the door wide. Chris shoved her in with one hand as he yanked the keys from the lock with the other. He swung into the driver's seat, jabbed the key in the ignition and twisted. Blessedly, the engine started on the first try. But he had to probe for reverse for what seemed an eternity. At last the gears ground into place and he let out the clutch. They shot backwards into the mews.

Scanning the mirror frantically as he shifted into first, Chris saw a running figure round the corner. He accelerated and ran through the gears, quivering in anticipation of the sound of popping glass. But it did not come, and he swerved the car into the street, the rear tires screaming, straightened out, and punched the accelerator down to the floor.

It took him a few seconds to realize that he was doing sixty down the wrong side of the road. He eased over to the left and braked as gently as he could manage, just in time to see a big red bus come lumbering around the bend in the other lane.

He gasped in relief and drew in a breath. It felt like his first breath in five minutes. He put some effort into it, and managed to breathe again.

He drove for some time with no sense of where he was going. Very slowly, the frenzied workings of his brain slowed, and the hammering of his heart eased. He became aware that he was leaning forward over the wheel, shoulders hunched and head down, in an instinctive, feeble crouch meant to fend off a bullet in the back. He straightened up. They were safe by now; it was time to survey the damage.

He turned into a side street and stopped the car.

"Brenda—how's the ankle? Think you broke it?"

She nodded dizzily; he doubted that she had understood his words. Then, abruptly, she twisted in the seat and lunged at him, throwing her arms round his shoulders, burying her face in his chest.

"Oh God that was so—awful." The words came out hastily, between racking sobs. "I was so scared. You—you saved my life."

Chris stroked her hair soothingly. "It's OK. We're safe now."

"Who were they? Why did they try to kill us?"

"Brenda, if you don't know, I sure as hell don't."

Her weeping became even more stormy. She gasped for breath and brought out, "I don't know anything—please believe me—please—"

"I believe you." He held her for some time, stroking her hair and murmuring comforting words. Finally she straightened up, wiping her cheeks, swallowing. But her breath still came uneasily, and her face was white and strained. He knew that now that she was calm enough to feel it, her ankle would be hurting badly.

He looked at his hands, which bore a few scrapes from the rough brick wall, as might be expected. But he was startled to see blood oozing from long tears in the black sleeve of his coat. He must have cut himself badly breaking the window, yet he felt nothing.

He looked around him. They were parked in a nondescript crescent: a cluster of plane trees surrounded by terrace houses in brick and stucco. "Any idea where we are?" he asked Brenda.

"There's a—an A-Z under the dash."

Chris picked up the London street atlas and flipped through the pages, looking for the map of Fulham.

"Where are we going?" Brenda asked. "What are you going to do?"

"I've got to find Sarah, but I don't know how to—" He broke off, in bitter frustration.

"Well, does she know where you live?"

"No, I never—" And then suddenly he remembered that she had sent him a telegram. It was as good an idea as any, and he consulted the map again to figure out how to get home.

Chapter 19

Despite the cool temperature and impenetrable overcast the paths of Holland Park this Saturday morning were crowded: There were old women with dogs, young women with perambulators. There was a foursome playing tennis, bundled in sweaters, the ends of their scarves swirling about their shoulders. Further up the long, sloping green, two men in bright jogging suits were doing limbering-up exercises. Glimpsed from a distance, they looked like antic windup toys.

It was all wonderfully soothing, and as Chris drove along the park and turned onto Duchess of Bedford's Walk, with its row of solid, handsome apartment houses, he felt better. Calm, almost. He parked the car at the side of his building, on Sheldrake Place.

As they were going up the path, the big front door swung open, and in a moment he saw the ruddy, cheerful face of the porter.

"Hi, Dutton."

"Good morning, sir." If Dutton saw anything unusual in Mr. Rockwell arriving home early in the morning in a dinner jacket, with a rag tied round one arm and a hobbling woman leaning on the other, he did not show it. "There's a young lady waiting to see you," he went on.

Chris bounded up the steps so that Brenda nearly stumbled at the momentary loss of support. He eagerly scanned the foyer. "Where is she?"

"Oh, I brought her in to give her a cup of tea. Poor young lady, she looks like she's come from the wars. Car broke down out in the country, she said."

Chris hastily settled Brenda in a chair and followed Dutton round the frosted-glass partition of the porter's lodge.

Sarah was sitting by the window, hunched over a steaming cup of tea. In the morning light, she looked dreadful. The fair skin of her forehead and hands was marred by a dozen scratches. The hair spilling from under the kerchief looked like a tangle of weathered rope. Her ankles were crossed and tucked under the chair, in an unconscious attempt to hide her torn and muddy hose.

"Oh, Sarah—"

At the sound of his voice, she looked up with a radiant smile and stood to be enfolded in his arms.

"Your—uh—car broke down?" he said, thinking of Dutton behind him.

"Right. Out in the country," she said sardonically. Her voice was lower and huskier than usual, and he could feel the heat of her forehead against his cheek.

"Kid, you're really ill."

She nodded. "Let's go up to your flat."

Dutton was rocking back and forth on his heels and beaming as they walked past him, pleased that his poor young lady had found a home. It was typical of Sarah, Chris thought, that she could pass muster with a Kensington porter no matter how disreputable she looked.

Brenda was waiting in the lobby, wincing as she probed her ankle. She rose shakily as they approached, her dark, plaintive eyes fixed on Sarah.

"Sarah, this is Brenda. Remember—"

"Yeah, I remember." Sarah was looking at her warily, as if she expected her to make a break for the door.

"She's not in this," Chris said quietly. "Wilson was wrong."

"Uh-huh. Let's go upstairs."

She had her hand in the crook of his arm, and Chris said, "You'll have to turn this over to Brenda. She needs it, and it's the only one I've got."

Sarah leaned over and gently examined his other arm. The blood was beginning to seep through the rag. "What happened?"

"I put it through a window."

She gave him a look, squeezed his good arm in concern, and then reluctantly stepped aside for Brenda.

As they made their way to the elevator, she cast a glance at the elegant hallway and laughed—a throaty chuckle. "We are a pathetic bunch. We really spoil the decor. I'll bet we get RGI evicted."

Chris laughed too, and Brenda looked from one to the other in amazement.

In the elevator Sarah wedged herself in a corner and closed her eyes. Chris pressed the button for his floor and looked at her. "What happened?"

"People were shooting at me. I was running," she replied without opening her eyes. "How about you guys?"

"Same thing."

"Same people?"

"God, Sarah, I just don't know."

The doors slid open, and they were silent as they made their way down the corridor to Chris's flat.

Sarah glanced about the beautifully furnished living room and said, "Very nice. Let's get you to the bathroom before you bleed on the Persian carpets."

With Brenda still leaning on him heavily, Chris led the way down the hall to the bathroom. He seated her gently on the edge of the tub.

Sarah bent over and raised the leg of Brenda's jeans. The ankle was hideously bruised and swollen.

"Can you do anything about that?" he asked.

"Sure. Didn't I ever tell you I was a candy striper in high school?"

"No, but it figures."

They grinned wryly at one another, and Sarah bent forward.

"Don't touch it!" Brenda exclaimed, shrinking back.

Chris looked at her. He sensed that his and Sarah's relief at seeing one another made her feel all the more frightened and alone.

"OK," said Sarah, getting up. "If you put some ice on, it'll ease the swelling."

But Brenda made no response, and Sarah turned to roll up Chris's sleeve. His forearm was scored with several shallow cuts, and she held it over the sink and began, cautiously, tenderly, to wash them out.

"What happened?" Chris asked.

"Wilson's dead," she answered, without looking up. Then she told him the whole story, in a flat tone of voice, quickly and without many details. She was trying not to recall the details.

Still it sounded like a nightmare; Chris could make no sense of it at all. "Those guys who were shooting at you—were they the ones who killed Wilson and the other man, or somebody else?"

"I don't know. I was too busy running."

"Did you see any of the cars clearly? Was one of them a black van, or a green Fiat?"

"I didn't see any of the cars. I could hardly see anything." She was wrapping one of the fine linen hand towels snugly about his forearm.

"How about the money? The killer took it, of course."

"I didn't look for the money. I was only trying to find you. . . ." For the first time her voice quavered and broke; she raised her eyes to his. "Chris, I thought—I thought—"

He put his arms around her and hugged her tightly. "Oh, Jesus. And I was sitting in Raspin's goddamn library, drinking coffee. What a rotten business this is—every damned bit of it."

She stroked his broad back and said, her usual wryness intact again, "There's worse to come. The cops are looking for me. They're not looking for anybody else."

He stood back and looked into her face. "They don't think—"

"I don't know." She grimaced. "Becoming a refrain, isn't it? I don't know, I don't know. I don't—"

She broke off, coughing.

Chris looked at her with concern. She was in far worse shape than Brenda or he; he marveled that she could maintain her composure.

"Kid," he said, "let's get you into some dry clothes at least."

She nodded and he turned to lead her into the bedroom.

"Don't leave me alone, please!" Brenda burst out. She looked from one to the other, and then covered her face with her hands. "I'm so scared."

Chris knelt beside her and put his arm around her shoulders. He felt foolish and helpless; all he could do for these two troubled women was to embrace one, then the other. But Brenda clung to him as if it really helped.

"It's OK. I'll find some clothes for Sarah, and then we'll—" He broke off; he had no idea what they should do next. "We'll find a way out of this."

He straightened up, Brenda releasing him reluctantly.

He led Sarah across the quiet, spacious apartment to the bedroom, with its oyster satin counterpane and matching draperies, and its view of the white villas that lined Holland Park.

"I'm going to have a heck of a time getting your trousers to stay on, Rockwell."

"It's OK. I bought you a skirt."

"A present!" She clapped her hands. "I'm so glad I didn't have to wait to see it."

Chris turned and looked at her. "Sarah, are you . . . all right?"

"What kind of question is that? Of course I'm not."

"I mean, you're getting a little giddy—"

"I think I'm still of sound mind, if that's what you mean."

Chris touched her shoulder and turned back to the closet. He got out the skirt he had bought her—a kilt in a muted tartan—and one of his own shirts.

"Thank you," she said, formally, and quickly stripped off all her clothes. He looked at her slender shoulders, her full, firm breasts. Her skin was so fair that he could see the delicate blue veins at the base of her throat. He turned away.

Sarah noticed. "What's with you?"

"Even at a time like this, my dear, you are distracting to behold."

"Thanks. I feel better already." For a moment she was silent; then: "About this Brenda creature. What do you think, really?"

"Really, I think it's a mistake. Wilson turned her on Dunbar, so he assumed she was shopping him. He was wrong."

"Chris, you wouldn't have spent the night watching her if you didn't suspect—"

"I spent the night watching her 'cause I couldn't think of anything else to do." He took a sweater out of the closet and pulled it on. "I mean, look at her, Sarah. She just hasn't got it in her to—"

"Because of all the caterwauling and simpering and clinging to you for dear life? I think that's an act. An overdone one."

"She's had a bad scare."

"So have I."

"Yeah, but nobody in their right mind is as brave as you are."

"There you go again—"

Sarah broke off on hearing a buzzing sound from the hallway. Chris winced.

"House intercom?"

He nodded and went past her as she hastily did up the shirt. In the hallway he bent over to the little grille, pressing the button. "Yes?"

"Mr. Rockwell," said Dutton's voice, "some gentlemen from your office to see you, sir."

Chris's thoughts raced. "OK," he said, "send them up." He looked up to see Brenda hobbling toward him, leaning on the wall. "Chris—how do you know they're really—"

"I don't. But if they're those trigger-happy bastards again, Dutton won't be able to stop 'em. And he might get hurt trying. Here, give me your arm."

"Oh God," Brenda whimpered as he pulled her arm over his shoulder, "there's not gonna be any shooting, is there? I couldn't stand—"

"Sarah—"

But she was already past him, pulling on her coat

and heading for the front door. She had it open by
the time he got there.

"Elevator coming up," she said, looking down the
hall.

"Other way," Chris called. With the instincts in-
stilled by his job, he had noted the stairs and the
back entrance without even thinking about it, and
he ran down the hall and pushed through the door.
Brenda, gasping with pain and fear at every step she
took, now seemed unable to do more than cling to
him, and he lifted her bodily and draped her over
one broad shoulder. They hurtled down the three
flights of steps, pursued only by the clattering echo
of their footfalls. Sarah, first to the landing, slowly
pushed the door open and peered out.

"All clear."

They came out in the back garden and ran along
the path to Sheldrake Place. Chris set Brenda down
beside the car, clumsily dug the keys out of his pocket,
and opened the door. Sarah scrambled over the seat
cushions into the back. Chris pushed Brenda in, got
behind the wheel, and started up.

"Relax," said Sarah, looking out the back window.
"I don't see anyone yet."

He took one deep breath and got the car moving.
At the corner of Duchess of Bedford's Walk, he looked
to his right and stopped. Double-parked in front of
the building was a white car with the scarlet markings of RGI. It was empty.

Sarah laughed. "How 'bout that. They really are
from the office."

"Should we talk to 'em?"

"What do you think?"

Doubts and fears swirled in Chris's mind. "Not if

we don't know who it is. The killings happened within a couple miles of a house full of RGI people."

He saw her nod in the rearview mirror. "Go."

Chris set off north. They passed through the meandering lanes of Kensington—walls of mottled brick, tall, somber trees, pretty little terrace houses painted bright colors. They reached a main road and Chris turned right.

Sarah was leaning forward with her elbows on the back of his seat. "Where are we going?"

"Toward central London. I'll welcome more specific ideas."

She kissed his shoulder and stared out at the passing traffic. Within a few minutes Holland Park Avenue, with its tall detached houses set disdainfully back from the road, was succeeded by Notting Hill Gate, with its rows of stores, and then by Bayswater Road: long whitewashed terraces to the left and the verdant sprawl of Kensington Gardens, brilliant beneath the dull gray sky, to the right.

"Well?" said Chris.

"I'm not coming up with anything." She turned aside to cough and then, abruptly, bent down. "Chris," she said, in a low, hard voice, "whose car is this?"

It struck him as an odd question, but at least it was one to which he had an answer. "Brenda's. Why?"

"Pull over. Now."

There was a wrought-iron gate to the right, and he turned into the park and stopped the car. "What is it?" he asked, turning around.

There was a British Airways flight bag lying on the floor behind Brenda's seat. Without a word, Sarah picked it up and spread the flaps.

It was full of money, neat bundles of highly colored twenty-pound notes.

"At last," said Sarah. "I've known this money since it was only blips. It started out in Atlantic Brands' bank. Then it went to another bank, in New York. Then a bank in Geneva. Then to the Midland Bank in Lombard Street. There Jack Wilson turned it into cash and took it with him out to Berkshire. What happened next, Brenda?"

Brenda shrank back against the door. She was looking not at the money but at Sarah's calm, implacable face.

"I—I never saw that before. I don't know how it got there."

"Really."

Brenda turned to Chris, desperately. "At my place—remember? There was that guy next to the car?"

"Yes."

"He must have planted—"

"He was trying to get into the car, Brenda. He was going to get the money, while his friends took care of us."

She grasped his arm in both her hands. "I wasn't there last night—when Wilson was killed—you know that, Chris. Tell her—please—"

He nodded. "I was with her all night, Sarah. I don't know how—" He broke off. Sarah's gaze had shifted to him, but her expression had not changed. Ghostly pale, haggard, suspicious.

He gently freed his arm from Brenda's grip. "I think I better take Sarah aside and have a talk with her." She was about to protest, but he cut her off. "I know you're OK—I just have to make that clear to Sarah." He smiled reassuringly and opened the door.

"I can hardly wait." Sarah tilted the seat forward

and got out, slinging the bag over her shoulder. She paused to take a last, hard look at Brenda. "If you put one foot out of this car—"

She left the threat there, slamming the door.

They walked a few paces across the dense, springy grass. "This is far enough," said Sarah, turning to watch the car over Chris's shoulder.

"What's the matter with you? You're scaring her half to death, and for no reason."

Sarah was fumbling with the epaulet of her trench coat, getting the strap of the airline bag anchored beneath it, as if she expected Chris to try to snatch it away from her. "No reason? There's only one thing we can be sure about: Wilson was killed for the money. And she's got the money. Therefore . . ."

"Look, I don't know how the money got in the car, but I do know she was at Leighton Hall when the killings happened. I had my eyes on her the whole time."

"Every minute?"

Chris hesitated. "Well, OK. For about half an hour Raspin made all the men hang around the dinner table and drink port."

"Oh, great. First you say every minute, now it seems there's a missing half-hour."

"That was before Wilson left, Sarah—"

"Well, maybe there were other times you lost her. Think hard, Chris."

"No, there were no other times." He looked at her carefully. Her face had gone even paler, though that hardly seemed possible, and she was shivering violently—perhaps from cold, perhaps from anger. "Sarah, you haven't slept in two nights, you're very sick, and after what you've gone through in the last twelve hours—"

"We're not talking about me," she said harshly, still not looking at him. "We're talking about Brenda. Wilson suspected her and now he's dead. These other people—I don't know what she's done to them but it's bad enough to make them try to kill her. And now there's the money. And you expect me to just take your word that she's OK?" Her eyes left the car and met his. "You're covering for her."

Chris was stunned. "I'm covering—"

"You lost her last night, and you won't say so, because you're convinced she's this dear, sweet little thing that doesn't mean any harm. Maybe you like having her cling to you and look at you like you're—like you're God or something."

"I was with her all night," Chris said again. "She couldn't have—"

"Yeah, that's something else I was wondering about. You said you were watching from your car, but when those guys came in the morning, you were in the house. There are lots of things that happened last night that I wonder about."

Chris fixed his eyes on the ground. "Sarah, you don't really believe that I've slept with Brenda, and I think it's sleazy of you to pretend like you do in order to bully me into saying what you want to hear."

She was silent for a moment. He felt her eyes on him, but did not look up.

"I didn't mean . . . I'm not trying to . . . Oh, I don't know *what* I'm saying. Raving—raving lunacy."

He gave a sigh of relief and reached out to take her hand. "It's OK, Sarah. Let's go back to the car. You're getting cold."

She grasped his hand and drew him closer. She was herself again now; the voice husky and humorous, the blue-gray eyes level and acute. "You know what your problem is? You're no fun to argue with."

"Sorry," he said, smiling back at her.

"Couldn't you slap my face? At least yell a little? No, you just stand there and calmly tell me what a—what a jerk I am." She shook her head; the playfulness had drained out of her voice. "God, Chris. I'm so sorry."

He put his arm around her and kissed her forehead. "Smart. Beautiful. Brave."

"What?"

"Just naming a few of your virtues. Good tennis player, too. Good taste in clothes. Speak French like a native—"

"*Je t'aime,*" she said, and further interrupted him with a kiss.

After a long moment they broke and turned back to the car. Chris glanced at Brenda, leaning against the window with her hand over her face. "Sarah," he said, "she's a very nice person, in a tough spot, and she's clinging to me only because—"

"Don't say any more, please," said Sarah. "Don't embarrass me."

"Sure. But I wish you'd give her a break."

She touched his arm lightly. "OK."

He opened the door and she clambered into the backseat. "Sorry, Brenda," she said perfunctorily, as if they were strangers who had bumped into one another. Brenda did not answer or even look at her, but fixed her yearning gaze once more upon Chris.

"It's OK," he said, patting her hand gingerly. Turning back to Sarah, he went on, "So it wasn't for the money. What was it all for?"

Sarah had to cough before she could answer. "You

know, last night at Raspin's we had this all figured out pretty well, remember?"

"Yeah, but that was before things went wrong at the meeting."

"Maybe they didn't go wrong."

"What?"

"Let's start at the beginning. Of all the bum notes in this whole job, let's start with the first one: that we both got mixed up in it."

"I was putting that down to our rotten luck."

"No. Think. Wilson sends to Inkwink for somebody to find out who's shopping him. At the same time Holman sends to Inkwink for somebody to find out how Wilson's getting the money for the payoff."

Chris looked at her sharply. "You think that's what he's doing? You think he knew all along?"

"I think that's the least of it. I think he knew what was going to happen out there last night."

Chris nodded thoughtfully. "What's he look like?"

"You can't miss him. He's unbearably handsome."

"Oh—the one with curly gray hair and glowing suntan? He didn't leave Leighton Hall all evening."

Sarah frowned and propped her chin on her hand. "I still think he knew what was going to happen."

Chris turned and started the engine. "Let's ask him."

Chapter 20

"Major Dunbar? I'm Superintendent Wells, Berkshire Constabulary. May I have a word with you, sir?"

They were standing on the doorstep of Dunbar's house in Knightsbridge. Dunbar had a bulky cardigan over his arm, as if he were just setting off for a morning's ramble across Hyde Park, but he glanced at Wells's warrant card and stepped back to let him in.

They went to a sitting room dominated by a huge, inchoate oil painting of the Battle of Alma. "Ghastly thing, isn't it?" said the major, following Wells's glance. "But my great-great-uncle was killed there so we've felt obliged to leave it up."

"Sorry to hear that, sir," said Wells.

They went through the usual English preliminaries. Apologies for delaying the major were made and brushed aside, tea was offered and refused, offered again and accepted, comfortable chairs selected, the dreadful traffic on the M4 mentioned and condemned.

"Well," said Dunbar, as if the idea had just occurred to him, "I suppose you've come about poor Wilson."

"Oh, you've heard about it then, sir?"

"Raspin rang me early this morning. Wanted me to know they're going on with their big gala down on the Thames tonight regardless, and not to be alarmed by the added security. And it's in the papers, of course. Now, what can I do for you, Superintendent?"

"Well, sir, Scotland Yard have informed me that

there's been some sort of incident in Fulham—at the house of Miss Wertheim."

"Good lord! She's one of my employees."

"Quite so, sir."

"Oh, you know that, of course. Was she—hurt?"

"We think not, sir. The reports are very confused, but there was shooting, and Miss Wertheim fled the scene in company with a man, described as large and bearded."

Major Dunbar frowned and scratched his white head. "See here, Wells. I think there's a connection here."

Wells nodded and waited patiently.

"There was a big fellow with a beard hanging about the place last week. Name of Rockwell. And he works for RGI."

"Yes, sir. Christopher K. Rockwell. He's a private detective from Greenwich, Connecticut."

Dunbar looked keenly disappointed. "Oh, dear. You're miles ahead of me, then. Private detective, you say?"

"You didn't know that, sir? You don't know what he was doing here?"

"I'm afraid not. He did seem to take an interest in Miss Wertheim, but that's all I know. Seemed a pleasant enough chap—*he* didn't shoot anyone, did he?"

"Not as far as we know, sir."

Dunbar shook his head. "Very baffling. Very baffling indeed."

He said nothing more, and after a moment Wells got to his feet. He closed his notebook and put it away; he had not written anything in it. "Well, thank you, sir. Sorry to have troubled you."

"I wish I could help you, Superintendent." Dunbar

rose to see him to the door. "Dreadful, isn't it? All
this violence about today. Not like when I was a
boy."

"Quite so, sir."

"It's all these foreigners, that's what it is. First
the Irish, then the Arabs, now we've got Americans
shooting up the place."

"Quite so, sir," Wells repeated. He had stopped
listening, and Dunbar saw him to the door and wished
him good morning.

Major Dunbar did not go out. He tossed the cardigan on a chair and walked back down the long
hallway. His steps were so slow and stiff that the creaks
and groans that accompanied him might have been
coming from his bones rather than the floorboards.
The room into which he turned had its shades down
and its furniture draped in dustcloths. Most of the
rooms in this large house were closed—had to be, Dunbar had decided, with the cost of keeping servants
these days.

"He's gone, Holman."

Holman rose up out of the gloom like a baleful
ghost. He had been crouching behind a table. "Who
was it?"

"Chap called Wells, from—"

"Wells! What's happening? Has he got anything?"

"No." Dunbar sat down in a wing chair, not mind-
ing about the dust. "Odd, really. It gave me such a
fright when he told me who he was and got out his
warrant card."

"What the hell's odd about that?" Holman was
pacing anxiously, hands jammed in the trouser pockets
of his handsome three-piece suit. "I spent half last

night giving a statement to that guy, and I was scared every minute."

Dunbar leaned over, his elbows on his knees. He went on, talking to himself rather than Holman. "It's odd that *I* should be frightened by a policeman. Just like a beggar in Trafalgar Square, or a Soho tart. For the rest of my life, I'll be frightened of policemen." He wagged his head thoughtfully. Then abruptly he straightened up. "He came to tell me—Wells, that is—about Wertheim. Those scum came after her, just as I expected they would, but Rockwell got her away. Don't know how he happened to be there."

Holman stopped dead. "Rockwell! Oh, that's terrific. Just terrific. What I came to tell you is, Sarah Saber—the girl I had tailing Wilson—she was there last night, when you—"

"Yes, I know. I read it in the papers."

"You know? Well, what are you going to do?"

Dunbar shrugged. "She couldn't have seen me, not to identify me. If she had done, she'd have gone to the police by now." In the same toneless voice, he went on. "You were supposed to see to it that she stayed away from Wilson."

Holman swung round and jabbed a finger at him. "You know why she didn't? She must have run into Rockwell at Raspin's house. They work for the same outfit."

"Oh? I didn't know that."

"I found out last night, at the police station. Man, I was hyper as it was, but when they laid that one on me—"

"How did it happen?"

"God, I don't know. The moment I heard what happened at the auction, I initiated the process of getting somebody from Inkwink to try and catch him embezzling the money. And the moment he got back from the auction, he must have turned to them too."

"So they're the lot that does the dirty work for RGI, is that it?" Dunbar had his eyes fixed on the floor again. "I wouldn't have thought it of Rockwell. Such a pleasant fellow. What's the other one like—Miss Saber?"

Holman gaped at him. "What's she like? What the hell kind of off-the-wall question is that? Dangerous, that's what she's like. Those two have joined forces, and between them they know enough to—"

"What? What do they know?"

Holman broke off. As usual, he had not thought it through. "Well—well, they'll know Wertheim's clean, and then they'll go looking for whoever really sold the marketing portfolio—"

"They don't know anything about the marketing portfolio, and there is no way for them to find out."

Holman's eyes flickered over Dunbar's face. Then he grinned, as if he had won a point. "*You* found out."

"No, Holman. You told me. I knew a great deal more than Rockwell and Miss Saber do, to begin with. But even so, I should never have got anywhere but for your stupidity. You must not be stupid again, Holman."

"Hey, look. This is no time for you to start putting me down. I mean, we've got a big problem here, and we've got to work through it together."

"Very well. I shall tell you what you must do. It will take a great deal of courage." Dunbar stood up and faced him. Holman's Adam's apple was bobbing up and down and his gaze was skittering nervously about the room. "You must do nothing."

"*Nothing?*"

"Go to the gala tonight, go to the meetings—carry on as usual. Brazen it out. I shall be doing the same. It won't be easy."

Holman stared in silence.

"Rockwell and Miss Saber can make guesses. They may even make the right guesses. But they cannot get any evidence against us, because there is no evidence."

Holman shook his head vigorously. "No. I mean, I can't do it. I can't deal with anxiety like this. We've got to do something, get it over with!"

"It'll never be over, Holman. We'll have the fear with us for the rest of our lives."

Holman was still shaking his head. "I know what's coming down with you. You've got guilt feelings you can't cope with. You *want* to be caught."

Dunbar looked at him in that unsettling way he had. "I'm not sorry for what I've done. But it will never be over. You must get used to that."

Holman could not bear having the old man's piercing blue eyes on him a moment longer. He shrugged and turned away, heading for the door.

Dunbar grasped his arm. "I do not mean to be caught. And I won't be unless you do something stupid. You must do nothing, Holman."

Hal Holman emerged into the cloudy day. He stood for a moment, breathing in the air laden with dampness and exhaust fumes, and looking about for his limousine. Then he remembered that he had come by taxi, as a precaution.

He walked to the corner of Brompton Road and flagged down a cab. Giving the address of RGI House, he sank back in the spacious backseat. On the short drive to Victoria Street he tried to think the whole matter over carefully, but the clicking of the meter distracted him. An amorphous man, he bore the imprint of a stronger personality for some time after he had come in contact with it. Do nothing, Dunbar had said. There is no evidence. Carry on as usual. The injunctions passed into his mind as if they were his own thoughts.

By the time he walked into the fifth-floor office that had been set up for him, he was really feeling high. His staff—all these bright, competent people at his beck and call—was at work in a tumult of clattering telexes and typewriters and buzzing telephones. A secretary rose as he passed her desk.

"Your calls, Mr. Holman."

"Oh—yes." He turned to face her, and she handed him a series of notes, with a comment on each one. The first ones were positive and supportive messages from his affiliate heads in Leisure Group. They were shocked at Wilson's death, in such scandalous circumstances; they remembered that Holman had always had doubts about him, and now that they thought about it, they realized they'd had doubts about him too. Holman accepted these messages eagerly.

Then she laid the heavy ones on him: Go up to Mr. Raspin's office. Call somebody named Chandler, at Inquiries, Inc. Mrs. Webb had called—there were six of those.

And finally, the worst one of all.

"Oh—there was a young lady rang you about ten minutes ago. She said she couldn't leave a number, but would ring back soon."

It came to Holman, with the swiftness and certitude of a disastrous but inescapable conclusion, that this was Saber.

Fighting off an anxiety attack with all his might,

Holman turned away and stumbled into his own office. He put his back to the door and stared at the telephone console on the desk. He was feeling threatened, and he knew he must take a positive step: He must get on the phone. Start calling people before they called him.

But Holman was very bad at taking positive steps. Whenever he reached a crossroad in his life and had to decide which fork to take, he ended up looking over his shoulder instead, back at all the wrong turnings that had brought him there. Decision was smothered by second guesses, regrets, reproaches. Reproaches of others, naturally.

Now he got as far as deciding that he must call Thea Webb first; he had not spoken to her since she had called him with her plan to make Wilson bring the cash to Leighton Hall. Then he thought: Yes, that was her idea. Just as it had been her idea to hire Saber to catch Wilson embezzling the money, and her idea to auction the marketing portfolio in the first place. It was *all* her fault. No, he did not want to talk to the bitch.

He sat down at his desk, with an uneasy sideways glance at the telephone. He repeated Dunbar's words to himself again: Brazen it out . . . There is no evidence. . . . But they were only faint echoes next to the threat of that mute telephone.

He *must* start returning calls.

He was prying the lid off his case of Valiums when the telephone buzzed. He jumped, scattering little blue pills all over the blotter. Then, reluctantly, he picked up the receiver.

"Call for you on line two-two-oh-four, sir. The lady won't give her name. Do you wish to take it?"

For a moment he thought he saw an out: Why

should he be expected to take a call when she wouldn't give her name? Then he realized that if she did give her name to the secretary, the situation would be even worse.

"I'll . . . take it," he said, trying to tune the quaver out of his voice. He punched the lighted button. "He-hello?"

"Saber."

Holman swallowed and gathered his resources for a prodigious feat of role playing. "Sarah! Thank God. We were afraid you'd been killed."

"Not quite."

"That must have been a really awful situation you were in, just awful."

"Yes, it was. It was considerate of you to try and stop me from following Wilson."

"Sorry? I'm afraid I'm not getting where you're coming from."

"You knew what was going to happen out there."

Holman cringed; he nearly sank down under the desk. "I see . . . I see. . . . Now set me straight here if I'm wrong, but what I'm getting from what you're saying is that you think I'm involved in some sort of criminal situation here."

"You got it."

He forced a laugh out of his throat. "That's just absurd. I mean, I know the feelings you must be experiencing, and don't think I can't relate, but that's just absurd."

"I've got Chris Rockwell and Wertheim with me. We want to meet you. We want you to do some explaining."

"Hey, that's just great!" said Holman, with genuine relief. This was not the worst; she wasn't sure. "That's what I want too. We can work through this problem together. Uh—you can't come here, of course. How about my place in Hampstead? Twenty-seven, Holly Mount. Say, two hours? It'll take me a while to get away—"

"One hour, Holman."

The line went dead.

Holman's relief and exhilaration lasted only until he had put the receiver down. Then the next ordeal loomed up before him: the meeting itself. Brazen it out, Dunbar had said. There is no evidence. They don't even know about the marketing portfolio.

But when he imagined facing Saber, and answering her first question, "Why did you call me off?" he quailed. The pretext he had given her now seemed as frail as wet paper to him. He remembered how it had gone down with Walter Raspin.

No. Holman's one great gift—his intuition for spotting people who were stronger and more clever than he, and knowing not to go up against them—told him that he must avoid this meeting at any cost. He could not face Saber, nor Rockwell and Wertheim—those two people whom he had never met, whom he had attempted to maneuver to their deaths.

But how could he avoid the meeting? He set his mind to the problem and once more was distracted into recriminations. It was all Dunbar's fault. How had he expected Holman to come up with a credible pretext for calling Saber off at that point in time? He should have refused, forced Dunbar to shoot her down along with the others. Then he would not have had this problem.

Suddenly Holman flashed on a plan. It was so bold that he began shivering the moment it sprang into his mind. If he could carry it out, make just one phone call, he would get clear.

With the rush of reckless courage known only to the cornered poltroon, he picked up the telephone and dialed a number in Brussels. It was a number he had long known, but had never used.

The line opened and he heard a few rapid words in French. "I want to speak to Lisle," he said. *"Parler à Lisle."*

Static and clicking noises—the call was being transferred. A new voice came on the line.

"You wish to speak to Monsieur Lisle?"

"Yes."

"Why should Monsieur Lisle wish to speak to you?"

Holman was about to say, "Re Martinique transaction," but then he thought: No, that's too close. Too damn close. "Eight hundred thousand dollars," he said, instead.

"What is your telephone number?"

He gave it, and the man hung up without a word. Holman picked up a Valium from the blotter and popped it, made two circuits of the desk, and then the telephone buzzed.

"A Monsieur Lisle for you, sir, on two-two-oh-eight—"

"Yeah," said Holman, and punched the lighted button. "Hello."

"Monsieur Holman?" said a precise, lightly accented voice. Holman, startled, was about to ask how the man had known his name, but then he remembered that his secretary answered the telephone with "Mr. Holman's office." Christ. Already he had come within a split second of making two mistakes, and he could afford none at all.

"Eight hundred thousand dollars, Lisle," he said, and was pleased with the calm, authoritative tone of his voice. He didn't know how come it came out that way. "You want it? I can help you get it. Interested?"

"I am interested," replied Lisle. "But we should continue this discussion in person."

"No way. This'll do."

"We shall have a car at RGI House for you in ten minutes. Will you be waiting in the lobby or shall we ask for you, Monsieur Holman?"

Holman swallowed audibly. "I'll be waiting."

"Very good. Look for a black van."

Holman was waiting not in the lobby but at the curb as the van eased out of traffic and pulled up beside him. There were two men in it. The one in the front passenger seat got out. He was a tall fellow with an impassive face.

"Mr. Holman?" he said politely.

"Yeah, right."

The man turned and shifted the side door of the van open. "Get in here—and we'd like you facing backwards, if you please."

There were no seats in the back of the van, so Holman crouched on the floor. He could see nothing, because the back windows of the van were covered with whitewash. The door slid shut, and he heard the man getting into the front seat. Then the driver pulled a U-turn that sent Holman sprawling on his side. For the next few minutes he was occupied with trying to keep himself upright as the van turned, stopped, and accelerated.

"Do we have far to go?" he asked, speaking for the first time.

"We're there," said the driver, as the van came to an abrupt halt.

The door slid open and he got out. They were in a mews, behind a row of tall whitewashed houses. The men fell in on either side of him and led him through a garage and into one of the houses. After going up some steps and through some corridors, they steered him into an office.

Behind the desk sat a little white-haired man. He had a bandage wrapped round the top of his head, and his thick bifocals rested crookedly on his nose because they were missing one temple. Lisle did not present a very impressive figure just now, in fact, and Holman felt his confidence take a jump. Boldly, he left the two men behind him and approached the desk to sit down in one of the chairs before it.

"I'm—"

Lisle nodded. "One of the vice-presidents of RGI. I know that, Monsieur Holman."

Holman fixed his eyes on Lisle. "Do you know I'm Wilson's superior?" He could see the uneasiness in the little man's face, and he pressed on, feeling stronger with each moment. "I'm aware of the situation Wilson got himself into with you people. I'm fully plugged in."

Lisle said nothing.

"You really blew it, Lisle. I guess you've figured out that last night you were shooting at the wrong woman? Wertheim got away long before you people arrived."

Now Lisle nodded. "Sarah Saber. She is your agent, then? I see."

"That's right." This was going well, thought Holman. He decided it was time for a little body-language. He crossed his legs easily and draped one arm over the back of the chair. "When you found out that Wertheim was under the illusion that she'd gotten away clean, you went to her place. And then you screwed up for the second time. A man got Wertheim away—and the money. The man's name is Rockwell, by the way."

Unconsciously, Lisle probed at his bandaged head. "Rockwell," he repeated.

"He and Wertheim have gotten together with Saber. They're to meet me in"—he glanced at his watch—"forty minutes. I've come to tell you where. You can have the money, and you can do what you want to Wertheim. Of course, you'll have to take care of the other two also."

Lisle shook his head. "No, Monsieur Holman, it won't do. Why should you contact us? Why should you want us to kill your own agent? You will have to do some more explaining, monsieur."

The bottom of Holman's confidence dropped out abruptly, as it was wont to do. He felt the calm, assured expression sliding from his face.

A moment longer and he would have begun to blubber. But just then the man who had driven the van stepped forward. "What the bloody hell do we care about that, Lisle? If we can get the money—"

Lisle interrupted quietly. "I thought we had agreed that I would make the decisions, Hardy."

"Oh, you've been making decisions, and lately I haven't liked them above half. We can have the money, and a crack at the Wertheim bitch, for the asking, and you're dithering about—" He broke off, shaking his head. "You stupid frog, I'm not taking orders from you anymore, and that's flat."

Lisle was looking at his hands. "Nicholls?" he asked.

"We haven't much time for explanations, sir," Nicholls replied, mildly.

"Very well. Where is the meeting to take place, Monsieur Holman?"

"My house, in Hampstead."

"They're not armed," said Hardy. "It'll be dead easy to take 'em."

"Right," said Holman, jumping to the aid of his unexpected ally. "It'll be easy. The address is Twenty-seven, Holly Mount."

Lisle rose. "Nicholls, fetch the other car. Monsieur Holman, you will ride with me."

Holman cringed. "Hey, wait a minute. I can't see any necessity—"

"You will ride with me," Lisle repeated.

Chapter 21

They had agreed, by a glance and a nod, that Sarah should take the wheel. Chris could not get used to being on the wrong side of the road in a car in which all the controls were backwards, and London driving, so different from the New York stoplight-to-stoplight dash, completely flummoxed him. But Sarah wove this little car through the thick traffic and round the winding streets with ease. He sat beside her, the A-Z open on his lap, navigating; Brenda was in the back, disconsolate and mute. The silence in the car, in fact, was broken only by Chris's directions and Sarah's coughing, which was so harsh that the very sound made his throat ache. He noticed that she was not smoking, a sure sign that she felt wretched.

They drove up Fitzjohn's Avenue, a broad street lined with Victorian monstrosities, great red-brick piles sprouting turrets and corbels in the most unlikely places. Then the road narrowed; the houses grew closer together and finally joined, and they were in Hampstead Village: pubs with big etched-glass windows, bookstores, sleek little boutiques selling antiques, clothes, furniture. Even on this glum morning, the traffic on Heath Street was down to a crawl and the pavements were thronged. Perhaps, though, "throng" was too indecorous a word to describe these people, who strolled along as if they did not have to get anywhere on time, and scanned the shop windows as if they could afford anything that took their fancy. They wore suede coats and silk scarves, cashmere jumpers and calfskin boots. Their faces had a benign, intelligent, well-fed look.

Sarah gave her throaty chuckle, which turned into a cough. "Gosh," she said, "I thought Connecticut was the last word in genteel wealth, but this place—"

Chris nodded. "Is this a classy neighborhood, Brenda?"

"What? Oh, I guess," she replied, listlessly.

"Well, I certainly can't imagine anything *nasty* happening here, can you, Chris?"

He pointed. "Here we are. Holly Mount. Left."

They turned and climbed a hill. Holly Mount was as quiet as Heath Street was busy. It was lined on one side by a steep grassy bank topped by fir trees, and on the other by a row of little houses with trellises and window boxes and trailing vines that looked as if they had been transported intact from some village lane.

"Lovely," said Sarah.

"Only the best for an RGI company house. Slow down. I want to take a look at the cars."

There was a solid line of them, parked with two wheels up on the curb.

"Twenty-seven—that's Holman's," said Sarah, as they passed a white stucco house surrounded by a high brick wall.

"Don't stop."

She accelerated and they climbed on, rounding a gentle bend in the road. Then she stopped and put on the emergency brake.

"Well?"

"Green Fiat parked in front of Holman's. That was one of the cars that was following Brenda."

Brenda plunged forward as if the car had come to a sudden halt. "Following me? When?"

"A couple of days ago," said Chris, uncomfortably.

"Those—those people were watching me, and you knew, and you wouldn't warn me?"

Chris did not turn to face her. "Well, I didn't know then whether I could trust you."

"You sure acted like it." Her tone was not accusatory, but deeply hurt. "Seeing me home and having tea and stuff, and all the time, you were—like—"

"I'm sorry. I should have trusted you."

At that moment Sarah, unasked, jumped to his defense. "Will you knock off this innocent-bystander bit, Brenda? Face it: You're a turn. You sold out your employer to that jerk Wilson, and you got what you deserved."

There was a moment's silence as Brenda stared at her, stricken. "Chris—tell her that's not fair. Tell her she doesn't know the whole thing."

He nodded. "Sarah, you don't know the whole story."

She was looking out the windshield, chin propped on her hand. "You saved her life, and I don't know where she gets the idea you owe her any apologies."

"I didn't—"

"Both of you, knock it off," Chris ordered. "We've got no time for this."

"Agreed," said Sarah. "Plan?"

"Plan!" said Brenda, choking. "Those are the guys who tried to kill us. We've got to—to get away from here!"

"Where do you want us to go, Brenda?" Sarah asked, in a carefully neutral voice.

"I'm not a—a professional like you guys. I can't *stand* any more of this."

Chris swiveled in his seat. "Don't you see? This means Holman's behind it. We've got to get our hands on him."

"But we can't go in there—we'll be killed."

"We're not going in there," said Sarah. "At least not just yet."

"Got an idea?"

"Yeah. I think I've got a way to split Holman's ranks."

"OK." He looked at Brenda again. "We won't take any unnecessary chances. Just trust me, OK?"

"I trust you." Brenda's big, disconsolate eyes fixed on Sarah. "But I don't trust her."

"I'm heartbroken," said Sarah, still looking out the windshield.

Holman had watched, in ever deepening horror, as the two men made their preparations: lowering the shades, clearing the furniture, taking down mirrors and glass-covered pictures. The quiet one, Nicholls, came up to him.

"We'll be needing some sheets."

"What for?"

"To spread on the floor."

Holman's insides writhed, and his throat burned with the effort of keeping himself from vomiting. "Linen closet—upstairs," he gasped, and turned to Lisle.

The little man was sitting in a straight chair by the door, legs crossed, hands folded over one knee. He still had his overcoat and hat on, and wore a mildly expectant expression, as if he were waiting for a train.

"I'll go upstairs," Holman said.

Lisle looked up at him, with his eerily magnified eyes. "I'm afraid that will hardly do, Holman. You must open the door, you see."

Hardy came up beside him. "As soon as they're

all in, you close the door, and then you fall flat on your face. Got it? You go right down on the floor." Holman gazed with sickly fascination at the gun in his hand—a small automatic with a long tube on the end. A silencer.

"I can't do it," he burst out.

Lisle looked at him in silence.

"I'd give it away. I just couldn't play the scene. Can't you get where I'm coming from?" he pleaded.

"Yes, I see," said Lisle. "You want them dead, but you do not want to see them killed. Quite understandable. But there is no choice. You must open the door."

Just then the telephone gave its strident double ring. Holman jumped.

"What do I do?"

Lisle shrugged. "Answer it."

Holman looked around dazedly; he had forgotten where the telephone was. Hardy pointed to an end table near the sofa. Holman trudged over, fumbled the receiver off the cradle, and raised it to his ear.

"Hello?"

"Holman," said Saber's voice, "meet me at Whitestone Pond. It's a ten-minute walk from your place, and I expect you there in ten minutes." She hung up.

Still holding the receiver in his hand, Holman turned and repeated the message to Lisle.

Lisle rose and stood meditatively stroking his white moustache for a few seconds. "Hardy, go down to Heath Street and fetch the van. Be quick."

"You think they're on to us, then?" Hardy was already making for the door.

"Yes, they're on to us." Lisle turned to Nicholls, who was standing at the foot of the stairs with an armful of sheets. "We will take the Fiat—"

"We're going to Whitestone Pond, sir?"

"Not as far as that, I suspect. Come on." At the door he paused and looked at Holman. He had forgotten him for a moment. "You, monsieur, wait here. You understand? Wait." Then they were gone, and the door slammed shut behind them.

Hal Holman stood in the middle of the room, his hands clenched, his breath coming in ragged gasps, his head empty. Panic rose in a great wave and engulfed him. He ran through the house, scrabbled desperately at the doorknob, turned it, and flung the door wide. He fled through the garden, without a backward glance.

Above Holman's house Holly Mount curved gently and, changing its name to Holly Bush Hill, looped around a green, which was lined by a high ironwork fence and cluttered with parked cars. Sarah had slid the Mini in beside the lofty fender of an old Jaguar. They were pointing downhill toward Holman's house.

"Here they come!" she exclaimed, as the green Fiat swung into view and rushed past. She let out the clutch and started downhill.

Chris swiveled and looked out the back window, willing the Fiat to sink out of sight over the top of the hill. It did not. It stopped and its backup lights blinked on.

"Damn it! They spotted us."

As he spoke he caught sight of Brenda, wedged in the corner of the backseat, eyes shut, locked in some storm cellar of her mind.

He turned round to another shock: The familiar black van was coming at them up the hill.

"Is that—"

"Yeah."

Sarah gave a vicious twist to the wheel and they mounted a narrow track, hardly wider than the car. They rushed along between a high brick wall set flush with the road on the right and a row of fir trees on the left. If someone's coming the other way—Chris shut his mind to the thought. Looking down through the trees, he could see their pursuers cross, and the Fiat stopped with a squeak of tires to turn around.

They whipped round a sharp-angled corner and along a row of muddy-brown brick houses. The street ended in a wide, straight, quiet avenue, and Sarah turned right, stamped on the accelerator, and rowed through the gears.

She had no sooner reached fourth gear than the straight road ran out. She downshifted and maneuvered the car through short, narrow streets that wriggled like worms.

"Any sign of 'em?" asked Sarah.

Chris was turned in his seat, partly to keep watch out the back window, partly because he preferred not to see how fast they were going. "Nope. They'll never find us in this maze. I think you can slow down."

He turned round, and saw that they were looping round a green lined with parked cars. "Hey," he said, "this is—"

"Familiar." She finished for him. "We've gone in a damned circle."

And then they were plunging downhill again, and Holly Mount straightened out below, and there was the green Fiat, coming up at them.

Again Sarah veered right onto the narrow hillside track between the wall and the fir trees.

"Chris, tell me where to go."

As they rounded the tight corner, a sign embedded

in the wall slid past: Mount Vernon. Chris tried to
focus on the jolting print of the A-Z in his lap. They
were somewhere in the corner of the map, where the
streets were so tiny and tangled that there was hardly
room for their names. He brought the book up until
the page was touching his nose; still he could not
read it.

"You'll have to stop."

Without hesitation she threw on the brakes and
the car lurched to a halt. The momentum carried
Brenda forward and slammed her against the front
seats. She gasped but said nothing.

Chris pinned Mount Vernon down with a finger-
nail. "Frognal," he said. "Next left. That'll get us
out of here."

He swiveled round as she gunned the engine and
popped the clutch. The rear wheels smoked and
skittered, and they were off. He saw the green car
rounding the turn fifty feet behind them.

When he faced forward again they were turning
into a wide, straight street that looked wonderfully
as if it were going somewhere. Chris was just taking
a deep breath when Sarah wrenched the wheel and
sent them into a little elbow-shaped street between
big red houses.

"What are you *doing*?"

She flicked him a glance. "Sign on the corner said
Frognal."

He squinted at the map. "It's Frognal *Gardens*!
That's a different street—it doesn't go—"

He looked up to see that his explanation was unnecessary: Frognal Gardens was ending in a tranquil
churchyard beneath tall pines. Sarah turned left.

"No, right! Right takes us back to Frognal!"

"They're in the way."

He glanced over his shoulder to see the green Fiat again bearing down on them.

"I'll go around," said Sarah, turning left.

They bumped over a curb and shot between two white pylons, up a cobbled pathway lined with rows of little houses whose doorsteps were set flush with the street.

"What do the white things mean?"

"They're supposed to keep out cars."

"Oh, well."

Even as she spoke a man stepped out his front door and directly into their path, his eyes fixed on a newspaper.

Sarah could not veer without running them into the opposite wall. She slammed her fist against the horn button. The man looked up in amazement and stumbled clumsily back over his doorstep.

"You sods!" he shouted as they went past.

The street ended in another that looked familiar. And then there it all was again: the sharp bend round the high brick wall, the fir trees on the bank. They were back at Mount Vernon again.

When they rounded the corner, the black van was driving slowly toward them, taking up the entire width of the track.

Sarah slammed on the brakes. With astonishing coolness she glanced down at the shift knob to read the gear diagram, notched into reverse, and took her foot off the clutch. The rear tires hopped and they lunged backwards a few feet, bumping into the side of a house and smashing the taillights. She spun the wheel left, and as she shifted into first, an arm swung out from the front window of the van. There was a thud and long cracks spread across their windshield. The bastards were still using silencers.

Sarah wheeled the car in a tight turn, its front fender clearing the brick wall by a hand's breadth, and then they were flying along, back the way they had come.

They reached Frognal again, that blessedly wide, straight street, but before Chris could say anything Sarah had turned right.

"Frognal, thank God."

"Yes. Only we're going the wrong way."

He took a quick glance out the back—no one in sight yet—and glimpsed Brenda, wedged in her corner again, eyes shut. He did not know how she was standing up to this; he was close to raving hysteria himself.

"The map, Chris. Where does this take us?"

He held the A-Z up, peering at it. "Holly Bush—"

"Yeah. Look."

He lowered the atlas. They were once more back at the car-cluttered green where they had been waiting in the first place.

Chris tossed the book down in the wheel well. "Oh, hell. Go straight down Holly Mount and we're back on Heath Street."

"Right."

Down the curving, sloping road they went again, past the tree-fringed knoll, past Holman's house. The road straightened out and they were coming down on the tail of the green Fiat.

The driver was damnably alert, and he swung the car broadside, blocking the road entirely.

A lane opened up to their left and Sarah dodged into it. They bounced over the curb and just missed clipping the front steps of a house. It was yet another track not ten feet wide, solidly lined with low brick houses. It curled sharply, and Chris said, "This *must* lead to Heath Street."

It took another curve and there was nothing before them but overlapping brick walls and an iron railing. Dead end. Sarah turned to glance at the gear pattern, looking for reverse—and then raised her eyes to Chris's.

"No time to get back. They'll be on us."

Chris pointed ahead. "Steps," he said. "Leave the car and run for it!"

Even as he spoke he threw the door open and ran back along the road, the way they had come.

"Chris, no!" Sarah screamed behind him.

As he rounded the curve at a dead run the green Fiat appeared. It was so close that he could recognize the man in the passenger seat, the little man in the fedora whom he had hit in Brenda's mews.

He tore his eyes from the car, searching for the gap he had glimpsed a moment ago. And there it was: a broad path between a brick wall and a trellis.

He ran into it, waiting for the shriek of the Fiat's brakes behind him, the thud of a gunshot. But he heard nothing—and then there was a steep bank of steps before him. He was down in a split second, out of sight, safe.

Sarah wasted one precious instant standing beside the car, staring at the curve round which he had vanished. Then she bent down, jerked the seat forward, and reached a hand out to Brenda. But Brenda did not take it.

"You'll never make it with me," she said, stating Sarah's thought. She knew she was doing so, and her dark eyes were full of measureless contempt, deeper even than her fear.

Then the Fiat swung round behind them, and Sarah turned and fled.

She saw bullets thudding into the brick wall before her, and then she dodged round it. There were steps and she hurtled down them. It was a steep path zigzagging between high walls, iron railings, and the locked back gates of houses. Down and down she ran, and suddenly the walls fell away and she was out in a road—a straight, sloping road. Across a strip of greenery she could see the crowds and traffic of Heath Street.

Hearing thudding footfalls, she swung round to find Chris beside her. She gave a moan of relief and threw her arms around him.

"Where's Brenda?"

"She—wouldn't come. They got her."

Chris said nothing. He broke their embrace, grasping her hand, and pulled her into a run.

"What is it?" she exclaimed, gasping. "They won't come after us now—"

"Don't count on it. You've got the money."

She had completely forgotten the heavy bag, still secured by her shoulder strap; had not even felt it thumping against her side as she ran.

The green tapered to an end as they reached the junction with Heath Street. She looked back to see a man at the foot of the steps. He had followed her and stood hesitating; even as she watched he broke into a run, after them. She was trying to make out if he had a gun in his hand when Chris yanked her to the side and she had to look ahead.

They leapt off the curb into the street. A car plunged to a halt, tires squeaking, the bumper a foot from her kneecaps. At the noise a couple of men

standing before a shop window turned to look at
them over their fleecy collars, with mild, curious
faces. They gained the crowded pavement, slowing
to a trot, dodging and weaving. She saw Chris's head
turn and followed his glance: Across the street, at the
corner of Holly Mount, the van had halted and a
man was clambering down from the driver's seat.
She looked ahead in time to see a terrier veer into
her path, nose to the ground. She leapt over his leash
and caught the beginnings of a startled remonstrance
from his white-haired mistress.

They had reached a corner, where she saw a purple-
tiled building with the circle and bar sign of an
Underground station. Now she hauled on Chris's
hand, pulling him in the entranceway.

They ran past the newsstand, paused, and spotted
the wooden doors of the elevator—just as they were
folding closed.

"There must be stairs—" Sarah gasped.

A frantic glance around them; she found the sign
with the word "steps" on the wall. Chris saw it at the
same moment. They rounded the angle of the wall,
running.

There were two broad, straight flights, and then
they were on a spiral staircase, wrapping round and
round a thick core of steel supports and cables. Their
footsteps rang on the narrow steel steps as they ran
on, down and down.

Gradually it penetrated Chris's dazed and frightened brain that this was not New York, where the
trains were only two flights below the street. Here
he had always taken elevators or steep banks of es-
calators to reach the trains. How much further could
it be?

Sarah's hand slid from his. He stopped and looked back. She was leaning over the rail, gasping and coughing. He climbed the two steps back and put his arm around her.

"Can't go on?"

"It doesn't matter," she said hoarsely. "Chris, the elevator's been down and up and back down again by now. They could be waiting for us on the platform."

"Go back?"

"Or they could be up there still."

Chris felt himself swaying. He let his knees buckle and sank down on the steps. Sarah settled beside him and took his hand again.

"They—" His voice echoed along the curving tiled wall, and he went on in a whisper, "they probably didn't see us go down the stairs—I think they were too far back."

"I hope."

"When they don't see us, they'll figure we got away. They can't hang around—it must be teeming with cops up there by now. Don't you think?"

"I hope," she repeated dully.

"This is the best place to be. If they come for us, we'll hear 'em in time to run."

Sarah made no reply, and he turned to her questioningly. "Unless—" she whispered—"unless they come from both directions at once. If they trap us here, we haven't got a chance."

There was no response to that. Chris pressed his wet palm against hers, and they waited, trying to quiet their breathing, straining their ears for the metallic ring of footfalls on the stairs. He could hear the sound—no louder than a sigh—of trains pulling into and out of the station; the low hum of the electric lights and the ventilating equipment; water dripping somewhere. Nothing else.

Abruptly, Sarah lifted her free arm and he jumped. But she was only sinking her face into the crook of her elbow, to muffle a coughing fit. She coughed until tears ran from her tightly shut eyes. He put his arms round her, trying to warm her.

They waited.

Finally it was Sarah who said, "I don't think they're coming."

"Jesus, I hope not. How long have we been here?"

"I don't know, but I've heard an awful lot of trains go past."

"Yeah."

For another moment they remained motionless. Then she stood up and said in a normal tone of voice, "I'm sick of this. Shall we go up or down?"

Chris got to his feet; his cramped legs tingled as the blood coursed into them. "Down. I'm too tired to climb."

"How far—" She broke off.

And then Chris heard it too: the metallic tap-tap-tap of footfalls. Someone was coming up the stairs. Running.

Chris swung round, grasping the railing with one hand and Sarah's arm with the other. She did not move. He turned back in astonishment.

"Listen!" she whispered.

He did—and his astonishment deepened as he heard that the runner was counting.

"Thirty-nine—forty—forty-one—"

They stood stock still, staring down at the point where the stairs swept out of sight beyond the steel core. The figure appeared; a young man in a rugby jersey, with sweaty hair curling over his ears.

"Forty-four—forty-five—forty-six—"

He looked up at them in surprise and stopped. "Oh—good afternoon."

"Good afternoon," Chris replied numbly.

He put his hands on his hips and breathed deeply. "D'you know, I've been running up these steps every Saturday for a year, and I've never seen a soul on them."

All Chris could think of to say was, "We're Americans."

"Oh, well that's it, isn't it? This is the deepest stairwell in the Underground system. Didn't you see the warning up top?"

"No, we didn't notice it."

The man was grinning. "Not to worry. It's only— Oh, bugger, I've lost count. But it's only forty-odd steps to the bottom. Long way to the top, though. Mustn't stop. Cheerio." And he was off again, arms and legs pumping rhythmically.

They watched him till he was out of sight, then turned to look at one another. Laughter bubbled up in their throats and they embraced.

Sarah locked her hands behind Chris's back, circling the whole girth of him, and rested her head on his broad shoulder. He was such an ample man—there was so much of him to cling to. He bent his head, and she felt the frame of his glasses, the short curly hairs of his beard against her cheeks. She turned her face to his and their lips met.

Moments passed unheeded. Finally, and without another word, they descended the last "forty-odd" steps.

There were a couple of dozen people on the platform, some pacing aimlessly, some reading, some staring up at the devastating underwear advertisements that decorate subway stations. No one's hand slipped beneath his coat; no one even looked at Chris and Sarah.

They ambled down the platform, feeling light-headed and thinking of nothing at all. There was a mounting rumble, a rush of stale air, and the big red train slid into the station and came rattling and whirring to a stop. People rose languidly and crossed the platform.

Chris and Sarah stood looking at one another. As usual in London, their air of confusion attracted a helpful stranger.

"This is the southbound train," said a young woman, slowly and clearly, in case they were foreigners. "Is that the one you want?"

"Well . . . I guess," Chris replied. He took Sarah's arm and they boarded.

Chapter 22

There were two of them. One was a seamy-faced man with a grizzled crew cut. He was draped in a raincoat that could easily have been mistaken for a gunnysack. The other was a taller, younger man who wore big steel-framed glasses and a smile that showed many teeth and no warmth.

"Mrs. Webb? Good morning. I'm Bill Chandler. This is my boss, Mr. Welch. May we come in?"

Thea Webb clutched her robe about her more tightly. Her pasty face seemed to grow still paler, her beady eyes still harder. After a moment's hesitation, she swung the door wide.

"Yes. All right."

There was a pause while the two men divested themselves of overshoes, coats, and hats. Mrs. Webb left them, retreating into her living room to pick up a pack of cigarettes from the coffee table. Beyond the sliding glass doors the balcony was under a six-inch-deep white blanket, and it was still snowing hard.

"Sorry to wake you so early on a Saturday morning." Welch was advancing on her, straightening the lapels of his glen plaid jacket. "But we're loking for some input on the Wilson problem."

"I'm afraid I can't help you," she replied, lighting the cigarette. "As I told Mr. Chandler last night, I don't know anything about it, and I haven't been able to reach Mr. Holman since then."

She glanced at Chandler. He was leaning in the doorway, looking at the telephone on the hall table. The receiver was lying off the cradle, as it had been all night. Chandler made no comment; instead he said, "Nobody seems to be able to reach Mr. Holman. He walked out of his office at RGI House about an hour and a half ago and dropped out of sight."

Mrs. Webb gave a shaky laugh. "Dropped out of sight? What on earth do you mean? Have they checked his house?"

"Yeah. We just got a call from Mr. Raspin. He sent somebody up there. Found the neighborhood full of cops."

"Cops? What happened?"

"The cops didn't know that themselves. They'd just gotten there, and they were taking statements." Chandler smiled. "One thing you find out in investigative work, when you've got a lot of witnesses to an event, they all tell different stories. So it's very confusing. But somebody was chasing somebody. A couple of the descriptions they got would fit Chris and Sarah."

"Chris and Sarah?"

Chandler's grin grew broader. "My friends at Inkwink. You remember Sarah Saber?"

"I believe you mentioned the name to me last night—"

Welch cut her off. "Anyway, Raspin's man proceeded to the house and was unable to locate Holman there. That's why we've come to you."

"To me?" Mrs. Webb laughed again. "But I told you last night, Mr. Chandler, Mr. Holman handled that himself. I know nothing about it."

"Yeah, you told me that, and I wasted a lot of time and woke a lot of people up finding out it wasn't true." Bill said this in the weary, emotionless tone of a man who had been lied to throughout his working life.

"Not true? What do you—"

Bill took a ragged piece of paper out of his pocket and read from it. "Sarah got her assignment Monday afternoon. Holman was in San Francisco from Friday until Wednesday morning. You, on the other hand, took a company plane from Fairfield to Richmond on Monday afternoon. Arriving four-thirty. And we've got a voucher for a flight from Richmond to La-Guardia, leaving at five, that Sarah took. Will that do, Mrs. Webb?" he asked, without irony. "Or do you want us to go to your staff and ask 'em what they remember?"

Mrs. Webb turned to face Welch. "So this is the way your famous Discretion policy works, is it, Welch? I've got a good mind to—"

"The Discretion policy is inoperative at this point in time," Welch replied stonily.

Bill was chuckling. "Gee, Mrs. Webb, I'm really impressed. It takes guts to attack when you're in this much trouble."

"You're in trouble, Mrs. Webb," Welch echoed.

Bill stopped smiling and said, "A couple of my friends are in danger over there in England, and I want some answers."

She stared at them in silence.

"Better decide, Mrs. Webb," said Welch, "while your input is still worth having."

Holman had committed the error a cannier conspirator would never have made; he had gone deeper without taking his accomplice with him. He had made it more risky for Thea Webb to stick by him than to sell him out.

She held on for one more puff of her cigarette, and then did so.

"I—I really don't know what Holman's up to now.

I have not spoken to him in a couple of days, just as I said."

The two men waited.

"But I do have some perception of his—his earlier activities."

"What were they?"

"I think he passed his copy of Wilson's marketing portfolio to a Cobi outfit and had them auction it."

"Why the hell would he do that?" asked Bill.

Welch held up his hand. "I think the highest-priority question at this point is: What Cobi outfit?"

"I believe he was dealing with a man called . . . Lisle."

"Oh sure, Lisle," said Welch.

"You know of this guy, Ross?" Bill asked.

"Yeah. Lisle's the name—one of the names—of a guy who works out of Brussels. Very reliable individual, I've heard, even if he is on the offensive side of operations." He paused for a moment, thinking. He had his toothy grin back again. "If we could contact him, I think we could explain to him that we share goals and could work together on this problem."

"As a matter of fact," Mrs. Webb put in, "I think I do know how Mr. Holman contacted him. . . ."

There was something wonderfully soothing about the London tube. The slotted rubber flooring, the sturdy plaid seat cushions, the handholds—knobs on the ends of springs—swaying with the motion of the car. The wheels made clickety-click noises, not the crash-batter-clang that deafened you on the New York subway. And then there was the illusion that you were getting somewhere.

Sarah's hands were folded over Chris's arm, and

her head rested on his shoulder, lolling gently with the motion of the car. She had not said anything, had not even coughed, in some time. Chris thought that she was asleep. But abruptly she spoke.

"I should have gotten her away."

She had been thinking about Brenda, of course, just as he had. "You had no time. I thought I'd confuse 'em, get 'em to come after me. They saw I didn't have the money and went right by me. You just didn't have time."

She was silent for a long time. Then: "If I'd stayed, offered to give them the money—"

"They'd have shot you both and taken it."

"Do you think they did—"

"No," said Chris, with more certainty than he felt. "They wouldn't shoot her, not when they haven't got the money yet. Getting away with it was the best thing you could have done."

She raised her head and gazed unseeingly out the dark windows. "Don't cover for me, Chris. I was scared for you and scared for myself, and I didn't give a damn about her. And she knew it. I was—I was really rotten to her."

Chris straightened up and turned to her. "Sarah. Listen to me. You could have been—a little more understanding, yes. But you could not have gotten her out of that car. All you could've done was get yourself killed. So forget it. We've got to think what to do next."

They were both silent then.

At last she said, "Chris, there *is* nothing we can do next."

He nodded bleakly.

"Think it's time for us to come in?"

"Raspin. We'll call him—see what he has to say."

She passed her hand across her brow. "Say, where are we?"

"Elephant and Castle."

"Was that the last station?"

"No, but it's the last name that stuck. I'm not very sharp right now. Any idea where it is?"

"Yeah. We've gone clear across London. We're south of the Thames."

The train began to slow. Darkness gave way to a white-tiled wall with a circle and bar on it that read "Clapham South." The train came to a jerky stop. They looked at one another.

"Let's go."

One escalator up, they came to a phone booth. They stepped in, and Chris pawed through his memory and came up with Raspin's office number.

"I'm terribly sorry, sir," said the airy voice on the other end of the line, "but Mr. Raspin's in conference just now. Is there anyone else who can help you?"

"Get Raspin. I'm Chris Rockwell."

"Oh. Oh, I see. One moment, please."

His call was snicked and buzzed to another telephone.

"That you, Chris? Have you got the money with you?"

The voice was not Raspin's. "Who is this?"

"Bud Nelger here, Chris. Have you and Sarah got the money?"

"Yeah. Listen, I want to talk to Raspin."

"I'm sorry, Chris. Mr. Raspin's tied up. I can—"

"Will you tell him it's me, for God's sake? He'll want to talk to me."

"Well, no, Chris. You see, your feedback just isn't necessary at this point. We have the capability to deal with the problem now."

"What?"

"The only role we need for you to play is—well, to be dead for the next couple of hours."

"What?" Chris repeated numbly.

"We'll send a car for you. Where are you, anyway?"

"Clapham South tube."

Nelger chuckled. "How the heck did you get there? Well, never mind. We'll send the car, and I'll come and have a talk with you soon as I have time." With that he hung up.

Chris put the receiver back on the hook. Sarah was looking at him in bafflement.

"What's going on?"

"They don't need us. All they want us to do is be dead for a while."

They were watching for a company car. Instead, a lofty old Rolls-Royce—Mr. Raspin's own car, no doubt —parked before the station entrance. There was no one in it but the chauffeur. He came straight up to them, where they stood leaning against the wall, touched the visor of his cap, and asked them to come along. They felt too listless to ask where they were going.

They sat back in the car, separated from the driver by a glass partition. There was a rich aroma of old, well-cared-for wood and leather. Chris slid a picnic table open and placed on it a couple of cheese and tomato sandwiches he had bought while they were waiting.

"I haven't eaten since dinner at Raspin's last night. How about you?"

"I had some tea this morning. And I think I had lunch yesterday."

They stared at the cellophane-wrapped sandwiches.

"Chris, I'm not hungry."

"Neither am I."

For the rest of the way they sat back quietly and only took note of where they were when the Rolls turned at a mews tucked in behind the creamy terraces of Chester Square. The rows of tiny houses were brightened by window boxes and brightly colored doors. The car stopped in front of a yellow door; Chris assumed that this was Raspin's *pied-à-terre*.

The chauffeur turned them over to a smiling maid in a black dress and white apron, who led them up to a bedroom and left them, saying she would be back in a moment.

There was a full-length mirror on the bathroom door. Sarah went to stand in front of it, sliding her coat off her shoulders. Weighted by the bag full of money, the coat thudded to the floor.

"Chris."

He stepped up beside her, and they looked in silence at their reflection. Chris was still wearing his satin-striped evening trousers, topped, absurdly, by a brown sweater. His hair and beard looked ragged, and his face was blank—drained of all animation by fatigue and confusion. Sarah looked even worse: Her shoes were still encrusted with mud, her legs bare, her kilt nearly covered by the tails of Chris's shirt. It fitted her like a burnoose. She had lost her kerchief, and her hair hung in dull, stiff tangles down her back. She raised her hands and turned them, looking at the angry scratches across their backs, then brought them to her pale face, touching her red-flecked cheeks, her puffy eyes.

She sagged against Chris and he put his arm around her shoulders.

"We've gone through all this, and for—for—"

She was interrupted by a knock on the door. The little maid leaned in. "Excuse me, miss, but I'm sure Mr. Raspin's daughter wouldn't mind if you borrowed this." She held out a black dress, draped over her arm. "You're of a size, I think."

A smile broke over Sarah's face. "Thanks. Could I use Miss Raspin's bathroom, too?" The maid assured her she could.

Chris found a comb on the dresser and did what he could for his hair and beard. Then he sat down on the bed, sunk in the dismal thoughts brought on by his confused and helpless state. The winter afternoon expired and the room grew dim, but he did not get up to turn on a lamp. He sat on the bed, hunched over, his arms dangling between his knees.

He was dazzled when the lights went on; he had not heard anyone come in. Bud Nelger was standing in the doorway, smiling. He wore a dinner jacket.

"Hi, Chris. Comfortable? Got what you need?"

"The woman who was with us—"

Nelger nodded and his thick forelock tumbled forward. "Brenda Wertheim," he said, pushing it back in place. "She's OK. We've dealt with that aspect of the problem."

"She's OK?" Chris straightened up. "How do you know?"

"Chris, I just haven't got time to explain the whole situation now. We'll send for you in a couple of hours. Where—" He broke off as he spotted the shoulder bag lying on the floor, half-covered by the raincoat. Stepping forward, he bent to pick it up, just as Sarah came in the door behind him.

She was wearing a long-sleeved black dress with a wrap bodice, and a narrow black velvet choker round her throat. Her hair fell free from a center parting to tumble, soft, gleaming, golden, about her shoulders. She had powdered her face to hide the scratches, and her big gray-blue eyes held all their usual humor and hauteur.

Nelger had frozen for a moment, bent over, staring back at her. "Oh," he said, "you must be Sarah Saber."

"I'll say she is," Chris murmured. She looked so glorious that his spirits rallied just to behold her. He leaned forward and snatched the bag of money away from Nelger.

"Hey, what the—"

"Sarah, this is Nelger," Chris interrupted, freeing the bag from the strap of the raincoat. "A Securitco colleague of ours. He says Brenda's OK."

"Oh, thank God!" she exclaimed. "But—how does he know?"

"He won't tell us that. Hasn't the time." Chris folded his arms over the bag.

Nelger got the point. "OK. We've established contact with Lisle."

"Who's Lisle?" asked Sarah, coming round to sit beside Chris.

"Let me guess: He's the man in charge of the people who've been trying to kill us. Right?"

"Well," said Nelger apologetically, "he was operating under a set of blurred perceptions, just as we all were."

"I feel better already. So what's really going on?"

"We haven't solved all the problems yet, but as soon as we get Holman—"

"Holman! He's probably on a plane to Costa Rica by now."

Negler nodded. "We thought that would be his

plan too, but then we realized he'd be unable to implement it."

"Why?"

"We found his passport at the house in Hampstead. We really didn't know where to start looking for the guy, so we just waited and hoped it would occur to him to call Lisle. Finally, he did."

"I see," said Sarah. "That's why we're supposed to be dead. Lisle told him everything came off OK and he was safe."

"And this"—Chris thumped the bag of money—"is the reason Lisle is being so cooperative?"

"Right. So if you'd just give it—"

Chris held up a hand. "You were saying about Holman?"

"Oh yeah." Nelger folded his arms and leaned back against the wall. He seemed to be warming to the story. "After he talked to Lisle, he called RGI House, just to be safe. The call was referred to me, of course." Nelger grinned. "Holman was playing ignorant, natch, so I broke the bad news to him. He said he guessed you must have been on the way to see him, although he hadn't talked to you and wasn't even at the house at the time. He sounded really shocked—"

"Did he say he was experiencing very heavy guilt feelings?" asked Sarah.

Nelger's grin grew broader. "Yeah—exactly. I don't know how he carried it off. I nearly broke up myself."

"You don't know Holman," she said. "It's hard to believe anyone so dumb could be so treacherous."

"Anyway, I offered—real casually—to send a car out to get him. He was at Heathrow, it turned out—

he'd gotten all the way there before he realized he couldn't leave the country. But he said no, he'd take a cab and come straight to the gala." Nelger glanced at his watch and straightened up. "Hell, he's probably there by now. I've got to get back, so—"

Ignoring his outstretched hand, Chris turned to Sarah. "You look great, kid. Thinking of going to a party?"

"Yes," she replied, smiling. "An RGI gala."

"Absolutely negative on that guys. I mean, don't you see why we don't want you there?"

"We want to be there." Chris tightened his grip on the bag.

Negler looked at them. Suddenly his hand darted beneath his coat and came out holding a sleek black automatic. He leveled it on Chris.

"No more games. Hand over the money. Now."

"No."

"What do you mean, no?" He looked down at the automatic and shook it, as if it were a flashlight that had failed to go on. "This is a gun."

"It's a very nice gun," said Sarah. "Walther PPK, official Securitco side arm. We just don't believe you're willing to shoot us."

"Oh." He looked at the automatic again and put it away. "Well, if you're going to be like that, I guess I'll have to take you with me. But Mr. Raspin isn't going to like this at all."

Chapter 23

A few people detached themselves from the theater-bound crowd to lean over the parapet of Hungerford Bridge and look down at the boat, aglow with gaiety and music.

Gordon Dunbar glanced up at their faces, pale in the reflected light. Like the Edwardian days, he thought: the poor gathered in a dark throng about some Park Lane house to glimpse the nobility as they left their carriages and ascended the red-carpeted stairs. Rather a letdown that we're all in trade.

Still, from a distance it must have made a fine show. The boat was a seventy-five-footer with glassed-in fore- and afterdecks, the sort that hauls tourists down to Greenwich and back in the daytime. Tonight it was strung from bow to stern with lights, a band was installed forward, and a number of waiters prowled the decks with trays of champagne glasses.

Tonight's entertainment was to be lavish: a cocktail-time cruise up the Thames, followed by a dinner dance at the Savoy. Dunbar glanced at his watch: They were due to cast off in half an hour. He decided to make another tour of the boat, looking for Holman.

Most of the guests were already here; the cabin—or whatever one called this glass-roofed enclosure—was crowded. The men were all alike in their evening clothes—the energetic gestures they made with their free hands, the eager, intent look on their faces. All the women wore slinky gowns, which seemed designed to show that there was nothing worn beneath them.

Quite untrue in fact. Dunbar, much against his will, had been made familiar with the intricacies of lingerie by the advertisements, and so he knew that these women were wearing a layer of seamless nylon to smooth and curve their flesh in the right ways. Even nakedness was an illusion these days.

There were people he knew, of course—Europeans whom he nodded at and whose handshakes he avoided. Europeans? Not really. They were a hybrid developed by the great multinational corporations—born in one country, living in another, and passing through an American business school in between. They attached American nicknames to their own surnames, and spoke a language not their own in an accent unique to their kind.

At least it was getter than the American accent, to which Dunbar could never accustom his ear. Those *r*'s, those flat vowels. "Oh, isn't the view fan-tas-tic," he heard a woman say, as he came out on deck again.

That was true enough, at any rate. The curve of the river showed London before them in all its glory. The clutter was left to subside into darkness, while the famous buildings stood out brilliantly in floodlight. It was a tourist's dream, the picture postcards made real. Downriver was Parliament, in all its warm brown intricacy, the Cyclopean eye of Big Ben, the lacy gray Victoria tower, and the blunt spires of Westminster Abbey beyond. Looking the other way, he saw a little of the long, low facade of Somerset House, but most of it was obscured by bridges. Far away to the east, the columned dome of Saint Paul's seemed to hang suspended in the night sky. Beyond it was a vertical scatter of lights, reaching so high up that Dunbar could hardly believe it marked a building. It did, though—the new development, the Barbican.

There was more of the new London straight across the dark, rippling river: the prefab concrete jumble of the National Theatre Complex, with that curious sign, like a giant neon paper clip, that they had put on the Film Theatre.

Dunbar turned away and walked down the gangplank to the dock. Charing Cross Pier had been redone for the occasion, festooned with scarlet and white streamers and lights, and the imperial standard, of course, the big red sign with the three initials on it. He was still looking for Holman, but he had not been on the boat, and he was not here either. Just as well; Dunbar could catch him as soon as he got out of his car, talk to him before he talked to anyone else. He would put some steel in his backbone. Not for the first time, he reflected that it was odd that such a booby as Holman had conceived such a bold plan against Wilson, and carried it as far as he had.

On the concrete apron beside the dock a big red trailer was parked. Telephone cables slithered from its base and guards stood at its door. Dunbar looked at it uneasily; this was Raspin's command post, and he had not ventured out of it all evening. He was not a gracious man, but nonetheless Dunbar would have expected him to be on the boat, greeting his guests, if all were as it should be. What were they doing in there?

Yes, he had better catch Holman right away. He turned and walked, with his slow, stiff gait, toward the "checkpoint."

That was what they called it. They had cordoned off most of the Embankment right down to Hungerford Bridge. Beyond the barriers, traffic crawled along in two lanes; within them, a number of men milled about, waiting for trouble. There were a few policemen, in their high helmets and long coats, but they were far outnumbered by RGI's private army of Securitco guards, in red-striped trousers and short tunics slit over their holsters. The thickest concentration of men was at the checkpoint, the break in the barriers where a long line of cars waited to let off their passengers. The Securitco men were checking the guests' identification, fumbling with flashlights, clipboards, and walkie-talkies.

A Rolls-Royce hove into view, cutting off the little white company car that was next in line. One of the guards leaned into the front window and then waved the car through.

Unusual, thought Dunbar. He turned and walked after the Rolls-Royce, as it lumbered through the crowd of arriving guests. As he expected, it stopped beside the trailer. The guards hurried to form a screen about it, like bodyguards protecting a politician. Still Dunbar recognized Rockwell as he got out of the backseat, followed by a slender blonde whom he took to be Miss Saber. They went up a step and into the trailer, followed by another man, and the door shut behind them.

Dunbar turned about and walked back the way he had come. They were having some sort of conference in there, and they surely meant to bring Holman before it. Dunbar had to talk to him first, prepare him as best he could. The major made a conscious effort to breathe deeply and evenly; he felt the keen edge of nervousness and dread.

Walter Raspin looked more severe than ever in his black dinner jacket. He was sitting at a tiny metal desk, and foil wrappers, neatly unfolded and smoothed out, were stacked in front of him like money. His eyes as he looked at them were like highly polished metal discs.

"Nelger," he rumbled, "what are *they* doing here?"

"It's OK, sir. Checkpoint says Holman hasn't come through yet."

Raspin glanced at his watch. "Where the devil *is* he?"

"I don't know. He should've been here by now—"

Nelger was interrupted by another voice—Bill Chandler's. Sarah looked about in confusion for a moment before noticing the speaker-phone on Raspin's desk. "Sarah? Chris? Are you there?"

Chris rushed up to the speaker as if to embrace it. "Bill! Where are you?"

"At Inkwink. Mr. Welch is here with me."

Prompted like a child, Welch piped in. "Hello, Sarah. Rockwell. Glad you—ah—Could make it. Mr. Raspin, maybe I should recapitulate for the benefit of—"

"Nelger filled us in on the way over," said Sarah. "Nice work, Bill."

"Thanks, honey."

Chris was setting the shoulder bag on a desk beside Raspin's. On it lay a red-covered typescript, as thick as a smalltown telephone directory.

"Is this it?" he asked. "What it was all about—the marketing portfolio?"

"Yes," said Welch. "We pried a copy out of Atlantic Brands and telexed it over. It's a brilliant piece of work—you can see why Wilson had to have it back."

Chris sat down and opened the folder. He was instantly lost in his reading.

"Bill," Sarah said into the speaker-phone, "are you sure you got everything out of Webb that she knew?"

"She's a tough old bird, but I don't think she held anything back. She doesn't know why that meeting took place, or why those guys got killed."

"Holman will enlighten us, I expect," said Raspin, glancing at his watch again. "Where *is* he? The damned boat sails in fifteen minutes."

The door opened and a diminutive gray-haired man, with a fedora set askew atop a bandaged head, stepped in. There was a Securitco guard right behind him.

"Monsieur Raspin? I have executed my part of the agreement—" Catching sight of Sarah, he broke off and lowered his eyes in embarrassment, as if he had walked in on her *en déshabillé.*

She picked up the shoulder bag and stepped across the room to face him. She was not a tall woman, but the crown of his hat was just level with her eyes.

"Lisle, right? Where is she?"

"Just outside—just coming from the car, mademoiselle," he replied, without looking up.

"She's OK? You haven't hurt her?"

"No, no. Her—uh—demeanor persuaded us within a few minutes that she did not have the qualities to execute such a plan. Even before Monsieur Nelger contacted us, we knew that there had been some mistake." He turned to Nelger and bowed.

Sarah interrupted this courtly gesture by shoving the heavy bag of money into his stomach as hard as she could. She was pleased to hear him gasp as she stepped out the door.

She immediately saw Brenda, clumsily getting out of a car with the help of a guard. She ran up and threw her arms around her.

"Oh Brenda! Thank God!"

Brenda was obviously startled: The beleagured, disdainful creature of the morning had been transformed into an elegant and gracious lady. But keenly in need of an embrace just now, she clung to Sarah as the latter helped her up the step and into the trailer.

Only ten minutes to go, now. Major Dunbar, still loitering at the checkpoint, looked back toward the dock. Men were hurrying across it to the gangplank, women waddling along beside them in their tight dresses and high heels. At the edge of the pier he could just discern the figures of a couple of crewmen bending over to cast off lines.

He turned. There was still a long black-and-white line—company cars and taxis—stretching out from the checkpoint. Holman must be in one of these cars— he couldn't be fool enough to fail to show up for the gala. Dunbar walked past the barriers.

"Hey you!" said a brusque American voice.

Dunbar started badly. It took a great effort to turn and face the Securitco guard who was striding toward him. "Sorry, but you can't go out once you're in. Security. Anyway, the boat's going in—"

"I shan't be sailing on the boat."

"Oh. OK then," said the guard indifferently, turning away.

Dunbar walked on, his heart still thudding violently, and realized that his steps were leading him not along the line but toward the cars parked at the side of the street. His own was one of them, and he unlocked the door and leaned in.

From the glove compartment he took his service revolver. It was the only piece of evidence against him; he should have destroyed it. I'll throw it in the river, he thought. If it turns out I don't need it now.

* * *

Chris did not look up from the marketing portfolio until Brenda had thrown herself on his neck with a sob of relief. Then he gave her only a wan smile and a pat on the shoulder, and turned away from her. His face, furnished as it was with beard and glasses, was difficult to read, but to Sarah he seemed both angry and deeply saddened.

"I've figured it out," he said.

They all looked at him, and there was silence until Raspin echoed, "Figured it out?"

"You read this thing, Mr. Raspin?" He snapped the cover of the portfolio closed and pushed it away.

"No."

"Oh, I have," Welch's voice piped in, from the speaker.

"Tell 'em what's in it, Welch." He got up and wandered aimlessly across the small room, his hands in his pockets and his head down.

"Well, many things, of course," Welch began. "But the most important concept had to do with the sherries. He was going to alter the product characteristics in order to fit them to user image perceptions—"

"You have an amazing memory for gobbledygook, Welch. Get to the point."

"Yes, sir," said Welch, as if Raspin had complimented him. "He was going to discontinue the dry sherries because of their low popularity potential on the American market, and push the cream sherry hard. His research indicated that consumers responded favorably to the name Dunbar's, but there was a counterbalancing perception that it wasn't strong enough to stand up to ice. Since a whopping seventy-three percent of new sherry drinkers reported they drink it on the rocks, he planned to make changes at the—the—"

"Solera," Chris supplied, without raising his head. "Where they blend different vintages to produce the finished sherry."

"Yeah. He was going to use newer wines, and fewer of them, to give the stuff more of a kick. Of course, that would cut production costs—"

"So he was going to lower the price?" asked Sarah.

"No, raise it." Welch's voice was tingling with enthusiasm. "His analysis of the market indicated that he could develop Dunbar's into a brand winner—a name that sells steadily despite fluctuations in the popularity of the brand. He had the first factor he needed—a prestige name—and he was going to add the second, a high price. He was basing a whole campaign on the theme: 'Dunbar's: the most expensive sherry you can buy.' You should see the ads, sir, they're—"

"How unbelievably shoddy!" Raspin bellowed. "Disgraceful!"

Welch fell silent so abruptly that one would have thought the satellite relaying his voice had fallen from the sky.

"The reason I didn't see it," said Chris, still looking at the floor, "was that it was too simple for me. Revenge. That was all Dunbar wanted."

Raspin gaped at him. "See here, Rockwell. You're not saying that Major Dunbar—people don't do such things!"

"This was only the last straw," Chris said, tapping the portfolio. "This came after they'd tricked him, and robbed him, and humiliated him." He stood silent for a moment, remembering. "It all must have hit him at once. He mustn't have known what Wilson

had done to him until I tipped him off about Brenda.
I did that. I didn't know enough to put it together,
but he did. And then he went to Holman. He found
out what they'd done to him, and he found out they
were all set up so he could kill them."

"But it couldn't possibly do him any good to—"
Sarah murmured.

"No. He killed them because he hated them, that's
all." Chris glanced at Brenda, who had shrunk against
the wall with her hand over her mouth and her eyes
closed. Learning how deeply Dunbar despised her
seemed to frighten her more than all the dangers of
the day.

"He must be insane," said Raspin.

"Maybe. But he almost pulled it off, didn't he? He
would've got away except that—" Chris broke off
abruptly. "Say, where is he?"

"Good God. He's been invited here."

Nelger snatched a walktie-talkie from the desk.
"Nelger here. Have you checked a G. Dunbar
through?"

A moment's pause, and the voice crackled over the
line, "Yes, sir. 'Bout an hour ago."

"Get to the boat, Nelger," snapped Raspin. "Take
some men, find him and bring him here. Do it as
quietly as you can."

Nelger spun and ran from the room.

Chris was through the door before it had closed,
and Sarah went after him. She found him taking a
gun from the guard outside. Turning to the other
one, she snapped, "Your gun—give it to me."

He handed the Walther over quickly enough, and
Chris was just a step ahead of her, striding across
the pavement.

"Where are you going?"

"If we don't get Holman, we haven't got a shred of proof against Dunbar. If he's figured that out—"

"They're not gonna find him on the boat," she finished for him. She kicked off her shoes and broke into a run, with Chris beside her.

The very last car in the line was a taxi; peering in, Dunbar recognized Holman's characteristic silhouette, his leonine curls. He wrenched the door open and leaned in.

Holman jumped—he had not seen Dunbar approach —and then his handsome face split in a grin. "Oh, hi, Dunbar. I'm not late, am I?"

"Where've you been?"

"Renting a tux at this place in the Strand. They had the heck of a time fitting me." He looked down over his white shirtfront and satin lapels. "I couldn't just turn up for the gala in a suit, y'know. It would be the wrong look entirely."

Dunbar took a deep breath. "Get out, Holman. We should have a talk."

"Surely," said Holman. "Walking's quicker anyway." He paid the driver and got out beside Dunbar.

They were under the bridge. Dunbar steered Holman toward the side of the road.

"Hey, where we going?"

"We must talk before you go in there."

Holman chuckled. "No problem, Dunbar. It's a wrap."

"What?"

"I've taken care of Wertheim for you."

"What do you mean, taken care of her?"

"I mean, she's wasted. Ditto Saber and Rockwell."

It was odd about fear. You got used to it, as you got used to everything. The shock rippled over Dunbar and then left him in command of himself, quite clear about what he must do next.

"I called Lisle," Holman was continuing. "Made a deal with him for the money. It's finished, Dunbar. We've gotten clear."

Dunbar pushed him back from the road, between two parked cars, right up against the great concrete piers of the bridge. He darted glances about him: There was no one nearby, and the nearest street lamp cast no light on them.

"You stupid bastard. They're here. Having a talk with Raspin. They were going to pick you up the moment you passed the gates." The handsome, confident facade of Holman's face crumbled. His shoulders hunched protectively.

"Got to—got to run! Let me go!" he whined.

"Coward. Fool. I can't leave you alive any longer."

Feeble to the end, Holman made no move to escape between the time—a split second—Dunbar's hands left his shoulders and closed round his throat.

It was Chris who spotted them first. He grasped Sarah's arm and pointed, and she could just discern the two black shapes in the gloom beneath the bridge.

No way to tell which was Dunbar, so she fired a shot down at the road. The dry crack of the report reverberated off the concrete. There was the pale smudge of shirtfront and face as Dunbar turned, and then the flash of a gunshot.

She flinched and lost sight of him for a moment; then headlights were veering crazily, and there was the shriek of brakes and the hollow thunk of colliding fenders. They ran after him across the Embankment, cars swerving and plunging on either side of them.

As they gained the opposite sidewalk, Sarah glanced

back to see a dozen figures fanning out among the
halted cars—policemen and guards.

They ran up a narrow street between the Underground station and the high concrete flank of the
bridge. Dunbar had a good twenty strides on them.
Abruptly he pivoted and disappeared to the right.

The next streets were empty and so quiet that they
could hear the ring of his footfalls. They ran along
shadowy arcades at the base of high, blank-walled
buildings. Chris could see Dunbar plainly, pitching
forward at every other step. He remembered the old
man's limp and wondered how long his leg could
hold up.

"Stay clear!" Sarah shouted, dropping away from
him, and Chris sheared off to the side of the street
to give her an open shot. In a moment he heard the
reports.

Dunbar wavered in instinctive reaction, but his
pace did not slacken. She had missed. Chris threw
all the strength he had left into his legs and rushed
headlong after him.

Sarah straightened up, lowering the gun. Men
came clattering up behind her; Nelger swept past
on her left without checking and she fell in beside
him.

"Dunbar?" he gasped.

She nodded, running as quickly as she could. Her
hose—Raspin's daughter's hose—were worn through
already, and her feet felt sore and cold.

They were in a narrow passageway now, passing,
to the right, the steamy, glowing windows of a pub
from which the muffled sound of singing came. Dunbar was charging up a steep bank of steps ahead.

Chris followed, thinking, I'm alone, and if he turns and fires, I've got nowhere to dodge. But the big man kept going, went over the top, and disappeared.

He heard the tumult erupt—screams of brakes, shouts, horns blaring—a moment before he reached the top. Then there was flat pavement before him and a barrier of people, a bus line, staring out into the street. He put out his arms and plunged through.

"Oh!"

"Here, what the—"

And then he was in the wide street, skirting cars slued broadside as others veered to avoid him, honking. He had a vague impression of big lighted windows and the bright marquees of theaters with crowds milling about their doors. This must be the Strand. As he reached the opposite pavement, he heard the shrill note of a whistle and glanced over his shoulder to see a policeman in white gauntlets running after him.

"You there! Stop!"

A clear thought passed through his frazzled brain: The policeman was not armed, so he did not have to worry about getting shot in the back. He ran on.

Dunbar was leaving a wake as clear as if he had been running through a wheat field: People pressed back against buildings or the curb, heads turned to stare after him. Hoping that no one would be stupid enough to try to stop him, Chris ran in pursuit. He caught glimpses of startled faces, and a drunken, cheery voice called, "What's your 'urry, mate?"

Ahead of him the lurching black-clad figure turned out of sight, and Chris followed to find himself in an alley beside the looming flank of a theater. There was only darkness ahead—and then he caught sight of Dunbar, briefly illuminated by the lights of a passing car.

"There he is!" shouted one of the Securitco men as they rounded the corner, pointing with his gun.

"That's Chris!" Sarah screamed, thinking: Two tall men in dark clothes, running—

"Atkins, McNally," Nelger shouted, "go on to the next corner and turn up—you'll get in front of them!"

With a fleeting hope that Nelger's grasp of geography was as good as it sounded, she plunged into the alley, in time to see Chris turn to the right, rounding the corner of a building.

Within a minute of crossing the Strand into Covent Garden, the pursuit degenerated into chaos. The district was a maze of short, narrow lanes, clogged by cars and knots of people bound for the theaters. Nelger's group broke up into pairs and trios of men dashing about at random, pursuing shadows, guesses, or each other.

Sarah found herself alone; she too had lost sight of Chris and Dunbar. But she had at least a vague idea where they had gone. Before her were the disused market buildings—enormous glass-roofed structures, decorated with columns and capitals and statuary, ghostly in the floodlight. They were boarded off, their courtyards turned into parking lots. She ran along the sidewalk, wincing as her bruised feet touched pavement, peering into the darkness.

Chris glimpsed Dunbar's white head and black shoulders over the roofs of parked cars as he zigzagged among them in pursuit.

At last the man brought up short before a blank hoarding. "Give up, Major!" Chris bawled. "You can't get away!"

Before the words were out Dunbar had turned and snapped off a shot, and then he was off again, running along the hoarding. Chris did not dare return fire—he was an atrocious shot—and he broke into a run after him.

From across the parking lot, Sarah had seen the muzzle flash. She brought up her gun, braced her left hand on her right, tracked Dunbar's silhouette along the hoarding, and squeezed off a shot. She missed, and then the other running shadow—Chris—came into her view. Too close. She lowered the gun and was about to dash across the street after them. But she never made it to the curb.

There was a trio of Securitco guards off to her right. They were frightened and confused; this situation had never figured in their training. They saw the flash of Sarah's gun, but they could not see her. They opened up anyway.

The fusillade blew out the plate-glass window of the café behind her, and she heard fragments shattering on the pavement around her as she sank to her knees and toppled over. Why am I falling? she wondered dazedly. I must be hit. She was dimly aware of the cold concrete against her cheek, of someone's shoe before her eyes. Far away—so it seemed—there were voices shouting. She could make out someone saying over and over again, "Don't move her!" She thought, I must be hurt badly. But shock and fear enveloped her like a fog, and her nerves could tell her nothing of where she had been hit.

*   *   *

Chris had heard the burst of firing, but his brain
did not register it. Dunbar was only ten paces ahead
of him, lurching so badly that Chris thought he must
surely fall at every step. But suddenly he whirled to
the right and disappeared.

Chris came to the gap in the hoarding and went
through. Big piles of bricks and lumber draped with
tarps, rubble pits, a line of columns: He was in one
of the vast market buildings now. There was a string
of bare bulbs along the ceiling, which did nothing
to illuminate the place. He stumbled across a floor
littered with debris and felt his way through a jungle
of scaffolding. There was a solid wall before him and,
running along it, he came at last to an archway. He
could see street lamps above a hoarding—that would
be the other side of the building—but he could see
nothing around him. He was blind and, because of
the racket he himself was making, deaf too. Instinctively he fumbled toward the lights.

A row of columns appeared out of the gloom. He
would be out of here in a moment. He broke into a
run and took two long strides before he banged his
shins into a roll of sheet metal and tumbled over, the
gun slipping from his grasp.

Getting his hands beneath him, he raised himself
and looked up—at Dunbar. He was standing five feet
in front of him, the gun leveled at his head.

Chris probed desperately, hopelessly, for the
Walther.

"Don't, Rockwell!" Dunbar pleaded hoarsely.

In the yellow glare of the street lamps he could
make out the sheen of sweat glistening on the man's
face. His chest was heaving and he leaned to one
side, all his weight on his good leg.

Chris rocked slowly back on his heels, raising his empty hands.

Dunbar turned and crossed the forecourt at a ragged run, his left leg nearly collapsing beneath him at every step.

Chris looked down at the Walther, lying a yard in front of him. It did not occur to him that he could pick the gun up and shoot the old man in the back. He rose to his feet and walked after him, waiting for him to drop.

Dunbar reached an opening in the hoarding, clung to the wall for a second, pushed himself off, and staggered into the street.

Chris heard the squeak of brakes as he rounded the corner, in time to see Dunbar stop, dazed, in the full glare of a car's headlights. Guns opened up behind the lights.

Dunbar flung his arms up, like a runner breaking the tape. The impact of the bullets rocked him back, and then he collapsed. There was a brief, eerie silence, in which Chris could hear Dunbar's gun clattering across the tarmac.

A door thudded; the car's lights swung away. As it turned he caught a glimpse of the bespectacled face of M. Lisle behind the wheel, and the indistinct shapes of the killers in the back. Then the car roared away up the street, its taillights glowed briefly, and with a last squeak of tires it swept out of sight.

Without looking at the body, Chris staggered back the way he had come.

Some minutes later he saw lights dancing about at the far end of the building. He did not call out, did not give them any thought at all until one of them shone full into his eyes.

"Hold it right there! Put your hands up!" shouted

a hysterical voice. Good God, Chris thought. They don't even know what Dunbar looked like.

"Dunbar's dead. I'm Rockwell." The light advanced, wavering.

"Take us to the body."

"Where's Sarah? The woman that was with us—where is she?"

"Oh—her. Back there aways. I think she's hurt pretty bad."

Chris's insides heaved. "Where? Where is she?"

The guard was still shining the light in his face, and he could just make out other men running up beside them.

"This guy says Dunbar's dead."

"Show us the—"

Chris snatched the flashlight away and grabbed him by the lapels. "Take me back to Sarah or I'll break your neck."

"OK—OK," said the man placatingly. They turned about and ran down the long rubble-strewn gallery.

Outside, across the tops of parked cars, he could see the café, and before it police cars with their blue lights spinning, a couple of white company cars, and a crowd of policemen, guards, and passersby. Despite his exhaustion, he broke into a dead run, leaving the Securitco man behind.

He shouldered his way through the ring of people. Sarah was sitting on the pavement, her back against the wall. He was vaguely aware of men crouching over her. The locks of her hair were clotted with blood and there was a dark smear on the glass-strewn pavement. But it was only when he knelt beside her that he saw the wound. Her dress was hiked up over a swollen thigh. There was a tiny hole in her skin, with black smudges around it but no blood at all.

"It's all right, sir," said an English voice beside him. He did not look around to see who was speaking. "Bullet went clean through and missed the bone. It's not serious at all."

Her head turned and she looked at him carefully, as if he were very far away and she was not sure she recognized him.

"It's OK," she whispered hollowly. "Don't worry. The blood's from m—minor lacerations." She was carefully repeating something the doctor had told her. "Glass."

"You dear, wonderful, beautiful . . ." Chris babbled on until a hand settled heavily on his shoulder. He turned to look up at the looming, helmeted figure of a policeman.

"Christopher Rockwell?"

"Yes."

"I must ask you to come round to Bow Street Station, Mr. Rockwell, to assist us in our inquiries." And then he added, "There'll be an ambulance round in a moment for the young lady."

Chris touched Sarah's cheek and then got up. He turned to see Walter Raspin, leaning against the fender of his Rolls-Royce, flanked by policemen.

"Holman?" Chris asked, as the policeman's hand closed round his arm.

"Fortunately for him, Dunbar managed to kill him," Raspin replied. "We're not supposed to say anything until our solicitors get here."

"Oh, give it up, Raspin! This is disaster for RGI, no matter what you do."

Raspin nodded. "Disaster."

Another bestseller from the world's master storyteller

The Top of the Hill

IRWIN SHAW

author of *Rich Man, Poor Man* and *Beggarman, Thief*

He feared nothing...wanted everything. Every thrill. Every danger. Every woman.

"Pure entertainment. Full of excitement."—*N.Y. Daily News*

"You can taste the stale air in the office and the frostbite on your fingertips, smell the wood in his fireplace and the perfume scent behind his mistresses' ears."—*Houston Chronicle*

A Dell Book $2.95 (18976-4)

At your local bookstore or use this handy coupon for ordering:

| **Dell** | **DELL BOOKS** | THE TOP OF THE HILL $2.95 (18976-4) |
| | **P.O. BOX 1000, PINEBROOK, N.J. 07058** | |

Please send me the above title. I am enclosing $ _____
(please add 75¢ per copy to cover postage and handling). Send check or money order—no cash or C.O.D.'s. Please allow up to 8 weeks for shipment.

Mr/Mrs/Miss_____

Address_____

City_____ State/Zip_____

Dell BESTSELLERS

- [ ] **TOP OF THE HILL** by Irwin Shaw $2.95 (18976-4)
- [ ] **THE ESTABLISHMENT** by Howard Fast........$3.25 (12296-1)
- [ ] **SHOGUN** by James Clavell $3.50 (17800-2)
- [ ] **LOVING** by Danielle Steel $2.75 (14684-4)
- [ ] **THE POWERS THAT BE**
      by David Halberstam $3.50 (16997-6)
- [ ] **THE SETTLERS** by William Stuart Long $2.95 (15923-7)
- [ ] **TINSEL** by William Goldman $2.75 (18735-4)
- [ ] **THE ENGLISH HEIRESS** by Roberta Gellis....$2.50 (12141-8)
- [ ] **THE LURE** by Felice Picano $2.75 (15081-7)
- [ ] **SEAFLAME** by Valerie Vayle $2.75 (17693-X)
- [ ] **PARLOR GAMES** by Robert Marasco $2.50 (17059-1)
- [ ] **THE BRAVE AND THE FREE**
      by Leslie Waller $2.50 (10915-9)
- [ ] **ARENA** by Norman Bogner $3.25 (10369-X)
- [ ] **COMES THE BLIND FURY** by John Saul $2.75 (11428-4)
- [ ] **RICH MAN, POOR MAN** by Irwin Shaw $2.95 (17424-4)
- [ ] **TAI-PAN** by James Clavell $3.25 (18462-2)
- [ ] **THE IMMIGRANTS** by Howard Fast $2.95 (14175-3)
- [ ] **BEGGARMAN, THIEF** by Irwin Shaw $2.75 (10701-6)

At your local bookstore or use this handy coupon for ordering:

Dell | **DELL BOOKS**
P.O. BOX 1000, PINEBROOK, N.J. 07058

Please send me the books I have checked above. I am enclosing $_____
(please add 75¢ per copy to cover postage and handling). Send check or money
order—no cash or C.O.D.'s. Please allow up to 8 weeks for shipment.

Mr/Mrs/Miss _____

Address _____

City _____ State/Zip _____